EMMA'S PEACE

Recent Titles by Elizabeth Daish

THE COPPINS BRIDGE TRILOGY
SHOP ON COPPINS BRIDGE
FAMILY ON COPPINS BRIDGE
EBB-TIDE AT COPPINS BRIDGE

EMMA'S WAR

OUT OF THE DUST

EMMA'S PEACE

Elizabeth Daish

This first world edition published in Great Britain 1995 by
SEVERN HOUSE PUBLISHERS LTD of
9–15 High Street, Sutton, Surrey SM1 1DF.
First published in the USA 1995 by
SEVERN HOUSE PUBLISHERS INC of
425 Park Avenue, New York, NY 10022.

British Library Cataloguing in Publication Data
Daish, Elizabeth
  Emma's Peace
  I. Title
  823.914 [F]

  ISBN 0-7278-4745-7

Typeset by Hewer Text Composition Services, Edinburgh.
Printed and bound in Great Britain by
Hartnolls Ltd, Bodmin, Cornwall.

For Derek

Chapter 1

Emma Dewar looked through the wide open gates of the Princess Beatrice Hospital in Southeast London and smiled. Everything looked the same. Grey-walled buildings, the long drive up to the front entrance past the porter's lodge and the car park for staff. Each time she returned to the parent hospital that had given her so much, she felt a thrill of anticipation. It was like coming home.

The taxi had left her by the gates and she walked slowly, carrying her suitcase and wondering what it would be like to work there again after a few months away in Surrey. She recalled her first day at Beatties, as the old hospital was called by staff and patients alike, and she couldn't visualise the timid girl who had put on stiff new uniform and presented herself on her first ward.

Emma walked confidently, sure of her new rank of Staff Nurse and the fact that she knew the old building as well as most of the senior staff, and some of the student nurses who had followed her to take a training at the world famous hospital.

The windows of the children's ward were slightly open at the top and she could see the pretty caps of two nurses who were making beds there. She hurried, as the case was heavy and she wanted to find her room in the Nurses' Home and unpack so that she could feel that she was really back again.

Soon, she would be working in one of the long Victorian wards and mingling with the other nurses and doctors in the daily life of the hospital.

She put the case down to change hands, as the grip was hard, and turned as someone touched her on the shoulder.

"I thought you were down at Heath Cross in darkest Surrey." Emma looked up sharply, then smiled. "Tony! It's good to see you. I wondered if there would be any of the old crowd back at Beatties when I arrived today. We all seem to have moved about since D-Day. I've lost touch with some of my set since they opened up the old School for the Blind near Leatherhead."

Tony Goldwater shrugged. "Have you been down there? It's all a bit primitive but at least the operating theatres are good and we do move the post-ops fairly quickly. Heath Cross was a shambles after the first flood of wounded and we took a lot of the heat off the staff there. I'm just up for the day to see Sir Neville and to lobby for new anaesthetic machines."

"I didn't know you were there. I've been at Heath Cross until today. We've sorted out most of the wards and they brought in Red Cross assistants to make swabs and mend gowns and gloves. The normal staff couldn't cope with that as well as ops. We were nearly cleaned out once the D-Day rush started and it was panic stations to get dressings sterilised." She frowned. "I've come back for a month or so to have a more varied experience in wards that I haven't even seen. I've had a lot of theatre experience and no kids or women's medical and my finals are looming up alarmingly. After that I have a few days' leave before I go back to Heath Cross. Surely the worst of it must be over now that our men are pushing back the Germans in France?"

2

"Not over yet. We win some and they counterattack, but over all, the tide has turned and we are going further into France every day. The liberation of Paris was a great boost to the Free French, but we have so many fronts, in Greece, Eastern Europe and the desert, and a war against Japan that still has to be won." She saw that the man who had driven everyone mad with his practical jokes and over-the-top humour was serious. His eyes held a sadness that she had seen in many faces as the war progressed and the reality of death and loss hit the public. "They don't expect so many casualties straight from the front," she said. "As the war goes into Europe, our people take over existing hospitals there and fly in equipment, surgeons and staff from the Forces. The ENT team at Heath Cross are agitating for a theatre of their own and when I go back I shall be working on a ward, not in theatre. If it's tonsils and mastoids again, I can bear not to be in theatre for a while."

"*Tout passe*," Tony said wryly. "I thought you, me and Guy and the others were fixtures in that ruin of a theatre. Looking back, I know it was a happy time, in between the horrors."

"Yes." She turned away and picked up her suitcase. "A lot happened that changed a few lives."

He took the case from her. "A body?" he asked with an exaggerated effort to lift it.

"Two at least," she said, laughing and relieved to see that the old Tony lurked somewhere under his new solemnity. "I was on my way to the Nurses' Home. I've reported back and have until supper time tomorrow off duty." She made a face. "Then kids, on night duty."

"Don't you like the idea? Every girl with a figure like yours can expect to have beautiful babies, so a bit of practice will be good for you."

3

They walked by Casualty and the main car park, and visitors came past, clutching bunches of weary flowers, bought at the gates when nearest and dearest suddenly realised that they had brought no gifts for their relatives.

"What's funny?" asked Tony.

"Nothing. It's nice to know that some things haven't changed. The woman who sells the flowers must be ninety! She buys white daisies in bulk and dyes them pink or that awful blue. They say she collects 'to sell again' all that are thrown out but are still fresh when patients leave and don't want to take their flowers with them. I don't believe it, but the ward maid on Gynae used to swear it was true."

"Where's Guy? I haven't seen him or David for at least a month. We seem to go round in circles. Now that we have the Sector Hospitals to staff, we could go for years never seeing our friends unless we make an effort to keep in touch." He eyed her with blatant curiosity. "You *are* seeing him, I suppose?"

Emma smiled. "Of course. I'm meeting Guy this afternoon but first I have to see Bea Shuter at lunch to catch up with all the gossip of the Princess Beatrice Hospital, which is quite different from the low grade stuff we have down in Surrey at Heath Cross."

"What's going to happen with you and Guy? He's a very good surgeon and will go places. He'll need you, Emma."

"I hope so," she said with a gentle smile. "I haven't met his family yet but we shall go down to Devon soon and be formally engaged."

"Why not marry him now? The war isn't over and anything could happen. You need to be together now." The sombre expression was there again and Emma knew how much he had suffered, with one after another of his relatives dying in Hitler's gas chambers.

4

"If I married a member of Beattie's staff, I would have to leave. They dislike married women as they think we should be completely dedicated to our work. Even Bea, who married her American pilot, has to keep to her maiden name here."

"Must go," Tony said. He dumped her case on the steps of the Nurses' Home and kissed her cheek. "Why aren't you a nice Jewish girl who makes chicken soup like my mother made?" he said lightly.

"Can't stand chopped liver," she said, and laughed. "In any case, Bea says that you have a girl. I'm glad."

"We have a lot of the past in common," he said. "Miriam has nobody left."

"Shouldn't you look to the future now? All this will be over soon; next year, perhaps, and we shall have peace for the first time for five years."

"Have you wondered what the face of peace will look like? Deprived and scarred and bitter, Emma. I think I prefer life as it is, before anyone counts the cost."

"Be happy, Tony," she whispered, and dragged her case into the foyer.

The room to which she was allotted as a senior staff nurse in the Nurses' Home of the Princess Beatrice Hospital was vastly superior to the one she had at Heath Cross. The Princess Beatrice was old and dignified and famous as a teaching hospital all over Europe, possibly the world, but the Sector Hospitals, set up in any building that could be adapted to wartime use, for surgery and the admission of hundreds of wounded from the bombings on London and the men returning from D-Day battles, lacked many amenities taken for granted in the parent hospital.

As Emergency Medical Service Hospitals, they were staffed by teams from all the leading London hospitals, each team with nurses and medical students in training, working in separate departments and wards so that they could continue to be taught in the manner of their own hospitals.

Heath Cross had been a Victorian mental hospital in Surrey that was taken over at the beginning of the war. It had never completely thrown off the overtones of the old sprawling mental hospital but under it had evolved a very efficient Emergency Medical Service Hospital.

Emma felt restless as she did each time she moved from Beatties to Heath Cross or back again to London. Seeing Tony again brought back so many memories of Heath Cross, of the long boring waiting for the balloon to go up before the invasion of Europe when the wards were ready but empty of patients, and the enforced leisure was filled by long off duties spent within a siren call of the hospital and twice weekly dances to old gramophone records.

It had been a bad time and a good time too, with hard work and friends from her own set who had begun training at the same time. Bea Shuter had worked with Emma in Bristol before they were old enough to do a full SRN training at a teaching hospital. A hundred years ago?

Emma wondered if the time at Beatties and Heath Cross would fade in her memory once the war was over and the twelve hundred patients trickled back to Heath Cross and the psychiatrists. Beatties could revert to the well- disciplined and sometimes harsh but wonderful training regime.

She smiled. It would never be the same again. Discipline had been relaxed when the Administration had lost total control of the trainees out in the sticks, and everyone had been called on to do far more than they would have been allowed to do in peacetime.

She knew that all the horror of the wounded of D-Day, when she worked in the the theatre where Guy Franklin

6

was doing surgery and Tony gave anaesthetics, had made a lasting impression on her and she had really grown up at that time.

Emma stared at the waving tree outside her window but saw nothing but Guy's face on that terrible night when it seemed that there would be no end to the convoys of ambulances bringing in the wounded from the Normandy beaches. He was tired and revolted and at the end of his self-control after twelve hours working on whatever ghastly wounds confronted him.

She had been the strong one then, seeing his need when they went off duty that morning, too tired but too stimulated to sleep. They were alone and walked on the Heath. She had taken the lead and they had made love among the young bracken, committing themselves to each other in passion and exhaustion and "the pain of too much tenderness".

She shrugged. The view of the back of A Block, the clinic for venereal diseases, wasn't as pretty as the view of the grounds, the poplar trees and the distant vista of the Heath that she had enjoyed for so many months in Surrey, but the smells and sounds of traffic by the hospital gates in Southeast London and the distant whine of trams were familiar and brought a kind of welcome and she felt at home.

Each place had its charms and she could see in her imagination the softly waving fronds of bracken that had made a bed the first time that she and Guy made love. At least that will never die, she thought. We have shared so much and suffered together and are really in love. Soon, when I've taken my exams, we can be married.

"Emma!" Bea Shuter burst into her room and slammed the door shut after her. "Am I glad to see you! This place is like a morgue after Heath Cross and I need a friend. Sister

Morgan keeps making snide remarks about girls who get married on the sly, to foreigners who could be anything but what they say they are back home, and who might get pregnant at any minute. I'd have to have a virgin birth or whatever it would be when a husband has been away for months!"

"I think she had a big disappointment over a Canadian major who had a wife tucked away in Toronto. She thinks everyone who came over the Atlantic must be a louse," said Emma.

Bea sat on the bed and held up the modest nightie that Emma had put ready for bedtime. "No wonder you wouldn't wear that fabulous black nightie that your old boy friend gave you."

Emma snatched it away. "I suppose you've worn it out by now! At least it went to a good cause."

"It made wonderful window-dressing but it's gone now." Bea chuckled. "I didn't know that Dwight was so earthy. After our last night together before he went to France, he bundled it up, smelling of Chanel Number Five and me. And him," she added reflectively. "He said he'd take it with him."

"He sounds like Napoleon, who wrote to his wife telling her not to wash before he came home as it made her more desirable. Or was it Nelson and Lady Hamilton? I forget."

"Not many of our set in London," Bea said. "Some at Heath Cross and two down with Tony and the urological team at the Beechmast School."

"I met him as I came in," Emma said. "He goes back this evening. Guy will be here soon but has to be back at Heath Cross tonight as he has a list tomorrow."

"You see as little of him as I do of Dwight," Bea protested. "Why don't you marry the man and have done with Beatties? You could follow him around, which is more than I can do with Dwight now he's in France at the forward air base."

"I want to finish my training," Emma said firmly. "I know I shall see less of him now I'm in London again, but I go back to Surrey in late autumn and if he isn't posted elsewhere by then, he said he'd rent a cottage where we can be together in off duty times." She sighed. "It's not good making do with the odd hotel bedroom. I feel like a tart and I long for a home where we can be together and shut the door on prying eyes."

"When do you meet his family?"

"Next month, when I have a long weekend off. We have to be very discreet and act like a virginal engaged couple, but at least we shall announce our engagement. Even Beatties can't object to an engagement."

"What about your Aunt Emily?"

"She's wonderful. I took Guy down to meet her and she eyed him up and down and said, 'You'll do.' We had the house to ourselves during the day as she went to work as usual, and it was heaven. Poor Guy saw nothing of the Isle of Wight beyond Ryde and Newport when we did her shopping. The restrictions there are less, but the coastline is still covered with concrete and iron. The fences take away all views of the sea in areas where they built a lot of Mulberry Harbour that was towed to France for the D-Day landings."

"Does she know?"

"Nothing said, but she gives me a few old-fashioned looks and she does approve of Guy. I have told her that we'll be married as soon as I finish my training next year and she seemed to like the idea. She said dryly, 'The sooner the better', as if she had an idea it might be urgent!"

9

"Back to the treadmill," Bea said. "You on nights?"

"As from tomorrow but I'm off until then."

"See you after duty this afternoon and for breakfast. I have a day off and you know you can never sleep before the first night on duty, so we can go up to town."

The black silk stockings, the cinched-in belt with the ornate silver buckle, and the neatly folded blonde French pleat had a last check in Emma's mirror, and Bea hurried out, back to men's surgical. It seemed to be her home each time she returned to Beatties, but this time as a senior staff nurse, wearing the distinctive frilled caps that were the envy of lesser ranks among the nurses.

They look as if they've been crimped with my Grannie's gophering iron, Emma thought as she assembled her own cap for the next day. Aunt Emily had it now and had shown Emma how the frills of the white starched aprons of the four Victorian girls in the Darwen family had been gophered after ironing.

"It took a lot of work but it was a matter of pride, especially with your mother. Clare was always vain and expected more than the others, but your Gran was fair to us all and never complained of her lot even when she was up half the night, ironing."

Emma paused in her unpacking, and faced the fact that sooner or later she must visit her parents in Bristol. Not with Guy, she had decided long ago. They would have to know when they married, but until then, she wanted no nagging from her mother about how girls of her age were lucky to get a man now that the war had taken so many, and she should snap him up and leave nursing. She'd heard it so often when Phillip, the boy she'd known from schooldays had wanted to marry her and she'd sent him away.

The leaves on the plane trees were dusty and she knew

that after a few hours in London, the hem of her white petticoat would be rimmed with grey, but as the weather was still warm at the end of summer, she picked out a white jacket and the pale turquoise summer dress that she knew would please Guy and hurried to meet him by the gate.

"Both early, as usual," he said and his smile was all that she could wish for. He kissed her briefly on the lips and held her hand as they sat in the back of the cab that he had waiting.

"How long have we?" she asked.

"Never long enough," Guy said. "I have to get back this evening and I'm hungry."

"So it's tea at Lyons and a quick look at the National Gallery and goodbye at Victoria? No car?"

"Someone drained the tank last night and even my concession coupons won't run to more until next week, but I brought some notes I can look at in the train."

"A pity you can't stay. I'm off until tomorrow night when I report to the children's ward."

"If only we had a place of our own. It's agony feeling you so close and knowing that all we can share today is a cup of tea and a toasted tea cake!"

"When I go back to Heath Cross," she replied gently. "We have more than many people, darling, and we have for ever when this is all over. Are we going to Devon next month?"

"Yes, they know we are coming but even that will be a bit fraught. I know my family and love them dearly, but they would be shocked if they knew we were lovers."

"If they love you, they will take one look at you and guess," she said, dryly. "It's a bit like Aunt Emily. While it is never put into words, the situation doesn't exist, but she made sure that we had lots of time alone."

"It was the happiest time of my life," he said, simply.

"Coventry Street Corner House all right, guv? The road's up in the Strand."

"Fine. In fact, if it's easier for you, put us down here." They walked past the boarded-up ruins by Leicester Square and the tired notices outside the Windmill Theatre that now bore proud stickers across the names of the artistes. "WE NEVER CLOSED" they read, and a few servicemen were already queuing for the next static nude show.

The Windmill, and the Whitehall Theatre where farces, comic and sentimental plays, and Phyllis Dixie shows made London and her adopted sons and daughters during the Blitz laugh and forget the war for an hour or so, had scars and lack of paint but were known wherever service- men and women talked of leave in London.

The list of available food was short and uninteresting. "Everything on toast," Emma said, and sighed.

"Not everyone has the imagination of Aunt Emily," Guy said. "The sausages, she would have put in one of those glorious toad-in-the-hole dishes she gave us and the eggs . . ."

"Don't!" Emma begged. "Do you think it possible that the Welsh rarebit could be more than semolina brushed with a tinge of cheese? On toast, of course."

"Egg and chips will be coming out of my ears soon. It's the safest and best thing I ever get in cafes at this time of day," Guy said, and ordered a double portion, while Emma toyed with baked beans, and a sausage that she tasted and then left on the plate.

The coffee was good and they lingered over second cups and Danish pastries which were fresh and filling. Guy looked up at the wall clock and raised his eyebrows. "Why does two hours with you seem like five minutes, and two hours back in my room at Heath Cross seem like

12

eternity?" Emma smiled wistfully. "Was it a mistake to go all the way?" he asked. "Sometimes it's too much to bear, knowing you, every wonderful part of you, and having to go away again. After you come back to Surrey, I'll rent a cottage near Epsom and we can live there. You can give up nursing and be there with me."

"I can't get away unless I'm married, Guy. You know that if I wasn't nursing, I'd have to do some other work. They do check and follow up people who try to dodge the system, and I can't be married yet as I do want to finish my training." She saw his frown. "It's a wonderful dream and I can't wait for the war to be over and to be married and have a family, but it isn't over and neither of us knows where we may be sent."

He forced a smile. "Like night duty with kids? Or back in the services for me?"

"That's impossible! I know you are in the Reserve, but you are needed here. They'd never take you for work overseas, would they?" The taste of synthetic sweetening from the Danish pastry was repeating, and Emma swallowed hard.

"There are rumours. There's an awful lot of clearing up to do over there and many hospitals need organising and good surgeons." He shrugged. "After Heath Cross, I am a very useable commodity, for work in the field as they say, and sometimes it really did feel like working in a field!"

"It brought us together," Emma said. "After the war we shall look back and wonder at all we went through, but now we have to plan for the future. When I am an SRN, we can go anywhere together and work together, here or abroad."

"You go all starry-eyed over the unpredictable future, but I can't see that far. I see as far as Devon and you coming back to Heath Cross in the autumn."

13

Emma shivered and it wasn't because the day in late summer was becoming cool. "You sound as if there's a chasm beyond that point. Come on, you'll miss your train and I must get back to meet Bea when she comes off duty. I think she has the blues. Dwight has been away for two months and she says the bombers are out every night pounding enemy positions, ever further east and they've lost a few Flying Fortresses."

"Come to the station, Emma." Guy grinned. "It's the only place where I can kiss you in public as if we are to be parted for years."

"You've be watching *Brief Encounter*."

"That poor bloke didn't make it," Guy said. "And she had a husband. You haven't anyone hidden away that I should know about? It cramps a man's style."

"You're the only one who wants me," Emma said with a wicked smile.

"Don't you believe it, and sometimes I can't believe my luck. That's our bus. I haven't time to search for a taxi."

Victoria Station was, as usual, teeming with people and several ambulances waited by one platform while a slow procession of carriages drew up.

"That's the platform for trains from the coast, rather like the old boat train when tours started from Victoria to the continent."

"I've never been abroad," Emma said.

"You've lived abroad on the Isle of Wight," Guy teased her" "Strange people over there but at least you understand the language."

"Do you speak other languages?" she asked, suddenly aware that good French might be a factor in sending doctors to France.

"I spent a summer in France and I can get by," he said

carelessly. "All I can say at this moment is *je t'aime* and that's *beaucoup*."

He kissed her and held her close, their bodies tense with longing and Emma felt as if she wanted to cry. "I'll ring tomorrow," he said at last and hurried to catch his train, while Emma watched the stretcher cases coming off the reserved carriages, escorted by Army nurses and military guards.

Guards? She looked again and saw a soldier with a rifle climb into one of the full ambulances, with an orderly and an Army nursing sister in a red and grey shoulder cape and smart cap. An armed guard by the platform eyed Emma with suspicion, and before she backed away, she heard a man on a stretcher call out in German.

Germans in England? Enemy wounded being cared for in English military hospitals? It was unbelievable. She tried to recall if they looked very ill and remembered only that there were no intravenous drips in position. Each man was well covered with army blankets as if the men were over the worst of their wounds or had to be shipped out in a hurry and were still to be assessed.

She hardly saw the broken walls and piles of ordered rubble by the roadside as the bus took her back to within a hundred yards of the Princess Beatrice Hospital, and she walked past the porter's lodge in a dream.

Bea was coming off duty for the evening and listened while Emma told her what she had seen. "It makes sense," she said. "I resent them getting better treatment than they gave our men but Dwight says they have little food and no decent field dressings. He's seen a few being interrogated. They are an unproductive burden, getting in the way of medical personnel trying to treat acute cases, eating and using up meagre resources. They take hospital space as our armies advance and the chronic cases clog up the system,

15

and when they are better, fill the prisoner-of-war camps which are already overflowing. More and more food and supplies have to be flown in and some of the Yanks are now complaining they are no longer fighter or bomber pilots, but grocery delivery boys." She giggled. "I told my darling husband I thought he'd make a good delivery boy and he said I needed my butt slapped!" She sighed. "If only he were here to do that."

"Any sign of leave?"

"He hopes to bum a lift from the RAF soon, just for forty-eight hours. I've asked Sister Dart who's been promoted to Admin and has a boy friend in the American Army, to arrange a bit of extra time off if he rings her direct. She's met Dwight and they got on well, so here's hoping!"

"Will you stay at your father's apartment in St James's?"

"No. Pa is very important now and has to have a pad close to Whitehall for his pet VIPs and whenever I ask if the flat is free, it isn't. Mostly Dutch and French diplomats and some Americans but on the whole not the sort I want to make small talk with when I have my wonderful hunk of a husband by my side, eager to be alone with me."

"So you'll be slumming at the Carlton or the Ritz?"

"Anywhere with four walls still standing, with hot water and good food," Bea said with feeling. "And a comfortable bed," she added, dreamily. "Room service and Dwight in bed is all I want."

"Listen!" Emma opened her bedroom door. "What was that?" she called.

"Staff Nurse Shuter wanted in the office," the nurse said. "Is she there? Sister said it was urgent."

Bea turned pale. "I wish I'd never agreed for Dwight to ring the office. My stomach does somersaults at the best of times when I have to report there and I dread wondering

16

if it might be bad news. Coming!" she said and put her uniform cap on again.

Emma began a letter to her Aunt Emily but couldn't concentrate. Suppose it was bad news? What if Dwight was shot down, injured or even killed? Her mouth was dry. What if Guy was recalled for service and had to go to France? She would feel as Bea did now, jumpy each time anyone in authority summoned her to the office, even if it was just to tell her that she was changing ward duties or was being transferred to one of the Sector Hospitals.

She turned to a textbook on paediatric nursing so that she wouldn't be completely ignorant when she went on duty to the children's ward, knowing that she dreaded it. To be in charge of a ward at night, when she had hardly known any small children and had changed only one baby in her whole nursing career, had made her ask to be on day duty for a while before doing night duty there. As a ward sister she would be in charge during the day and she wouldn't have to depend on a roving night sister for support if anything went wrong.

She had been told curtly that it was about time she learned to deal with babies, and must be professional enough by now to cope with any age or sex in any hospital situation.

"Emma?" The call could have been desperation or joy, but was certainly loud and clear. "Help me pack a few things. He's *here*! What luck that I have a day off and a morning after that with an afternoon extension, by kind permission of my friend in Admin, bless her." She opened a drawer and looked at the neatly folded underwear, then stirred it as if not sure what she was looking for but knew that she must pack. "The car comes in half an hour. No, less than that," she yelped.

"Get changed," Emma said and pushed her away and

17

opened the door to the closet. "Wear the grey suit and the gold blouse. You may eat somewhere smart tonight. Men get hungry, so it won't be all love and Champagne."

"Hark at you! What happened to the girl who had never been kissed, never been . . ."

"I had you as a bad example," Emma said calmly. "Get your toilet bag and that new bottle of scent and anything else you might need in bed."

"Crikey! Nearly forgot. Dwight would divorce me if I got pregnant just now."

"Clean panties, bra and waist petti, the Hedy Lamar nightie, handkerchiefs and spare stockings and some lighter shoes for indoors, and you'd better take a warm coat. Love never feels the cold, Aunt Emily says when she sees my goose pimples, but they aren't attractive and the evenings are getting colder."

"Yes, Granny," Bea said, and hugged her. "What will I do without you after the war? You and Guy must come to the States to work. I shall insist."

"You have exactly six minutes," Emma said sternly. "Less lipstick and a touch more face powder to hide that disgusting healthy glow. Anyone would think you were meeting someone important." She thrust the case into Bea's arms. "Give him my love; lots of it," Emma said.

"Not too much!" said Bea. "He'd fancy you if I wasn't in the way!"

"Have a lovely time."

"See you soon." Bea ran down the stairs and the Nurses' Home was silent. Emma shrugged and went down to supper and to listen to music in the common room.

A porter glanced round the music room and beckoned. Emma went to answer the phone and to her surprise, found Aunt Emily speaking.

"Is anything wrong?"

18

"Well, I don't know. Can you hear me? I can hear you as if you were in the next room," Emily said with faint surprise.

"I can hear you too. What's wrong?"

"It may be nothing but your mother wrote and said your father has been ill. She said very little about him, as usual, but grumbled that she'd had to give up certain activities for a week or so and said what a lot of work he had caused her. She said she wouldn't be telling you as she was sure he was putting on an act to get sympathy, but reading between the lines I think he had a heart attack."

"You think I ought to go?"

"Not in a great hurry, as he's over whatever it was, but soon. I've never had much time for your father and I know it hasn't been easy for you, Emma, but if anything happened, you'd feel guilty and your mother would have a moan to keep her tongue busy for years."

"Thank you for letting me know. I dread going there but I was thinking of going on my nights off. I shall have three nights off together, so I can stay there for at least two days, depending on transport."

"You're a good girl, Emma. Just don't let Clare make you promise anything you know you can't do, like giving up nursing to stay with her. We all give in to what we hate when emotions are high and Clare is good at getting her own way." She paused but Emma sensed that she had more to say, so she didn't reply, and Emily went on. "Get leave soon, Emma. You ought to see him soon."

"You have one of your presentiments?"

"Yes. If he's had a heart attack, the chances are that he'll have another, especially if Clare nags him and makes him feel guilty. She never could make for a calm atmosphere, even as a child, amd you know from your own

19

nursing experience that a contented mind breeds health in these cases."

"I have no intention of giving up nursing. If Guy can't persuade me to do so, then my mother hasn't a chance," Emma said firmly.

"I'm glad he's tried, but time enough to make an honest woman of you when you've earned your stripes, as they say." There was a hint of a chuckle as Emily hung up and left her niece with no chance to retort.

Emma looked in her diary. If she asked for her first nights off soon, on compassionate grounds, she could go to the Island and still be able to set aside the time for the Devon visit in six weeks time. She had asked to count that as a few days from her annual holiday, to make sure it was firmly booked and wouldn't be changed as normal off duty might be. She sighed with relief. Nothing must interfere with that.

Chapter 2

The railway station on the outer ring of Bristol was even less attractive than Emma remembered from her first glimpse of it at the beginning of the war. Grimy gas holders dominated one side and the roofs of depressed-looking houses the other, black with soot from the steam engines that passed by their windows. The station platform was muddy and littered with scraps of paper and rubbish. She wished that her train had come into Temple Meads, the busy mainline station in the centre of the city, but repairs and reconstruction after the bombings made some platforms unusable and many trains into Bristol were diverted to the smaller branch lines.

It was quite a long walk to the bus stop and she knew she would have to change again if she wanted to get nearer to her parents' house in the suburbs. When it arrived, the bus was nearly empty and she sat at the back where she could keep watch on her case stowed away in the luggage rack.

Empty spaces and the fragile façades of bombed buildings were beginning to mellow. Nature covered war's shame with lichen and buddleia and the odd rogue dog-rose so that the rubble was partly hidden. Fresh damage had been caused by the arrival in that spring, of 1944, of Hitler's secret weapon, the pilotless flying V bombs, that buzzed overhead, cut out the engine and dropped

21

in an arc to do indiscriminate damage. It had become second nature to hear the bomb and note where it was when the engine stopped. If it was overhead, there was no danger as the falling arc of movement would take it further away, but any that stopped short of the watchers might easily, as they said in London during the Blitz, "Have your name on it."

Women walked about the poorer districts in a mixture of mud-coloured clothes in an attempt to suit the weather, looking uniformly shabby. Emma felt almost too smart in her blanket coat and velvet beret, both of which she had made from unrationed bedcovers and scraps from an old dress of Aunt Emily's.

The change of bus brought a change of scene. The houses were newer and ranks of shops were full of people queuing for whatever was off ration. She glanced into her purse to make sure she had the emergency ration cards that she could use when away from the hospital.

The road leading to the house was unmade. Houses being built before the war were now in limbo, and would stay uncompleted until the hostilities were really over, but the roads and sidewalks fronting the completed houses were finished and the pebble-dashed buildings looked neat and modern. The barrage balloon on the concrete pad on the rise of land above them was tethered close to the ground and the anti-aircraft gun was shrouded in camouflage netting that hadn't been removed for business for several weeks.

Emma pushed open one of the double gates leading to the short drive which led to the back door and a shed housing bicycles and garden tools. She pressed the bell and the sugary chimes announced her arrival but there was no human sound from within. She found her key and opened the door, and called, "Anyone at home?" but knew that the house was empty. Although she was relieved, she felt a sense of anticlimax. If both her mother and father were out, then perhaps Aunt Emily's presentiment was unfounded and Clare Dewar had exaggerated to gain attention. The small room she used when at home was tidy and cold. She unpacked the few things she thought would be needed and went downstairs, after peeping into the other bedrooms.

A small fire was glowing under a layer of coke and Emma put more coal on it to make the sitting room habitable, then saw the note on the table.

"As you will be here, I'm going out until this evening. There's bread and cheese and cake and you can cook the sausages and beans in the fridge for your father when he comes home. I'll see you later, but if I didn't get out of the house sometimes, I'd go mad. If only I could go away and live in a room of my own, I'd be content. He'll come home by car, but I have to take the bus."

No . . . "looking forward to seeing you, good of you to come all this way". The bitterness was almost tangible. Emma grabbed her purse and key and hurried out of the house. At the end of the next road was a shop, a Post Office and a fish and chip shop, and she was hungry. She pulled her bike from the shed and hoped she was in time to buy something hot before the shop closed. She also took some old newspapers to give the proprietor as wrapping paper was scarce and it would keep the food hot while she cycled home.

It was a good idea, as the fish and chip shop had run out of newspaper and unless customers had their own or a container to put the fish in, they couldn't be served. The small piece of greaseproof paper round the fish would be inadequate.

"Can I have all that?" The woman serving looked pleased. "I'm serving this lady first as she brought paper but there will be enough for you if you don't want to go away to fetch your own, and you can think yourselves lucky!"

Nobody accused her of jumping the queue and Emma rode back with the smell of rock cod and chips trailing the bicycle.

She laid the table for one while the fish was keeping hot in the oven and made toast from the grey National bread, spreading it with Marmite to give it flavour.

Gradually, the room warmed up and she could relax with good food and the silence of the house. I wonder why my mother was anxious to know which train I would take, she thought. "Come as early as you can," she'd said, but must have known that she wouldn't be there to greet her. Emma washed the dishes and saw with wry amusement that a bowl of potatoes sat on the draining board with some raw carrots and a scraping knife, obviously a hint for her to clean and peel them for the evening meal. She looked in the larder and found a packet of dried milk. She had brought six eggs with her that had been a present from an ex-patient, so she made a batter of eggs, dried milk and flour as she had seen Aunt Emily do, and when she heard a car stop by the gate, and saw her father climb out slowly, the sausages were browning nicely in the crisp batter, the vegetables were ready and the beans hot in the oven.

"What are you doing here?" Alan Dewar said. "Clare didn't send for you, did she?"

"No, I had nights off, which makes it worth coming all this way. I have tomorrow off and go back the day after." Neither of them showed any sign of pleasure at the meeting and they didn't touch.

He picked up a piece of paper from the sideboard

and swore softly. "She said she'd get my tablets from the chemist but the prescription's here."

Emma glanced at the clock and went to the phone. She rang the local chemist and asked if they'd have the tablets ready if she came at once as she had the prescription with her.

"We close in fifteen minutes, but we can do that." The chemist repeated what she read from the prescription and Emma put her coat on again.

"I'll be back in time to give you your supper," she said. "It's not quite ready yet, so sit down and relax until I come back."

A drug to steady the heartbeat and capsules of nitro-glycerin to break under his nose if he has an attack, she thought. Both essential to have at hand if he had the severe heart condition the drugs indicated.

The hill seemed extra steep and she pedalled furiously, but she was in time to collect the drugs and was soon home again. Her father dozed by the fire, his face thinner than she recalled and his mouth had a faintly cyanosed rim. She dished up the food and made tea, as she knew that this was what her father drank at every meal. She laid three places and almost as if she had received a signal, as soon as Emma raised a spoon to the toad-in-the-hole, the door opened and her mother returned.

"Just in time," Emma called. "Supper's ready."

"I had a sandwich with Mrs Hammond," Clare Dewar said, then sniffed and came into the room. "I hope you didn't use the only two eggs I had in the larder," she said accusingly.

"Of course not. I brought some with me," Emma said. "Sit down and have some while it's hot." She served her father with the best portion of crusty batter and browned sausage and pushed the dish of puréed carrots and baked potatoes towards him.

"This is the nicest meal I've had for ages," he said, and helped himself to more. Emma noticed that her mother ate her fair share and more, even though her resentment showed in that Emma had managed to do what she wouldn't dream of doing, cook a decent meal from very few basic ingredients.

"So you found time to visit us at last," Clare Dewar said when Emma began to clear away the plates.

"I'm on nights now, which makes it easier," Emma replied mildly and tipped a few soap flakes into the washing up bowl, vigorously swishing them round until they dissolved. She filled the encrusted dish with cold water to soak away the batter and picked up the dish mop.

"You found time to visit Emily," her mother went on and Emma silently cursed Ivy, the woman who wrote to Clare only when she had something to report that might cause friction. "Who was the nice-looking man you took there? Very superior, Ivy said, and obviously fond of you. She saw you shopping in Newport and saw you get on the bus to Shide but when she asked Emily who he was, she wouldn't say."

"Ivy still writes to you? I wonder she finds the time after spying on her neighbours."

Clare Dewar looked annoyed. "Just as well she tells me a few things or I'd never know," she said. "You never tell me about your friends and as for your father, I could be deaf or dead for all he cares."

"Someone from the hospital needed a break and so did I," Emma said. "Aunt Emily was pleased to put him up. It's nobody who you will meet so calm down. Did you have a good day? Was it something special?"

"I went to the pictures with Mrs Hammond and we had

lunch at Caroline's cafe. She says I ought to please myself more now that your father's over his turn. I thought I'd go mad when he was in bed. The doctor made him stay there for over a week and I had all the running up and down stairs and cooking to do. If you'd stayed in Bristol and done your training here, you could have helped out in your off duty."

"Well, I'm here now and I quite like cooking," Emma said. "You don't have to stay at home during the day, do you? Dad is back at work now, so everything is back to normal as far as him needing any special care, except for his medicines," she added with a glance towards the dresser where the tablets were still wrapped in white paper from the chemist.

"Did you get his prescription? I left it on purpose as I think he can overdo all that. A few days without the tablets won't hurt. Mrs Hammond says that after a while they do more harm than good and he'll feel he's an invalid."

"Mother," Emma said, endeavouring to sound reasonable. "He needs to have those tablets and may need to take them for the rest of his life. The glass phials must go with him wherever he goes as they are what might save his life if he is suddenly taken ill, so promise me, you will do as the doctor says and *not* what that horrible woman tells you!"

"You mustn't call her that. Mrs Hammond talks a lot of sense."

"She knows nothing of medicine and feeds you with old wives' tales that are dangerous. Dad is ill and will be for a long time, but with these tablets he can cope with his condition. With care, he can live for a long time. I was glad to see that someone gives him a lift to and from work. He really should never ride his bike again, especially up that hill." She saw that her mother

27

was unconvinced. "I'm serious, Mother, and I *do* know about such things."

Clare Dewar tightened her lips. "You always did take his side. I think he's a sham half the time and does it to get at me. If only I could go away and live in just one room, that would be heaven. I don't like Bristol any more than I liked that house he took me to when we were first married, up north by that canal."

"You were keen to have this house," Emma reminded her.

"The house is all right," she admitted, "but it takes such a time to get anywhere here. It's half an hour on the bus to the town centre and then a long walk to any of the cinemas that are left."

"At least you weren't bombed," Emma said. "Do you still go to the clothing centre?"

"Twice a week. It's easy now as the stocks of clothes have grown again and there are fewer families in need even after the doodlebugs, but I go there for company and we have a good laugh." She glanced sideways at Emma to note her reaction. "It's awkward you being here, as tomorrow is a big day. Lady Cousins is coming to talk to us about emergency centres she visits. You can come too if you like."

"I think I've wasted my time coming here," Emma said. "I was alone all day even though you insisted that I came as early as possible, and tomorrow will be no better. I thought I could take you out somewhere but I can see that you don't want to do that. I'm going to bed now as I was on duty last night and have had no sleep." She picked up her cardigan and made for the door, deciding to warm her feet by the fire before she went upstairs as the evening had turned chilly and there was no heat in her bedroom.

"You can fill the coal scuttle before you go up," her

28

mother said. "He used to do it but the doctor told him not to lift heavy things so I have it all to do. It's all very well for the doctor to say he needs to be kept warm. I have the work to do and coal fires aren't really necessary until November or December if it's mild. She looked at the clock and seemed embarrassed. "I did say I'd look in for five minutes to see Mrs Barker up the road, so if you're going to bed, I think I'll do that."

"Go on then," Emma said. "I'll get the coal and set the table for breakfast, but after breakfast I'm going back to London. Why not face the fact that we have nothing left in common? You resent it if I stay away and have no time for me when I come here. I shall spend my next days off in Devon with a friend. You may have a letter from Ivy later when I go to see Aunt Emily but it will be a long time before I come to Bristol again."

"Don't talk to me like that. Mrs Hammond says . . ."

"I don't want to hear what that bloody woman says. She's brainwashed you."

Emma slammed the door behind her and picked up the brass coal scuttle, digging furiously into the heap of fuel in the coal house at the back of the kitchen. She was close to tears and longed to hear Guy's voice and to feel his arms round her. She filled two extra buckets and stood them in the kitchen, then went into the warm sitting room where her father sat reading the *Evening News*.

"That was a beautiful meal, Emma," he said. "Take after Emily, I expect, but not your mother." He gave a wry smile. "Emily was the best of that bunch in my opinion, but your mother was a good-looker in those days and seemed the one for me." He heard the front door slam and knew that his wife had gone out. "I want to show you something," he said, and fetched a metal box from his bedroom.

29

"What's that?" asked Emma.

"Your mother thinks it contains just my war medals and a few bits and pieces from the other war, so she never asks about it," he said. "I want you to see these documents." He took out several stiff manilla envelopes. "When I married your mother, I promised that she would never want and that I'd provide for her until she died. I took out several insurance policies and when I die, she'll be better off than she is now." He eyed his daughter shrewdly. "You know I haven't long, don't you? When I'm gone, Clare will make a lot of fuss, saying that I have left her with nothing. I know her too well not to know that. I want you to see what I have done for her and I've sent a letter to the solicitor who arranged the buying of this house. He'll see to everything and he has a copy of my will. A lawyer came to the factory and made out simple forms for a lot of us when the bombings were bad, which will be legal and easy to prove."

"Why tell me?"

"You must never feel your duty is with her. She'd wring you dry as she has me. She'll be fine on her own and you must keep away. Get yourself a nice man and enjoy your work, but forget about us. I suppose I've been weak not taking notice of you but if I was nice to anyone, we had rows, and I like a bit of peace."

"You must take care and be sure to take the tablets," Emma said. "I'm glad that you go to work by car now. Do as the doctor says and take no notice of that awful friend of Mother's and her half-baked ideas." She yawned. "Can I get you some cocoa before you go to bed?" she asked.

"That would be nice. I'm a bit done up tonight. Put this box away in my wardrobe under the magazines. It's a relief that you have seen the papers."

It was nearly eleven when Mrs Dewar came home and

found the house in darkness, the fire banked up and the table ready for breakfast. The rest of the eggs that Emma had brought were in a bowl by the stove, as if waiting for whoever wanted boiled eggs. She put them in the larder. "They'll do for his supper," she said, and in the morning, she made porridge and cut bread for toast and didn't offer either her husband or Emma anything more.

"You needn't go back," Clare Dewar said. "We could go out this evening if you like. I've wanted to see that new musical at the Hippodrome but I hate coming home on the bus after dark."

"I'm going back," Emma said. "Why not go with your friend?"

"She has a relative coming to stay for a day or so," Clare said as if she had heard bad news. "I shall go there the day after tomorrow but after the meeting this afternoon, I shall have nobody to talk to."

"You could do some cooking. Make a nice cake or some jam tarts for Dad. I brought some jam and put it in the larder."

A car horn sounded and Alan Dewar picked up his newspaper and hat and went to the door. He waved to the driver to let him know he had heard him arrive then turned to Emma. "Remember what I said." He took her hand and squeezed it. "Goodbye, Emma."

Impulsively, with a feeling of finality, Emma kissed his cheek.

"Goodbye. Take care of yourself," she said.

"I should have known better than to leave you two alone last night." The resentment was palpable. "I suppose he grumbled that I neglect him and that he's much worse than I admit?"

"No," Emma said quietly. "He talked about the past and showed me the medals he won in the last war and

31

said that you had been very pretty and the one person he wanted to marry." Emma regarded her mother with a serious expression. "He's stayed with you all this time, even when you don't get on together. He's given you what he could and it's a pity you don't give him any credit for that. I think he's ill and if you want to keep him well, you'll look after him better and be a bit warmer."

Mrs Dewar poured more tea with a shaking hand. "You don't know what I've missed in life," she said. "I stay with him out of duty but I wish I could go away in one room and be independent."

"Where would you go?" Emma asked relentlessly. "You've never trained for a job and you escaped war work because you took in a lodger from the factory for six months and had the RAF phone here until they fixed their own office up by the barrage balloon. Aunt Emily has worked hard for years and never grumbles and you might have been better if you'd had more to do."

"Coming here stirring up trouble and being all over him as if you really cared about him," Clare Dewar said in angry embarrassment.

"If you've finished with the teapot, I'll wash up and pack," Emma said. "I doubt if I shall come here again unless there's an emergency, but I'll write sometimes."

She put her clothes in the suitcase together with the few things she'd left in the room from earlier visits and looked round the bedroom that to her was as featureless as a strange hotel room. She took down the picture of the shepherd boy and the brass rubbing that she'd done on a school trip to Westminster Abbey. The gaudy soft toy that Phillip had won for her at a fair on the Island, she left, as it had no place in her future, and she picked up the few books that were all that remained of her sojourns in Bristol.

There was no need for souvenirs of the Home on the Downs, apart from a photograph she had taken of the place. Bea Shuter was her souvenir of that time but even Bea was changing and might soon be gone to America, if the war ended soon. She called goodbye to her mother but there was no reply. On the dining room table, she left her emergency ration card which had three weeks' rations to come and quietly left the house of no good memories.

If the war ended soon? She felt every bump in the road as the boneshaker bus wheezed along to the station. The sun shone on the gas holders and the empty houses. Emma wondered if they minded being exposed to bright light when they looked so sad and shabby. Someone had taken pictures of such scenes by moonlight and achieved a degree of softness and elegance from the gaunt remains and gave them a spurious beauty, but exposed today, it was as if she saw a glamorous nightclub after the revellers had left and the windows were opened to let in light and dispel the rank odour of stale drink and tobacco.

On Victoria Station, she bought a sandwich and tea from a mobile stall and munched the heavy bread and fish paste without noticing what she ate. The queue for the one working telephone was long and she gave up waiting, beginning to think she might have done better to stay in Bristol for another day, but as she came closer to the Princess Beatrice Hospital, she relaxed, her doubts dissipating and her spirits rising.

"Is Mr Franklin available?" she asked over the phone when she got through to Heath Cross and the villa where Guy had a room.

A murmur of voices came and another voice asked who was ringing. "Emma? Guy will be back this afternoon, but try Orthopaedics at Beatties. You may catch him as he's done a case there today."

"Is that David? I thought I recognised your voice. If he comes back and I haven't managed to find him, will you ask him to ring me? I'll be in my room all day."

"Sure. When are you coming back here? We miss you."

"That's the nicest thing anyone has said to me today," Emma replied.

"It's true. I miss you a lot." There was a fairly heavy silence and she laughed, dismissing his serious tone as banter.

"How's Lindy?" she asked and smiled to herself. David had enough to occupy his mind and time with the pretty but vulgar nursing assistant who filled his leisure hours but had an eye for other men.

"Fine," he said shortly. "Try the theatre now and you may catch him."

She raised her eyebrows as the phone went dead. David wasn't very happy. She rang the theatre and after a short wait she heard Guy's voice. "Where are you? I thought you were lost in the bosom of your family."

"I found it was a very inhospitable bosom," she said, "so I came back early."

"Great. I've got the car and we can go to Dorking and stay the night. I'll pick you up at six and we can eat at the Punch Bowl. I'll book dinner when I book the room."

"Wonderful. I was afraid you'd be too busy."

"I'll tidy up a few notes here and phone Heath Cross and tell them I'm unavoidably detained until tomorrow." His voice was eager and full of laughter and Emma closed her eyes and savoured the welling up of love that his voice brought her.

She showered and changed, adding a thin sweater to her summer dress and packing a skirt and jacket to wear that evening. She found the slim gold ring and turned it on

34

her ring finger, as always half-ashamed to act as a married woman when staying in a hotel with Guy.

"No thanks. I had coffee when I was writing the notes," Guy said when Emma came out of the small kitchen carrying a mug. "Didn't want to waste any time," he said softly, and his lips were warm as he enfolded her in a tight embrace. "It's all settled. I rang the hotel and booked a room and dinner." He reached over to the table and took two chocolate biscuits. "I'm starving. There wasn't time for lunch as an accident case wouldn't wait." He regarded a biscuit with interest. "Bea again?"

"Dwight supplies the entire Nurses' Home, but secretly we'd rather have the biscuits that Bea's father sends. They are Swiss and absolutely delicious and these taste all the same. They look nice but lack a certain something." She giggled. "I wish he'd stick to sending Spam and canned sausages, and nylons, of course."

"I won't have you accepting nylons from Yanks," Guy said sternly.

"You wouldn't like to see my legs in thick lisle, would you?"

"I like them anyway you choose to show them," he said. "But thick wool might be an idea to wear on duty to stop all those randy soldiers eyeing you."

"On the children's ward? Bea is the one who nurses soldiers here and they adore her."

"I'll bet they do," Guy said dryly. "It must be torture to have girls like Bea and you nursing them and having to keep their hands to themselves."

"We develop a technique," Emma said, and closed the biscuit tin firmly. "They end up thinking we are nuns or frigid and are inclined to pity our menfolk, if they think we have any."

"That, I don't believe. However, things are changing at Heath Cross. We shall have more long-term patients from the forces now that base hospitals have been set up in France for the acute cases." He looked serious. "Just as well they didn't send all their psychiatrists away when they turned out the mental patients. They'll need them now, and there might be a lot of men who are unhappy and far from home who want female comfort. It can be fraught, as care and compassion can be mistaken for something deeper and so they suffer yet again."

"I have come across that," Emma confessed. "Usually, as soon as they are ready to go home, they change back to what they were before their illness and really want to forget everything and everyone to do with hospital, but one or two try to keep in touch when they leave. One civilian casualty of the fire bombs wrote reams of stupid stuff to me and even tried to come back to see me again, but I had moved down to Heath Cross and my faithful friends, bless them, didn't tell him where I was."

She ran up the stairs to fetch her case and Guy waited in the hall.

"That isn't likely to happen again," she said when they were in the car and driving down to Surrey. "I may work on a ward again next month or whenever they send me down to Heath Cross, but now that I'm more senior I shall not do the more intimate things for patients that sometimes cause trouble."

"How do you feel about nursing German prisoners of war."

"You're joking!" she said but remembered the casualty train at Victoria.

"It's on the cards. I've seen some in other hospitals and there's a lot of work to be done there. As German supplies have got worse, field dressings have become very primitive and a lot of first-aid has to be redone. Several wards at Heath Cross are now given over to wounded servicemen of our own and we had some seconded to us from Macindoe's burns unit to wait between grafts in an atmosphere with which they are familiar, and to have cautious psychiatric help, so we have even more teams of doctors now."

"It will seem strange," Emma said.

"I'll be glad when you go back to Heath Cross," Guy said. "My RAF contacts tell me that a new wave of a worse type of flying bombs has started. It's officially the V2 but is much more powerful and doesn't have that minute after the engine cuts to give warning. The first one landed in Chiswick on September 1st last week, and they intercepted a lot along the south coast, but they obviously have the range of London."

"We all thought that once Paris was liberated last month the Germans would crumble, but they seem even more determined to fight now. Dwight goes on many missions as we push east in Europe and there's talk of him going to some islands in the Pacific to make a base against the Japs. Bea dreads it and it's just as well she's busy. Even the fact that he's been promised leave soon indicates that he'll be moving away even further."

"If I am called up again, you'll be there when I return? Dwight and I are the lucky ones," Guy said when they had finished dinner and were in the pretty, countrified bedroom.

"Have you heard anything?" Emma asked, trying to sound calm.

"Not exactly, but David is going to Paris to set up liaison with the French medics and my languages are good, too."

"Don't!" she whispered. "You are much too valuable here."

"Cheer up. I doubt if it will happen. The war should be over soon, you'll be an SRN and we can get married." He kissed her throat and caressed her body. "I wish we were married now. This is wonderful but until we really tie the knot I shall never feel that you are completely mine."

"I am yours," she whispered. "No ceremony will make any difference."

"Till death us do part?" She stopped his words with a deep and desperate kiss, and their love-making had an edge of sadness.

Chapter 3

"It must be the Pacific," Bea said. "Dwight said he was issued with tropical kit and told to prepare to ferry a bomber a long way. He certainly wouldn't need that in Eastern Europe."

"What about North Africa?"

"No. American forces are massing in the Pacific islands and Montgomery seems to be the man for the desert and Rommel's lot." Bea tipped her case out over Emma's bed.

"Do you mind?" Emma said as an open lipstick rolled under her pillow. "You didn't pack. You just threw things in there."

Bea giggled. "Dwight nearly missed his Jeep. We were in bed when the porter rang to say it was time to go. I don't think my husband is wearing underpants." She held up a pair of Y-fronts. "He shot out of bed and dressed, and left me to pack my things alone and to ring for a taxi to get me back here. Just as well, as it saved last goodbyes and we both hate that." Her face was pale. "I adore that man and if anything happened to him, I'd go mad and kill myself."

"Nothing will go wrong," Emma said in a soothing voice. "You'll be in America next year and this will all be a bad dream."

"Everything could go wrong! He's flying over the sea,

he might be shot down or killed in action and they haven't even had time to have all the right jabs against the diseases they may find there. At least, they have had the jabs but some take a week or so to settle and be effective." She regarded Emma with envy. "It's all very well for you. Guy is safe, and apart from the odd V2 which we all might meet, will be in no danger."

"He hinted that he will be called up from the Reserve to help in a field hospital near Paris. David has already had his orders, but I think he volunteered." Emma looked puzzled. "I can't think why David wants to go. He's doing interesting work here and has a good social life. He's very nice under that casual exterior and I've been glad of his company at times when Guy has been busy."

"I saw him on the ward when he came to see Sister with a parcel from her friend at Heath Cross. She was off duty, so we drank her very good coffee, ate my biscuits and had a long chat." Emma was glad to see the tension slackening as Bea became amused. "He's suffering from wounded pride but also a lot of relief which he hasn't accepted as yet."

"What do you mean?"

"Belinda has ditched him for a very cockney petty officer who has tattoos everywhere."

"I don't believe it!"

"It's true and I'm not really surprised. The man is good-looking and is a strong character who will not let her get away with any shenanigans behind the potting shed with other men. I think she did that to make David jealous and when she finally saw that he wanted her only for passing pleasure and would never marry her she decided very wisely to look elsewhere."

"Poor David."

"Not at all. He'd cooled off a lot and is secretly glad it's all over. It was only a physical thing and she made him

40

laugh when life was grim after Dunkirk." Bea laughed. "Lindy is very smug. She shows her engagement ring to everyone who wants to see it and many who don't, and is buying any spare clothing coupons to get a wedding outfit."

"Do we send a present? I like Belinda and she deserves to be happy."

"What will go with pale blue?" Bea asked. "A horrid but wise choice. The blue rayon suits I've seen are cheap and cheerful but I wonder if she knows they crease like mad." She closed her eyes. "I can see it all. Lindy with an extra layer of pancake make-up, purple lipstick, a half-hat of dyed chicken feathers and a silver paper horseshoe for good luck dangling from her wrist."

"That's not fair. You really are a snob, Bea. I shall send her the new pink blouse that is too big for me. My mother bought it and didn't like it, so handed it to me as if she was doing me a great favour, but it's never been worn and I can parcel it up in white lining paper with a few gold stars stuck on for decoration."

"It's a very good blouse and will make everything else she has look cheap, but I'm sure she'll be pleased." Bea blushed. "I know I say awful things but I sent her some coupons. I hardly need mine as Dwight and my pa send me clothes, so I can spare them. She did a lot for David when he was low and I hope he never forgets, but it wasn't a healthy relationship and I'm sure he'll be back to normal in a few weeks."

"Yes, he'll have another girl friend," Emma said, smiling.

"You think so?" Bea gave her a long, reflective look. "A few flirtations perhaps, but nothing serious. He knows who he wants but he hasn't a hope in hell."

"He told you that?"

41

"Yes, but he didn't need to. I could guess."

"Who?"

"My lips are sealed. I make a good mother confessor."
Bea swept up her scattered toilet things and the crumpled
clothes and went to her own room, and Emma put studs in
her clean cuffs and pulled the frilled cap into shape before
changing for night duty.

After breakfast at eight in the evening, which was
enough to prove just how up-side-down night duty would
be, Emma walked to the end of the long corridor to the
swing doors opening on to a short hallway and then on to
a ward where the lights were already dimmed over the cots
and child-sized beds, except where screens surrounded
two beds and bright lights emitted through the cracks.

With an air of confidence which was far from her real
feelings, Emma advanced to the central desk where the
Day Sister was writing the last of her report. Most of
the beds were occupied and on her way to the ward,
the sounds of weak crying had come from one of the
side wards. Emma was aware from the trolley laid with
gowns and masks outside the door, that the child was in
isolation, probably infectious.

"Most of it's straightforward," Sister said. "Four post-
op tonsils and adenoids who are fine and will probably
demand ice cream for breakfast as promised. Nothing like
it to make a cold compress on the way down, and the most
popular medicine they'll have here. The others are either
bomb casualties recovering and in for a few more days
or medical cases waiting for test results. Two babies who
had Ramstedt's operation for pyloric stenosis are in one
sideward with a Special Nurse giving them two teaspoons
of saline and glucose by mouth every fifteen minutes.
Night Sister will decide when they can take more at less
frequent intervals but you must check that the Nurse has

everything she needs. She will be relieved at midnight for her meal by a nurse from Women's Medical and the day staff will of course take over in the morning."

"Who is in the other sideward, Sister?"

"Two D and V babies," Sister said cheerfully. "Rampantly infectious but barrier nursed and on sub cuts. One has badly scoured buttocks which we are treating with tannic acid compresses, but I hope we can change to castor oil and zinc cream as soon as possible as the tannic acid is sometimes too drying. They have a Special too, and nobody working in the ward must go near the diarrhoea babies. Watch the house physician as he is inclined to slip in there and not wash his hands afterwards. He swears he touches nothing in that room but looks on from afar, but unless we have stringent rules we might have a disaster, and we've never had cross infection in this ward yet! Make him gown up and you must keep away from those two, as you might have to feed the pylorics at times."

The night was less daunting than Emma expected and by morning she was exhausted but pleased with herself. She had changed small babies and they had gone to sleep peacefully, instead of, as she had expected, crying all night after her ministrations. She had soothed the swollen weals of giant urticaria with cool camomile lotion and felt a growing tenderness for her patients.

The two tiny forms of six-week-old baby boys, strapped as if crucified to wooden crosses to prevent them tearing at their dressings, made her want to weep but she took a turn in spoon-feeding them and changing the small nappies. The sunken fontanelles were filling up and the babies, who had been dehydrated when breast milk couldn't pass their stomachs through the pyloric obstruction, were by morning on quarter strength premature baby food every half an hour, and growing increasingly hungry and strong.

The infusions of subcutaneous saline in the other side-ward were working well as the slack muscles absorbed the needed fluid, and one baby was well enough to have saline and glucose by mouth.

Emma gave report and glanced back at the neat and quiet ward. She knew that she could now cope with sick children, but did that mean she'd make a good children's nurse or a good mother? As if she read her thoughts, the Day Sister smiled. "You are good with them because you aren't sentimental about children. They sense your honesty and respond to it. It's the ones who say they adore every little snotty-nosed scrap who fill me with despair," she added. "Never believe that babies are incapable of dominating a situation. They take advantage as soon as they are born!"

Bea came to wake Emma with coffee before she went on duty again the following night. "That really was our last leave together for a while, I had a letter today that he must have posted the morning he left me. I feel limp and a part of me wants sit down and cry but we've been far too busy to have time to mope. I wish that Guy was Orthopaedic Registrar here again. We had a haematoma under a plaster today and it came from a badly tied ligature after a complicated fracture. The plaster was a mess and the pressure had built up almost to crush syndrome level, so now we have to test for possible kidney failure." She shrugged. "I'm glad I don't really like the soldier concerned. It's a bit like a case I nursed early in my training but now I can look at this one with complete detachment."

"I think I might grow to like kids' ward," Emma said.

"Well, don't go all broody and want one of your own!"

"No chance of that. I'll wait until I'm qualified and Guy

and I are married, so that I can relax and give any child I have a loving background and my full attention."

"So long as you don't smother it. Neither of us has done badly in spite of cold parents and if we go the other way, we could do as much harm as emotional neglect does," Bea said. "In my case, I think I would have kicked against a normal upbringing, so my marriage worked out fine. My mother still refuses to have me around when her young gigolos are there, and we seldom see one another." She laughed. "When I have a baby, I shall take it to see 'Grandma' and watch her suffer. I shall dress him in the terrible clothes that American males wear from an early age and hope he burbles with an American accent."

"You never change, Bea," Emma said affectionately. "Have you thought, you might have a girl?"

"Dwight would like boys, so I shall have to visit a witch doctor to make it happen, when it happens, but as from today, I'm a chaste Penelope who will wait for her hero to return and not give in to other suitors."

"He will return safely," Emma said firmly.

"Thank you for that." Bea looked serious. "You had an Irish grandmother, didn't you? I think you too are a bit fey."

"My aunt is. She warned me that my father might be ill and although she hasn't said so and hasn't seen him, she thinks he may die soon."

"Has she looked in her crystal ball for Guy?"

"She doesn't do that. All she said when I told her we'd get married as soon as I qualified, was, 'Make it soon,' but I think that's to spare me insults from anyone who hears that we are lovers." Emma poured more coffee and tried not to think of Emily Darwen's dark eyes that had seemed to hold deep secrets when she said the words.

As she became accustomed to night duty, Emma felt less

tired during the day and spent less of her time sleeping. It was possible to have the morning off duty, to go to the West End by bus or to walk in the park, or to sleep when she came off duty and have time off later, if Guy could meet her. She started sewing, using the precious material that she bought in good stores such as Liberty's, so that anything she made would be of good quality and last for a long time. Not a bottom drawer, she told herself, but she made sure that the garments were pretty enough for a bride, and daydreamed of the time when she could be a real wife with a husband who shared her home.

News from the various war fronts was mixed, with successes and failures but the general thrust of the war seemed to be with the Allies. On the rare occasions when Guy came to the hospital and they had an hour or so together, eating in local cafes or sitting in the music room with other members of staff, Guy kept her supplied with news of friends down at Heath Cross and the changes appearing there.

"I heard from David," he said. "He's busy but wishes he was back here. Sent his love to you, by the way, and his hearty congratulations to me as I told him we would get engaged when we go to Devon. It's only two weeks away now," he said and she wished that they were alone instead of sitting sedately apart listening to Mozart with six other people.

"Does he hear more about the war from where he is?" she asked in an attempt to sound composed.

"There's talk of another assassination attempt on Hitler but they botch it each time. General De Gaulle is in Paris making a provisional government and they think he'll be proclaimed the Head of State soon. It was expected but some top brass aren't all that keen on him. Our bombers and the US air force are pounding away at German towns and bases, and the Baltic countries are seeing which way the wind blows and making truces with the Russians who seem to be doing rather well. Bulgaria has actually declared war on Germany, and with the Russians breathing hot air down their necks, who can blame them? Hitler has to spread his troops a bit thinly now that Russia is taking a lot of his attention and they say he is doing what we did at the beginning of the war, making men too old for active service into a Home Guard."

He frowned. "There are rumours that the people of Warsaw tried to rise up against the Germans and are being crushed with the utmost brutality. Thousands have been killed and a witch hunt is on to kill more. They probably heard of a few German defeats and thought the time was ripe for rebellion, but they got it wrong."

"Bea hears very little from Dwight and misses him a lot, but at least she can talk about him in public," Emma said wistfully.

"We could get married, darling. I know you want to get your State Registration, but is it worth it?"

She moved restlessly. "You know how much that means to me, Guy, and I'll be of far better use when we can be together, wherever we go as two professional people." She smiled. "We can get married the day after I have my results. This place can bleat as much as it likes and throw me out if they don't want a nurse married to a junior consultant in the same hospital."

"Aunt Emily would like to see you safely married," he said.

"I know, but she never nags me about it and I think accepts that she'll have to wait before she can dance at my wedding."

"Did she say that?"

Emma laughed. "Not in so many words but she's put

47

aside the crochet bed cover that she's been making for years. She said she'd finish it when I got married. She still has about two months' work to do on it."

"I'll ring you about the time when we go to Devon. I'm saving up my petrol coupons so that we can drive down, and I can't wait for them to meet you." She walked with him to the car park and they held each other close in the shadow of the gatehouse.

"Not much longer," he said at last. "This *bloody* war! I want to take you to France and Italy, if there's any of it left after it's over, but our honeymoon will have to be in Great Britain. Even Southern Ireland is out and we can eat corned beef and Spam anywhere!"

"At least we have a week away together soon," she said to console him. "I don't know Devon, so I hope the petrol holds out for a few days. I want to see as much as possible."

"We'll explore the countryside. Exeter isn't very accessible after the bombing but there are many smaller towns unharmed. If you can face a few hours shopping with my mother in Exmouth, or wherever she wants to go, she'll love you for life."

"That sounds good. What will you do while we shop?"

"Go with my father on his rounds. He likes that and sometimes I can help, out of my vast experience." He laughed in a self-deprecating way. "After the blood and gore of Heath Cross, at least I can face the odd farmhand mangled in a thresher."

"It's a pity you are so good with orthopaedics," Emma said. "I can see you in general practice with an adoring clientele and grateful patients leaving eggs and rabbits on your doorstep."

"It's a bit like that with my father," he said, smiling. "In a way, I'd like to follow him but I just can't see what

48

will happen after the war." He shrugged. "I've been told that I am good at my hospital work and will make a good consultant, which is a far cry from country practice, so I suppose that is my niche in medicine. As Milton said, I must not . . . 'Have that one talent . . . lodged with me useless . . .' I may find that it is my duty and I do enjoy surgery, but I know that my father would prefer his son to come into the practice with him."

"It must be wonderful to come from a loving family," Emma said. "I hope they like me."

"They will." He took her hand. "Come on, I hate to leave you. We've just time to go down to the ABC cafe for coffee and then I must go back."

The cafe was half empty and the windows steamed up but the tables covered with oil cloth were clean and the coffee hot. Guy lifted the lids over the slots where hot food was ready to take and brought back a helping of treacle pudding, but Emma refused it saying that she would fall asleep over report if she ate it. She watched him with amusement as he swore he hadn't tasted treacle pud for years, and teased him, saying that she would refuse to cook it for him after they were married, in case he put on weight.

"If that's true, I wonder why I love you," he said. "I shall expect my wife to obey very whim. I shall marry Aunt Emily. She would never be so cruel as to refuse me puddings."

"She wouldn't have you," Emma said. "She is a one man woman who has refused a good many proposals from men who have tasted her cooking and seen her comfortable little home."

"I can't think why she never married."

"She loved a man in the first war and he died away in France, not of wounds but of typhoid fever, which somehow seemed unfair. Most of the family had no idea that she loved her Arnold, and my mother dismissed his death as a piece of news that had no relevance to anyone in the family. Emily just settled down to looking after her mother and has had a fairly good and contented life in spite of being a spinster. Her generation accepted fate more easily than we would do," she added. "I suppose death was everywhere and many in big families died, so it was accepted as an act of God."

"If I died, would you marry someone?" Guy said.

Emma looked troubled. "What a thing to say! I haven't married even one husband as yet and I can't think of anyone to take your place."

"It could happen," he said sombrely. "I heard today of two old friends who were killed in raids over Germany."

"But you aren't on active flying service and the bombing here seems to be concentrated on the southern counties with mostly V2s, so surely the danger is less now than when London was the main target?"

"Come on. I have to go and so do you. News of Patrick and Mark and this heavy pudding that I wish I'd never eaten, are making me depressed! We shall all emerge from the war intact and ready to enjoy life," he said firmly.

"I shan't see you again until we go to Devon," Emma said when they kissed goodbye.

"Afraid not. I have a lot of loose ends to tidy before I go on leave, but I'll ring tomorrow." He put a hand in his pocket and drew out a small box. "I bought this and hope you like it. I thought it much nicer than the modern rings and these antiques are snapped up quickly so I couldn't ask for your opinion. If it's not right, we'll buy one when we are on leave. Take it to fit on before we go to Devon and if it's too big or not right for you, you have time to have it altered."

Emma looked at the ruby and turquoise ring and kissed him. "It's perfect," she said. "But I'll examine it carefully and see if it's a good fit. If it's loose, I know a jeweller who was a patient at Beatties who will fix it for me."

Back in her room, Emma slid the ring over her engagement finger and admired it from every angle. The rubies glowed and seemed to give out warmth. As she slipped the ring on to a gold chain and hung it between her breasts, she wondered who had worn it and how it came to be sold. She remembered the necklace and bracelet that Aunt Emily had, a present from her brother who went to America and became a movie star. Such precious things usually were handed down to the next generation and Emma knew that one day the golden jewellery would be hers and she would keep it forever, giving it to her own daughter if she ever had one.

She touched the ring and it felt secure and friendly against her skin. I shall never sell this, whatever happens, she thought, then wondered why she had the thought, as the need would never arise.

The next few nights fled in a sudden burst of activity on the ward and exhausted sleep during the day. Her copy of *The Complete System of Nursing* by Millicent Ashdown, with its practical and sensible instructions about most known medical conditions, became her bible. She read other paediatric notes and books, eventually blessing her time on the children's ward for insight into conditions she previously knew nothing about.

The day before Emma was due to go on leave, Aunt Emily phoned.

"Are you there?" she asked.

"Yes this is Emma Dewar," Emma said for the third time. "Aunt Emily?"

"Oh, it is you. I had a feeling that something might be

wrong and telephoned your mother." She paused as if to gather her thoughts. "You know what I'm like, but this time I think there's real trouble there. Clare said that your father is in hospital again and seemed very put out as she thought he was better."

"She hasn't told me," Emma said. "Is he very ill?"

"I think he is. He collapsed halfway up that hill on his bike and was taken by ambulance to the Bristol Royal Infirmary. Clare says he is half asleep and she can't get a lot of sense out of him, but if I was ill, she wouldn't get a lot of sense out of me, either!"

Emily waited and Emma said slowly, "You think I should go?"

"I think you should ask Guy to ring the hospital as he's medical and they'll tell him more than just say he's as well as can be expected."

"That's right." Emma gave a sigh of relief. "He knows a registrar there and he might help with information."

Guy immediately contacted his friend and rang back. "Bad, I'm afraid," he said. "He's had another attack since admission and is sinking fast. I think you should be there, darling. It's a blow to us both but you need to be there at once. Go tomorrow and let me know how things are."

"But Devon and our week together," Emma murmured.

"I know. It's shattering but you'd not be happy if you didn't do your duty."

"I suppose not."

"Remember, I love you and if there's anything I can do, just call. Do you want me there with you? I could come down the day after tomorrow."

"No, Guy. I must go alone. My mother doesn't know about you and I'd rather keep it that way."

Emma remembered that she had removed all her

belongings from her room in Bristol and had to pack, but her clothes were ready for the holiday in Devon so she had only to put in a toilet bag and a kimono and shut the lid of the suitcase.

I might have to stay for days, she thought with horror, and knew that she dreaded the visit even if her father survived and recovered, but she had seen too many heart cases similar to his not to know the outcome.

Why was he on his bicycle? she wondered as the train took her through windswept countryside and bleakly leaf-stripped trees. Her parents knew that the doctor had ordered him to give up cycling and to take everything more slowly. She was aware that if her father couldn't have a lift to work he would rather risk the bike than stay at home to be nagged.

To be on the other side of hospital life was odd and frustrating and she decided that she would have greater concern for fraught relatives in future. Once again, she blessed her grandmother who had left her enough money for a small allowance and hailed a taxi outside the railway station to take her to her destination.

The house looked as usual, neat, and the net curtains were clean and well-hung in the front windows, but the house was empty. Emma went upstairs to her old room and to her amazement found that there were clothes in the closet and a coat spread over the back of the chair as if someone was living there. She peeped into her father's room and saw the stripped bed and the pile of clean linen on the tallboy. She brought her case upstairs and put it in the empty room, then went down and made some tea. When she had telephoned to say she was coming, her mother had said nothing about a visitor using the small room.

A note on the dining room table told her to go to the

hospital and she took her bicycle from the shed and cycled there, thinking it might be quicker than waiting in the cold for infrequent buses.

The ward was quiet and Emma explained who she was and asked to be shown her father. The nurse took her down between the lines of beds in the long, open ward, and stopped by closed screens. She smiled nervously as if she dreaded being asked about his condition and left Emma on the wooden chair by the bed. The fact that she had been admitted at once, outside the normally rigid visiting hours, indicated that he was very ill and on the danger list.

She touched his hand and looked down at the face she hardly recognised. His eyes flickered open and he gave a half smile. "Good. Good." His speech was slurred but intelligible. Emma squeezed his hand and smiled but said nothing, sensing that the usual platitudes about getting well soon would be an insult. She bent lower to catch his words. "Remember what I said?"

"About the papers?" she asked gently. "I'll do as you told me, when the time comes. I have the address of the solicitor and he'll see to everything. Are you comfortable?" She cast a practised glance over the supporting pillows and found no fault in them. This was a good ward, well-run under careful supervision. "Would you like a drink?"

He shook his head. "Thank you for coming. It's a weight off my mind." For a second there was humour in his eyes. "I shan't keep you long." He closed his eyes and his breathing grew deeper as he slept.

Emma sat by the bed until the Ward Sister came to check his pulse, then followed her to the office. "He asked for you," Sister said.

"I came as soon as I heard," Emma said. "My mother

54

told me nothing as she's inclined to ignore anything painful and doesn't believe that he's as ill as he is."

"He's resting more peacefully than at any time since he was admitted. You've been good for him. Can you stay?"

"I start a week's leave today," Emma said wryly. "I can sit with him but I can't stay with my mother as there is no room." The thought of occupying her father's room was abhorrent and she had no wish to meet whoever was in the spare room.

"Dr Sykes mentioned you. Your fiancé rang him and he told me that you are working at the Princess Beatrice in London. Fetch your gear and there's a room vacant in the Nurses' Home. I'll clear it with admin as you are one of us." Her smile was so friendly that Emma wanted to burst into tears, but she just nodded and murmured her thanks and relief.

Chapter 4

"Did you come straight here?" asked Clare Dewar. "I was out today." She looked at the suitcase at Emma's feet. It was later that evening, and Emma had fetched her case from the house, relieved not to meet her mother there and brought it back to the hospital. She had been with her father all day apart from a brief break when she went out to buy a sandwich. She had been invited to have supper with Dr Sykes in the medical dining room and then would sleep in a room provided for visiting staff in a Victorian house beyond the hospital. Being engaged to a colleague of one of the registrars of the BRI obviously carried weight.

"I've been here for most of the day after I saw your note," said Emma. "I came here on my bike and found somewhere to stay, cycled back and collected my bag."

"Found somewhere to stay? You'll come back with me tonight," Clare Dewar said. "Found somewhere to stay indeed, when there's a room waiting for you in your own home." Her complacent smile vanished. "I suppose you were upset when you saw that your room was occupied? You can have your father's room. It just needs the bed being made up again."

"That's his room and if they find that he can go home, he will need bed care, as he will be an invalid," Emma said firmly.

"He won't be coming home," her mother said, but sounded almost guilty.

"We can't know that," Emma said gently. "You have to take things day by day and hope that he'll be better, even if he is as ill as this."

"I can't look after him. I've told the Sister that I can't nurse him as I've had to take in someone billeted on me by the government. I want him kept in hospital, in the one nearer our house." She worried the finger that had a blackened half nail, a relic of a childhood accident. It had always annoyed her and was usually kept out of sight under one of the many pairs of gloves that preserved her vanity. "They asked how many rooms we had and I said I had to keep one for my daughter who is a nurse."

"That hospital has only just been converted from a work- house! It's going to be good one day, they say, but as yet it's not as good as this one. He'd be in the old poor law ward! I know they don't call it that now but it's a dismal place and will be until they can rebuild after the war," Emma said.

"If you are so upset, you can give up nursing and come to look after your own father," Clare Dewar said.

"If he wasn't as ill as he is, I wouldn't be here now," Emma said. "I told you that I would not be coming to Bristol again to stay, except in an emergency, so you have plenty of room even if you have taken a lodger."

"Mrs Hammond said that they are expecting a contingent of Irish labourers to work on the airfield. The government are billeting them on people whether they want them or not. She advised me to get a girl from the offices up at the factory and say I had no spare rooms. They say they come home drunk and wet the beds," she added defensively.

"So you have a girl who is out all day and has a midday

meal in the works canteen," Emma said. "I bet she makes her own bed, too, and helps bring in the coal."

"I find the money useful."

"You've never been short of that," Emma said.

"If he dies, I shall be left with nothing." She paused to let the drama sink in. "If I hadn't been such a good manager, things would have been different. He never looked at the bills. I sometimes wonder what he did with the money he had left after he gave me the housekeeping. He never let on just what he earned. He said that men from his part of the country never told their wives everything, and he could be stubborn. There are things that even I have never winkled out of him. Widows get nothing much and the mortgage on the house would be too much for me. We thought an expensive house would be a good investment, but I can see now that I shall be in one room, living on bread and cheese when he dies."

"You told me once that you have an insurance policy," Emma pointed out. "And I'm sure that Dad would not leave you without means. I've nothing in common with him and haven't for years. I owe him nothing. My legacy from Gran payed for my extras at school and my start in nursing, but he's honest and has always seen that you never went short even during that period, before the war when he was unemployed and was moving around chasing jobs."

Her mother stood up. "Well, I must be going."

"Have you been in to see him?"

Clare Dewar's face went pink. "I peeped in but he was asleep and when he's awake he never speaks. I have to get back to get supper for my lodger, Maureen."

"You'll look in to let him know you were here? You can at least say good night."

"We'll look in together before we go home," she said.

58

"Are you ready? That case looks heavy and the buses will be crowded at this time of the evening."

"You don't listen, Mother," Emma said with studied patience. "I have no intention of sleeping in that room and I'm never going to sleep in that house again. I have made arrangements and shall stay here, so you will have to go home alone, but see him first. I'll come with you."

They left the ward waiting room and Emma parted the curtains drawn round the bed. Her father had slipped down from the pillows and looked uncomfortable, so Emma called a nurse to help her lift him back up the bed. He sank back with a sigh and moved his lips but no sound came.

Clare Dewar sat down self-consciously on the hard chair by the bed and stroked her injured nail. "I can't stay any longer," she said after five minutes, as if she was in charge of a convoy of lorries instead of going to wait for a bus. "I have to get back through the evening traffic. I'll be back tomorrow, but rest now and have a good night's sleep," she added brightly. "You'll be better in the morning." She glanced at the box on the locker by the bed. "He refused to come here without his medals," she said, as if he couldn't hear her. "You might as well have them. I don't want them or the other rubbish he kept from the last war."

Emma glanced at the drawn, parchment-coloured face and wished her mother would shut up, but she saw that he was watching her and so she smiled. He murmured something, then one eyelid closed and Emma realised that he had given her the wink of a fellow conspirator.

She picked up the box to take with her and gravely she winked in return and felt closer to him than she had been for years.

After more grumbling, her mother went to find a bus

and Emma said good night to the Ward Sister. "He's had his medication and there's no change, so why not go with Dr Sykes now? He rang through and said he'll be in the office in Out-patients reading notes and can take you over as soon as you are ready. Goodbye. I hope we don't have to call you in the night but I have the number of the house down the road."

"Let's go out for a meal," Paul Sykes said as soon as Emma had left her case in the room put at her disposal.

"I don't want to take up your time," Emma began. "Already I can't thank you enough for getting me a bed for the next night or so."

"You'll be doing me a favour," he assured her. "I am a friend of Guy's and glad to entertain his pretty fiancée. It's been one hell of a day and we can both do with the break."

As they walked up Park Row, Emma looked about her with mixed feelings. Many buildings that she recalled from her time in the Home on the Downs were there, some intact, others boarded up and derelict. The space where the old Prince's Theatre had been, lay dark and covered with weeds as if a building exuding life and laughter and colour had never been there.

Paul mentioned the house off Whiteladies Road where she had eaten with Phillip, Maeve Evans and Tony, and sometimes with Bea. "Is that still open?" she asked and found a lump in her throat as a wave of nostalgia swept over her. "I thought it would be closed a long time ago as they served a lot of black market food and sold illegal whisky."

"Not as good but still there, down to the last encrusted bottle of brown sauce and the torn oilcloth tablecovers," he said. "Perhaps we deserve better. There's a new place and they say it's quite good so long as we stick to fish.

I can't bear to contemplate yet another vienna steak. Mostly fish there, which is fairly safe if it's really fresh and I hear it is."

The plain walls smelled of fresh distemper and the wooden floor was polished, giving off a faint mixture of lavender and paraffin, soon lost under the appetising fishy smells. They ate in near silence, each realising just how much they needed food.

Emma was fascinated to hear snippets of information about Guy's student days, and Paul was an amusing companion. Gradually, she relaxed and when he asked about her time in Bristol she was able to share her lighter memories and found herself laughing.

Over the so-called trifle, a piece of sponge cake soaked in fruit squash with custard over it and a dab of synthetic cream, Emma realised that her life up to the present time had been in several definitely separate periods. No other person knew about all of them and even Guy knew little of her life in Bristol at the beginning of the war. She found herself talking about happenings that she had never thought to tell Guy and yet she was telling Paul about them because he knew the city and her old haunts. He had even heard of the Home on the Downs and was fascinated to hear what really went on beyond the beautiful grounds, inside the thick stone walls. It made him a familiar friend after only an hour or so.

But Paul knows nothing of my life at Beatties, she decided, and my mother knows nothing of Guy or my work, just as she knew little of my work in Bristol.

Paul talked animatedly, as if he too needed to reminisce, and Emma thought of the soldiers she met on trains who opened up to a stranger because they knew subconsciously that they would never meet again and so their confidences were released but secure.

61

She had put on her engagement ring when she changed to go out for the meal, as proof that she and Guy were engaged, and for consolation because he was far away and she had given up her holiday with him in Devon. She wondered if Guy would object to her wearing it before they announced it to his parents. He would be with them by now, enjoying the warmth of family life and slotting back into an environment that she envied.

"We'd better get back," Paul said. "I have a night round to do, so I'll come with you to the ward to see how your father is, then you must go to bed. It's been a long day for you and a worrying one, I think."

"Thank you, Paul. You saved my life," she said.

"Any time. I really enjoyed your company." Suddenly, they were stiff and uncertain, as if they had stepped over the first barrier of friendship and were far more intimate than was possible after such a short time. The ring was tight under her glove and she smoothed it through the leather almost as her mother smoothed her torn nail when she was worried or angry.

The hospital was quiet except for the muted drone of traffic that passed endlessly by the front entrance. The ward was in twilight gloom and the blackout curtains were drawn, excluding the starlight.

Paul led her firmly into the ward past a rather disapproving night nurse who could say nothing to prevent a doctor of Paul's seniority bringing a visitor at that hour. Alan Dewar lay still, his face ashen and his eyes closed. Paul glanced at his chart and said softly, "He's sedated. Get some rest while you can."

Emma sank into bed and into an exhausted sleep. Images of half recognised shapes and people flitted through her dreams and she woke suddenly, groped for the bedside light and her watch. It was four in the morning, the time the ancients said was the hour when death claimed his own, and many times she had known this to be true. She sank back into an unsettled sleep and was awakened by the bell calling off-duty staff for breakfast.

Dressed and surprisingly fresh, she went down to the front hall of the house and met a porter coming in with a note for her which confirmed her suspicions that her father had died in the night. The porter was an elderly man, too old for active service and had seen it all before. However, his manner softened as he saw her face. "It happened about four," he said. "Get something inside you, Nurse. They don't want you up in the ward now. Have something to eat and I'll tell you when they want you in the Chapel of Rest. I rang his wife and she said she will come in later, about eleven. There'll be forms to sign and she'll want to see her solicitor. The Registrar of Deaths comes in later in the mornings to save people having to find him if they are strangers to the city."

"Thank you," Emma said and managed a weak smile. "I'll have some coffee and ring the solicitor. I expect I shall be dealing with him more than my mother will." She wanted to be rid of the documents and to leave them in responsible hands before her mother appeared. It would do her father no harm now if his wife thought he had left them with the lawyer instead of giving them to her, and Emma had no desire or the strength to submit to more nagging on that score. She made a note of what her mother could expect in the way of income from the various policies and was surprised at the total.

She walked back from the solicitor's office in Broad Street, buttoning her coat high against a sneaking wind but enjoying the freshness of the air after the spent atmosphere of the room where she had slept. Her eyes were dry until she took off her coat again and combed her hair, and she felt as if she would never cry for her father. It wasn't a bereavement, it was an end to something that had never had substance.

Suddenly, tears came, and she knew they were not for him, but rather for her and the fact that she had never loved him.

It was nearly eleven and Emma walked to the main entrance of the hospital and asked if her mother had arrived. She waited and made an appointment for her to see the Registrar of Deaths, Births and Marriages at half past and when Clare Dewar arrived at half past eleven, had no time to talk but took her along to the office.

The formalities over, Emma told her that she'd been in touch with the solicitor and he had certain papers for her to sign before he contacted the various insurance firms, and he'd need copies of the death certificate. "That won't amount to much," Clare Dewar said.

"You'll find it does," Emma said quietly. "Dad told me that you'd be well off once he was dead, and one policy would wipe out the rest of the mortgage."

"I don't believe it. I'll end up in one room, alone," she replied dramatically.

Emma gritted her teeth. "You've said for years that all you wanted was one room where you could be independent and alone. Now you'll have a whole house full of rooms and you can be alone in all of them!" She picked up her coat. "I'll walk with you to the solicitor's office now and then take you somewhere to eat."

"Don't walk so fast. I can't keep up with you," Clare Dewar said, but she said no more, as one look at Emma's face told her that she had reached her limit of patience.

"The funeral is tomorrow," Emma said when she rang Aunt Emily. "I'm glad they didn't waste time. I want to get away from here. Mother is all in black and is doing a poor widow act but secretly, I think she's pleased that he's gone and she will be quite well off."

"Don't be bitter. She's been like that all her life and she'll not change now. Just don't make her any promises you can't keep, Emma, and leave Bristol as soon as you can."

"I wish I could come to you, but that's impossible. I have to get back on duty soon and Guy will wonder what's happening."

"Does he know?"

"Not yet. I've never let my parents know about him and I don't want him involved now. I'll ring him this evening. I have the Devon number. Are you coming to the funeral?"

"No. It would be hypocritical to say we ever really liked each other, and I couldn't stomach seeing Clare doing the Dying Swan act all over again! I'm glad he left her secure but I don't want to see her just now. Tell her I'll write but I've just got up from the 'flu so I can't travel now."

"Are you all right?"

"Don't sound so worried. I'm fine, but tell her what I said and bring that nice man down again soon, but for heaven's sake don't say I want her to visit me! If she asks, I shall say I work all day and don't cook any more than I have to, and she should go to Cowes to stay with Lizzy, who has nothing to do."

Emma found herself smiling. Emily was so practical and warm. She set out the change she would need if she telephoned Devon and found that she hadn't enough small coins, so she went out to buy toothpaste and get more change. As she passed the car park, Paul Sykes

65

called to her. "I'm sorry," he said, simply. "Anything I can do?"

"You helped me enough the other night," she said. "The funeral is tomorrow and then I'll collect my bag from here and hope to escape back to normality. I can't stay here any longer and I must go back." She turned down the corners of her mouth. "My holiday is over."

"Some holiday! What does Guy say? Will he be there when you return?"

"I haven't told him. I'll ring him in Devon later and tell him that I'm leaving here tomorrow."

"When you get back here, give me a ring on the in-house phone and I'll run you to the station if you're taking the late train."

"That would be wonderful," Emma said quietly. "I think I was dreading that bit, getting to that awful station, more than I'm dreading the funeral."

"Well, at least the weather is dry for the funeral," he said and hurried away into the hospital.

At first, Clare announced that she'd be too upset to go to the cemetery, but a phone call from one of Alan's colleagues made her curious to see who would be there from the factory. She pulled on black gloves and sat with Emma in the back of the shabby taxi that was all that the undertaker could arrange for them to follow the hearse.

"Fancy!" Clare said after the church service. "I never knew he had so many friends at work."

"Did we really know him?" asked Emma.

"Don't be silly. I'd been married to him for years and knew him inside-out." She gave Emma a sharp nudge. "That's one of the directors. Wait until I tell Mrs Hammond who was here."

"I wonder she isn't here today," Emma said dryly.

"She's away," Clare said with regret. "She'd have loved it and it would have been company for me as you say you intend deserting me after the cemetery, but she'll want to hear all about it. I think you could have worn black to show a bit of respect," she added.

"I once had some black underwear," Emma said.

"You never did! Don't be rude, Emma."

The vicar droned over the grave of the man he'd never met in church and knew only by name; the flowers were set by the grave and Mrs Dewar examined every card, exclaiming with pleasure at each one and with surprise at some beautiful lilies that came from Alan's department in the factory, until the taxi driver asked when she would be leaving as he had another fare to collect.

"I wanted to see them as I shall have no opportunity to come here again," Mrs Dewar told him, but climbed into the car and sat back to enjoy the ride home. "It was easy to see just how respected my husband was," she said, and Emma felt slightly sick, as she saw how her mother would make the most of the situation and the huge bunch of lilies would be mentioned for months to come.

"Where do you pick up your next fare?" asked Emma.

"Clifton," said the driver.

"Then you can have an extra fare," Emma said. "I'm going to a house near the BRI, so that's on your way."

"I managed to get some ham," Clare Dewar said in an aggrieved tone. "I thought you'd be staying."

"No, Mother. I said I'd catch the late train back to London and I have to go back on duty."

"Your father wouldn't like that," she said.

"Was he ever allowed to have an opinion? He certainly can't care now."

"You've got hard, Emma. That's what nursing has done for you, and the people you meet have made a real snob of you. You never told me who you took to the Island with you."

"Goodbye, Mother. I can't keep the driver waiting so I won't come in. I didn't bring anything with me. My luggage is in my room at the hospital. I'll write."

The car lurched forward. "Glad to be out of it, are you, miss?" Emma took a deep breath. "Yes," she said.

"Families are worse than friends," the driver said. "My wife has dozens of 'em and they gather like vultures when there's a funeral."

"Not many vultures today," Emma said lightly. "My father had few relations and my mother doesn't come from this part of the country." She asked to be put down at the top of Park Street where she could buy something to eat and look round the remnants of the Museum that had lost most of its treaures to storage or bomb damage. The art gallery had taken a hammering during one of the raids and now was an empty shell, with no-one concerned about its future.

The cheese omelette was passable and the bread fresh and she drank coffee to while away the time in a cafe in Park Row. Thoughts of her father refused to go away. She couldn't remember sitting on his lap or being kissed by him and she knew nothing of his background.

She had been to the town where Alan Dewar had lived for most of his life, only once as a child, with her mother protesting about the cold and finding fault with their boarding house. She couldn't recall meeting anyone who was an aunt or uncle or grandmother, but her father had absented himself at times to meet people who her mother refused to see, and the journey home had been full of silent disapproval. Maybe he did have people who had known him years ago and might once have been close. They might care that he died.

She paid the bill and walked past the University tower to College Green and the Cathedral before going back to her temporary lodging to tidy up, rest for a while and collect her bag. She was tempted to telephone Guy but decided to wait until she returned to Beatties, suddenly shy in case one of his family answered the telephone and she had to ask for him. What would she say? Take it for granted that they knew about her and Guy being engaged and assume a false familiarity with his family before they had been introduced?

"Coward," she called herself but knew that she could contact Devon through the impersonal switchboard at the Princess Beatrice and the girl on duty would be willing to ring Guy, thinking it was an offical call. She took her case to the front door to be ready when Paul came to fetch her and waited, dressed for the journey and eager to get away.

"Is that all?" Paul swung her case into the back of the car and settled her in beside him. He drove well and used side turnings to avoid the worst of the traffic, and they found themselves among depressing streets of houses with broken windows and flaking paint. "Not the area to linger in," he said. "Tarts seem to manage even during wartime or perhaps because of war." He grinned. "Some of my regular patients come from here. I'm not a surgeon like Guy. I thought I'd opt for the quiet life and be a physician, but I couldn't have been more wrong. Guy can cut 'em up and say goodbye once they leave hospital but we have to follow up chronic cases and see many of the same people time and again." He sighed. "It's difficult not to get involved with their personal problems. Some of them have terrible lives and the women from back there are usually riddled with gonorrhoea and some have syphilis and appear at our special clinics with monotous regularity, for us to treat them and advise them to stay off the game."

"But they don't. We have the same problem and there seems no short-term treatment for VD," said Emma.

Paul laughed. "Minnie, one of my regulars, goes straight from the clinic back on the street, reeking of antiseptic and her genitalia gloriously coloured purple with gentian violet, as if she carries a certificate of safety! I often wonder what her punters think!"

"You must be a good doctor, Paul."

"I like to think so, but it's frustrating not to do more. Some day, new drugs will cope with many of the things we find beyond us now and I can't wait. Sulphonamides help a lot but they aren't the complete answer."

He stopped the car on the incline leading to the railway station. "We've got here early. Stay in the car for a few minutes. Platforms are the draughtiest of places. What will you do when you marry Guy?" he asked.

"I'm taking finals after Christmas and then we'll be married."

"After that?"

"I hope to stay on at Beatties if they relax the married nurses' rule."

"And if they don't?" he asked bluntly.

"I don't know."

"What does Guy say?"

Emma looked uneasy. "I don't think we've looked that far ahead."

"I hear the train whistle. It should be here at any moment." Paul carried her case to the platform and waited until the train slowed down and stopped in a flurry of smoke and dust. He opened the carriage door and she turned to look over the open window to say goodbye.

"Thanks for everything," she said.

"I may come to London for a seminar on diseases of the nervous system," he said. "May I get in touch?"

"I shall insist on it! I owe you a good meal and loads of thanks," she said. "Guy will be pleased to think we met and he'll want to see you when you come up to London."

The journey back seemed shorter than when she came to Bristol dreading what she would find when she saw her parents. She read a magazine and when she had put it away, thought of the past few days with increasing detachment. Paul's care had been a comfort and she could imagine him with patients, his calm eyes and humorous mouth making them feel at ease and as if he could and would help them.

I've spent a fortune on cars, she thought as she checked to see if she had enough money to take her back to Beatties. I can afford a taxi now as Paul took me to the station, and it was with intense relief that she dragged her case up the steps of the Nurses' Home.

A note in her pigeonhole was from Guy. "I wanted to phone you but you were very sure you didn't want me to telephone your mother, so I came back early. If you are back by seven-thirty, be at the door ready to go out." It had that day's date and Emma hurried to change.

"Darling!" Warm arms held her and Guy's lips were tender and hungry and what she needed more than anything. Emma burst into tears.

"Was it really bad? I should have insisted on coming with you. I didn't know that you were so fond of him," he said at last when the storm was over and she hiccupped inelegantly into his shoulder.

"Bad enough, Guy, but I wasn't crying for him. It was

seeing you again and knowing that I have at least one human being who I truly love and who loves me."

"For ever," he said. "Come on, hunger makes you depressed. If it's any consolation, I didn't enjoy Devon. The family have colds and it rained all the time and I missed you. My God, how I missed you."

Chapter 5

"They surely aren't shifting you again?" Bea eyed Emma with disgust. "It's been good having you here and I'll miss you. I haven't heard from my husband for ages. Too many grass skirts and hula dancers," she added. "I reminded him of the nice little present that Captain Cook's men left for the good people of Hawaii and I think he's in a huff." She smiled wickedly. "He's Dwight the White Knight and I believe it, but he likes to think I could be jealous."

"Tell you later," Emma said. "She wants to see you now. Maybe you are to go to Heath Cross too."

"More likely the other place. They say it's as dead as a dodo there and more difficult to get up to Town. Tony seems to like it, but he's the exception. He works hard and says he might get married in the spring if the war goes well."

"He's a very good anaesthetist and Guy thinks he'll go into private practice with the ENT firms who are pioneering the labyrinthectomys and fenestrations." Emma laughed. "I never thought I'd want to stay out of Theatre, but standing for hours in semi-darkness while the surgeon grubs around in a tiny hole with miniscule instruments, using a microscope to see what he's doing in the ear, isn't my idea of fun."

"Guy is staying at Heath Cross?"

"Yes, that's the best of it. He'd already decided to rent

73

a small cottage so that he can escape at times and I can join him for days off, and now we can use it for off duty and days off without the bore of having to get back to London."

"Who's 'we'? Can anyone join? I don't use the St James's apartment now and it would be nice to slop around and play music and read sometimes; and write letters to my love," she added dreamily.

"Go and find out your fate," Emma advised. "Even if it is the old School for the Blind, that will be closer to Heath Cross than London. It may be promotion and I shall have to call you Acting Sister. They are giving sisters' caps and bows to anyone with good SRN passes, to stop all their hard work being wasted when girls leave as soon as they qualify, to go into the services. If it wasn't for Guy, I'd rather fancy myself in naval uniform. Those tricorne hats are lovely."

"We'll have to wait until after Christmas for that," Bea said and hurried over to the administration office. She returned more slowly, looking puzzled.

"Siberia?" asked Emma helpfully.

"Heath Cross with you, but I can't think why. She said they have to open a few wards that they closed after the convoys eased up. We had fewer emergencies fresh from the European Front, but all the news points to the fighting pushing further across France and Eastern Europe, and our men, like David, are moving in to existing hospitals that they can take over and use."

"Guy mentioned German prisoners of war. Evidently, there are so many of their wounded that they clog up the field hospitals and need to be sent away. Many of them need further surgery and all need nursing care as their first-aid before they were captured became almost nonexistent. A lot of treatment has to be undone before they can get it right."

"Why should we have to do that? Look what they did to London and Coventry and Exeter, and we both know all about Bristol bombings."

Emma smiled. "Calm down, Bea. You are married to a bomber pilot who has done as much damage to them as they did to us. Trade Coventry for Dresden and neither side has a lot to shout about as neither city was a military target."

Bea looked angry. "They don't treat their prisoners well. Men who have escaped and returned home have a bitter tale to tell. I nursed a glider pilot who had half of both feet amputated through frostbite when he escaped. He said when he was captured in a field, it was the women who scared him. They wanted to lynch 'the terror bomber', and he had to be protected by soldiers until he went to the *stalag*, and then it wasn't exactly a load of fun!"

"Our job is to heal," Emma said. "If we bothered with the morality of our patients, we'd want to stop nursing half of them!"

"Well, I shall pretend I speak no German and understand even less." Bea's eyes sparkled. "In that way I can be a spy! Think of all the military secrets I'll learn."

"Knowing our luck we'll nurse the ordinary squaddies and the other hospitals will get the high ranking officers with sabre scars on their faces, beautiful manners, and orders from Hitler strapped on their chests."

"There must be a conspiracy against us," Bea agreed. "I think it's because Beatties' nurses are too intelligent and attractive to risk them being sullied by lecherous officers."

"We haven't seen any yet and we may have to nurse

civilians again," Emma reminded her. "Get packed. We have to be at the entrance in two hours. The porters are coming for our cases half an hour before that."

Bea climbed on to the coach clutching a large framed photograph of her husband, but Emma was aware that her own engagement ring must stay on the thin gold chain round her neck, giving no hint of her relationship with Guy. "This coach could drive itself there by now," Bea said. "At least I shall have a bit more social life as Dwight's godfather is back at the house on Epsom Downs for conflabs with top brass, and I have an open invitation. So have you," she added. "The General likes you and thinks Guy is one hell of a guy, if you get my meaning."

An electrically driven store's wagon droned along the long corridor and the wind picked up spirals of dust and dead leaves in the empty garden patches by the wards. Emma and Bea went to the administration block to receive their instructions.

"At least it's day duty and on wards we know," Emma said as they unpacked in the villa set aside for senior nurses and sisters. "I have Sister Sinclair. What's she like?"

"Not Princess Beatrice trained and I assume turned down for the forces as she's a bit long in the tooth. Very efficient and very smartly dressed, with hair that looks as crimped and blue rinsed as Sister Cary at the Home in Bristol."

"I hope the resemblance ends there," Emma said with feeling.

"She's fine. A bit of a snob but a very good sister." Bea put her expensive perfume on the dressing table with the ebony and gold manicure set and the picture of Dwight. She looked pensive. "I wonder how she'll cope with the prisoners? Rumour has it that her name was originally Snitzler but her family changed it to

Sinclair just before the war and came to England from Austria."

"Did Tony Goldwater tell you that?"

"His family knew hers but he never contacts her as he wants to forget the past in Germany. He doesn't really have a lot in common with her apart from that, and Tony, who loves everybody, does not like her, which tells me a lot."

"At least she'll speak German," Emma said with relief. "I'll be hopeless."

"Don't worry. You'll need only two or three phrases and I'll teach you the most important ones like, Have you had your bowels open today? . . . Where is your wound? . . . Does that hurt, I hope? . . . How many British soldiers have you killed?"

"*Bea!* Don't even think it. What a good thing you and Sister Sinclair are not on the same ward or there might be mayhem if she shares your dislike of them."

"She does, so be as quiet as a mouse when you first meet her," Bea advised. "Not all Jews are as tolerant and philosophical as Tony, though I can't see why he is, after losing all his family in the gas chambers."

"We don't have to go on duty until tomorrow so why not whoop it up in Epsom tonight?" said Emma in a determind effort to take Bea's mind off German prisoners, who they had not even seen and might not be nursing when they went on duty the next day.

"No Guy?"

"He's away on a course, so we're on our own."

"Good. See you in an hour, after we've unpacked properly. Wrap up warm as we shall walk and get up an appetite. We could ring the General and be invited to dinner there." Bea bit her lip. "Dwight would approve but I really don't want to talk about the war tonight."

"All that rich food is bad for us," Emma said. "We'd never enjoy our fish cakes for breakfast here if we had lobster tonight."

"Don't! Do you think they have any left from last time, growing a gentle film of green algae? I'll telephone Hunters Lodge and tell them that we are here but resist an invitation tonight as we are exhausted by the move down." She gave a sweet smile. "In that way, I'll have done my duty to Dwight's godfather and they'll be convinced I'm starving and send down some lovely cans of food and biscuits and things. The General acts as if he was responsible for Dwight being sent away, but I know it wasn't in his power to stop it. However, a bit of guilt brings home the bacon, *and* the tins of sausages and chicken!"

"I'll finish unpacking," Emma said. "I have a key to the cottage and Guy asked me to have a look at it in case I don't like it. It's on the edge of the town, not deep in the Surrey countryside, so we can get there easily from here."

"I love looking at other people's houses. If they left it furnished, I can be as rude as I like about their decor without upsetting you!"

The lack of street lighting was not important as the moon was bright and full over the damp heath, but the paths were muddy and they walked along the side of the main road into Epsom. They passed the small church and Emma looked up at the gaunt tower as they paused to listen to voices singing. "They are rehearsing carols," Bea said. "Carols?"

"Work it out. We aren't all that far away from Christmas. I lose track of time now."

"I wonder where Dwight will be this year? I have a dream of a cottage with a huge log fire on Christmas Eve, and just Dwight and me, finding out what's in my stocking," Bea said demurely.

78

Emma sighed. "I may be back on nights by then, and you know the tradition at Beatties, that staff do not ask for leave over the Christmas period. Patients come first and we make it as good a time as possible for them."

"Come on, I'm frozen and have a date with the Marquis of Granby as soon as we've seen the cottage."

"I've been on duty for Christmas for every one there's been during my training," said Emma.

"You should have had one free. They do allow that," Bea said. "I had the one they grudgingly handed out and another one when my father entertained VIPs at the apartment, but that might have been because he pulled a few strings."

"Don't pity me. I was glad to stay and had a lot of fun each time. Much more fun than if I'd gone to Bristol, and the patients enjoyed it."

"Well don't ask me to parade with my cloak showing red side out and holding a candle, doing the rounds of the wards on Christmas Eve."

"I enjoy that and the candlelight makes everyone look gentle and fresh. Some patients said they'd never forget it and it helped to make Christmas special."

"Yes, they do like it and I suspect that some have no real celebrations in wartime at home back in Peabody Buildings and the like." Bea peered at the road name and saw that it was the one they wanted if they were to find the cottage. "I'll tour the wards but I refuse to sing to German prisoners unless I can sing *Fight the Good Fight*, or *Onward Christian Soldiers*."

"This must be it." Emma rubbed away the damp covering the name on the gate. "Rose Cottage! How original," she said, and pushed open the wooden gate.

Bea looked approving. "Detached and quite big," she said. "But there are a lot of houses lying empty. The owners have fled from the war and are only too happy to rent them out at a very low price. I think I'll buy a house before the end of the war as a base for us in England and a good investment. My father said he'll find something and if he buys it he'll pay very little." She laughed. "He could reduce a Turkish carpet seller to tears with his hard bargaining."

"Guy did warn me that I ought to come here first by daylight as there is no electricty until next month, but he's left candles and an oil lamp and matches inside the door and there's a gas fire that works."

"Nice! Very nice," Bea said as the candle flared and Emma lit the lamp. The main room had old beams and a wide, deep hearth in which kindling and logs were set ready to light, and in the morning room was the functional gas fire which she lit. They would be in the house for such a short time and it was unnecessary to light a real fire.

Bea was already opening doors and the drawers in the kitchen. "There's an old-fashioned walk-in larder with a marble shelf and the back door, which is locked, leads into a conservatory," she said, peering through the glass door.

"It's well furnished," Emma said, bouncing on a well-sprung settee. They explored the upper rooms and she opened a window to look at the garden. "Mostly grass, Guy said, and a man still comes in to tidy it once a month."

A pile of new bed-linen and blankets in the airing cupboard made Bea smile. "I'm glad he has his priorities right. Log fires and comfortable beds. I do envy you, Dewar," she said, slipping back to the formal name of duty and Emma knew that she was upset.

"I'd rather be really married, like you and Dwight," Emma said slowly. "A part of me still feels guilty and I can't talk about . . . us, freely to anyone but you."

80

"But you have him here and Dwight is thousands of miles away."

"He'll be back and you'll forget the partings. I wish I could really look forward," Emma said. "Guy never talks of the distant future. He wants to be married and refuses to look further than that. It was a blow that I couldn't get to Devon, but somehow I don't want to go there until we are ready to be married."

"Well, this place should help. I hope you aren't keeping it all to yourself."

"Guy did suggest that you should come here whenever you want to have a bit of peace. We can study revision when he is away and when Dwight comes back you can have the cottage all to yourselves."

"He said that?"

Emma smiled. "He also suggested that you might like a key and one of spare rooms, so make yourself at home, unless you have something better in mind." She held up a key fob and waved it under Bea's nose.

"Gimme!" Bea said and put the key in her purse. "I have no intention of thanking you as I shall have a duty to perform. I shall be your chaperone. We are now a party of three; four when Dwight comes back and I am your chaperone when people find out about this place, so that it doesn't get called Guy's love-nest but a respectable haven for traumatised staff."

The gas fire spluttered and went out. "That's another thing. When you come here, bring plenty of shilling pieces as the fire is on a meter and gets very hungry." Emma turned off the gas tap firmly. "Talking of getting hungry, I'm starving, so we ought to get something to eat. I shall come back in daylight and put hot water bottles in all the beds to air them before I make them up with bedding. The owners really did leave everything as if escaping a

81

massacre. There are stone hotties and a couple of rubber ones in the utility room. It's sad to think they had to leave. Guy said they went to Canada and might stay there after the war. They suggested that he might like to buy it just as it is, furniture and all. I think it would be a good base for him and for me, as it's near London but far enough away to have privacy."

"May I bring some things tomorrow? Books and writing materials and a few records? I see that there is a rather ancient record player and a few classics here and I have loads of modern stuff that Dwight will enjoy."

"Have one of the double bedrooms and feel free," Emma said, "but keep quiet about the place as we don't want it a hostel for itinerant medics."

She locked the front door after carefully dousing the oil lamp and they walked into the town. The snug of the Marquis of Granby was furnished with graceful, faded velvet-covered chairs, and some new cretonne-covered stools by the bar which as Bea said would look better when covered with bums.

They sat on bar stools and looked into the glass-covered counter where a rather fat but well-roasted belly of pork rested on a bed of lettuce by a huge bowl of Russian salad.

"I'm glad the Russians are our allies," Bea said as she cut the succulent pork and ate it in the Amercian way with a fork in her right hand. "I can praise their salad even if they have more potato than anything. The mayonnaise isn't bad and there's plenty of it."

"The wife of the publican does all the cooking and she has the same touch with food as Aunt Emily. That rabbit pie looks delicious. She makes a little go a long way, and still serves tasty dishes."

"I think we are going to be busy soon," Bea said. "I

noticed three medics here who were at the old Blind School with Tony, and there's another coming in now." She sipped the good coffee and nodded her approval. "Do you think the lady of the house sells her virtue to the Americans for this? It's really good. The Marquis of Granby would be really pleased."

"Who was he?"

"I don't know. I've seen several Marquis of Granby pubs in the Home Counties but I have no idea who he was as yet."

"You mean you are going to find out?" Emma was amused.

"I'll have to as my dear husband is into British history in a big way, and if he sees the name, his eyes will glaze over. The States are so young that they think anything over a hundred years old is ancient and he's struck dumb by the old churches and buildings he sees over here, which I've passed by a hundred times and never really seen. Even my father's apartment thrilled him as it had echoes of the old diarists and parliamentarians of whom he had only read. He kept muttering about the old clubs in St James's, Pepys and the Royal Society and I had to look intelligent and nod wisely."

"You have no time for that if you're to do revision. Finals are looming up and we ought to get down to some work."

"One good thing I learned from my pa was to delegate and have someone to blame for not doing it right. I shall recruit one of those idle, peppermint-fresh blondes who act as personal secretaries to the General and his ilk, and let her sweat for me. They are so *keen!*"

Emma glanced along the wide mahogany rail and saw that one of the doctors was trying to attract her attention. "They're leaving and want to know if they can walk back with us," she said. "Who is the dark one? I've not seen him at Beatties."

"Some bod from St Mary's, I think. A team came down the last time I was here to try out a new drug, on service persomnel only, as it's so expensive and rare and they have priority for treatment. I believe it's revolutionary and will cure everything if it turns out as they hope."

"Guy mentioned it. It's called penicillin and I believe it was discovered ages ago, but has only now been researched in depth by Fleming at St Mary's and some doctors overseas. He said it was a bit difficult to obtain in the vast quantities needed for civilian use. It is far from pure as yet, but has done a lot to clear up streptococcal infections, and when used for infected war wounds has made a lot of difference to fast recovery. As yet, it is kept locked up as if it is a dangerous drug, and they have to sign for use to make sure of every drop."

Bea picked up her purse, and they paid the bill, then joined the doctors by the door. "Might as well have protection from the foxes," she said and smiled sweetly at the man from St Mary's who was introduced as Desmond Clarke, one of the penicillin team. They walked briskly and Emma tried to find out when the wards would be ready to receive patients and who they would be. Desmond was laconic about penicillin and stressed that as they hadn't done really in-depth clinical trials, he could say little that was scientifically official, but results were good and the drug, although crude as yet and causing pain at the site of injection in some cases, seemed to have no known side effects.

"What cases benefit most?" asked Bea.

"Wounds that are septic; pneumonia clears up quickly with no crisis, and other things show promise." He grinned. "We tried it on soldiers who had a dose of

84

gonorrhoea and they were clear in a few days with no residual infection that we could find, and we have a few syphilitics that we have under treatment here at Heath Cross. Some of the ones infected years ago that now have the general paralysis of the insane, are stable and early cases show that the spirochaete has been killed without the use of malaria therapy or mercurial inunctions."

"They are civilians," Bea said.

Desmond shrugged. "We need guinea pigs and these patients are not at risk but supply us with valuable data. The wages of sin are paying off now if we can eradicate VD."

"If you are here, does that mean we shall use it?" Bea asked shrewdly.

"Yes, we have supplies ready," Desmond said, but with an air of wanting to finish the conversation.

"If we have Germans in our wards and you use penicillin on them and not on our British civilians, you'll raise a terrible stink," Bea went on. Her voice sounded calm but Emma recognised the ice in it that meant she was about to blow her top.

"We thought of that and supplies are now at some of the main London hospitals for civilian use," he said defensively.

"Enough to treat everyone who needs it? Enough to save a lot of lives that might be lost without it? Will our lovely people from the Buildings get any? Or just a small supply to be a sop to the public, with a rider that we have to be careful in case there are side effects, but jam tomorrow if they live that long?"

He shrugged. "We do our best and at least we're on the way to a very exciting era."

"I suppose so, but you'll have to be careful or you'll have angry relatives demanding the new wonder drug that they've heard about, for their dying loved ones, and I hope you handle it personally and not leave it to the long-suffering sisters to deal with."

"Fierce, isn't she?" Emma heard as they left the doctors and went on to their villa.

"Great nurses, both of them, and don't eye the other one, she's taken too, worse luck." Emma blushed. It was always a shock to discover that men other than Guy lusted after her.

She glanced at the hall clock and saw that it was late. She bit her lip and wondered if Guy had rung from Guildford where he was staying in the college hall of residence.

Half way up the stairs she heard the phone ring and ran down again. "Emma?" Guy laughed when he heard her voice. "Sorry I didn't ring earlier but we were discussing a new procedure and I couldn't get away. I hope you didn't wait about. That's the worst of these sessions. We talk shop all the time and don't get any exercise or relaxation."

"Well, forget that now. Bea and I went to the cottage and I'm thrilled with it. It felt so homely even when it was bitterly cold in there. We lit the gas fire and explored by lamplight," she went on, her pleasure spilling over the phone.

"Will it be habitable by the weekend after next?"

"You'll be away for all that time?"

"Afraid so. I am going back to Beatties to lecture the students on the uses of penicillin and to see a few patients, so I can't see you until after that time."

"I miss you," Emma said.

"Miss you, too. I'll ring tomorrow evening. Good night, my darling."

Emma walked slowly up to her room. The cottage would be fun and more, as soon as she and Guy made it their home for brief periods of time, and in the Marquis she had dreamed of marrying and living there to be near him, free of work and hospital convention, and making a real home, but what if she was able to give up nursing to marry him? There would be long bleak periods when she saw nothing of him and would have to wait around for his telephone calls and visits as she couldn't follow him from hospital to college and back again.

Bea and other wives with men far away, missed them desperately but were able to concentrate on their work and friends. They could live their own lives on a fairly even plane, with ecstatic reunions at intervals, almost fresh honeymoons, but Emma could feel a kind of restlessness. She couldn't settle to anything if her life was as disjointed as it would be waiting for Guy, keeping the cottage and the bed warm and waiting and waiting. She would want to be with Guy as much as possible and if they were married, he would expect her to be there waiting. Guiltily, she saw disadvantages and knew she was right to stay and finish her training.

It seemed strange to work on a ward again at Heath Cross as most of her past experience there had been in the operating theatres. Emma thought back to the trim wards and highly polished floors and open fires at Beatties and wondered why the floors of the Heath Cross wards couldn't be covered with linoleum rather than be left stained and sealed but bare. The empty ward showed up the lack of comfort, but as she helped make up beds, covered with the bright red and blue military blankets, an orderly brought in a huge vase of foliage to brighten Sister's desk, and lit coke fires in all three sections of the ward, it began to look reasonably inviting.

Sister Sinclair checked the drug cupboard's contents with Emma and made a note of what might be needed in addition to the usual remedies and dangerous drugs. There seemed to be a huge supply of surgical dressings and gauze and heavy Winchesters of antiseptics and sterile saline. Emma counted thirty metal boxes of Tulle Gras, the gauze dressings soaked in petroleum jelly and Balsam of Peru that were invaluable when there was a danger of dressings sticking and making a wound bleed again when the old dressing was removed. So, there would be a lot of surgical dressing to do, she decided, but remembering what Bea had said about Sister Sinclair's opinions of Germans, she refrained from asking her what kind of patients they were to expect.

"Go off duty, Nurse Dewar. I shall expect you early tomorrow morning. We are expecting our first convoy of Krauts." Sister Sinclair's eyes were cold as she faced the nurses. "Remember Nurses, whatever you think or feel, you must be correct in your behaviour at all times. We shall do our duty, tend them and send them on their way to the north or to camps if they are well enough. We do not fraternise with any of them, neither do we talk to them when we do dressings." She looked at each nurse in turn as if to fix her words firmly on every one of them and asked if any of them spoke German.

"I do, Sister," said a junior nurse.

"You will listen but say nothing in that language unless the military need an interpreter. As you are not senior enough to do dressings, you will have little contact with them individually. The ward will be under military orders and we shall have a guard posted at the end of the ward, day and night. In the case of any harassment or difficulty, you may call him and leave it to the soldiers to sort out, and tell me of anything you find offensive in their behaviour."

"You, too?" Bea asked when she met Emma in the villa.

"We had a pep talk about behaviour but I can't think that any of us will be exactly buddies with them."

"I think the talk was to make sure we treat them fairly, but keep a distance," Emma said mildly. "But it was an effort for Sister Sinclair to mouth the words, and I think she may have a very low flash point."

"So do I." Bea looked angry. "The first one who puts up his hand in salute and says Heil Hitler gets a bedpan emptied over his head."

"What a good thing you are too senior to deal with bedpans," Emma said. "But I shall want a little help with a few essential phrases, so long as you don't give me the wrong ones!"

"Promise," Bea said. "I feel generous as I had a letter from Dwight today and he's fine. I'll write out a few things and their meanings and you can put it up in the duty room for the staff. I think you are sharing our nurses' changing room as yours will have to be an office where officers will interview individual prisoners before they leave Heath Cross."

"It all sounds terrible. It makes our wards like prisons."

"They are prisons, ducky, and don't ever forget it. We are nursing prisoners of war who have fought our men, women and chidren and destroyed the lives of thousands, even in their own country."

Chapter 6

"Some of them are filthy," Sister Sinclair said. "Before we can dress any wounds they must be bathed or we'll spread infection." She pulled the junior nurse back from the first bed. "I think that some have lice, too," she said. "Any ambulant cases must be taken to the sluice room and stripped, then made to shower thoroughly and wash their hair." She went from one bed to the next and checked who could be taken in wheel-chairs to the shower room and who must have bed baths.

"What about their clothes?" asked Emma.

"Fumigation for everything," Sister said firmly. "The ones still in uniform must take their possessions from their clothes and put them on the lockers by the beds. The clothes will be taken down to the basement for treatment. The ones in hospital pyjamas are men who have been prisoners for some time and may be cleaner." She gave instructions to the three Junior nurses about bed baths and told Emma and the junior Staff Nurse to lay up dressing trolleys and go from bed to bed as soon as the patients had been washed.

Emma knew that many of the men needed to have crude dressings renewed but saw the sense in the delay, and helped with the bed baths. At last, the ward was full of slightly damp-haired German soldiers, some smelling strongly of sassafras from the lotion applied to kill head- lice. A dinner wagon arrived with hot food and the dressings were delayed further until the afternoon. Some of the men grabbed anything they were given and ate almost savagely, as if they were afraid that someone would steal their food. Others seemed too apathetic to care, and ate sparingly. The jugs of water put on lockers were emptied, and gradually, the atmosphere improved, with one or two of the men beginning to talk to their neighbours.

"Go to lunch, Nurse Dewar, but first change your apron and sleeves. I think we have been careful and shall have no trouble with any more infection than there is already in those terrible dressings, but I'll ask the House Surgeon to make a note of the ones needing priority with treatment, and I'll write up the charts." She told the junior nurse who spoke German, to go too, so that Emma would have someone with her to translate if required when Sister was out of the ward for her lunch later.

"I feel as if I'm crawling with bugs," Bea said as they picked up their plates of beans and sausages. "How did it go with your *oberführer*?"

Emma giggled. "She is a bit like that, but very much keeping to the book and treats them fairly, and she's a terrific organiser. We haven't started dressings, but now I can go back on a warm cloud of sassafras and Dettol and get a few done. Sister has demanded more senior staff or medical students to help as we'll never get done today if we don't have more hands. I'm sure you are in the same boat."

Bea nodded and pushed a jar of good jam over to Emma to help down the soggy bread. "The thing that gets to me is the guard at the end of the ward, complete with rifle and ammo. The patients look so normal once the dirt is gone and they've got over their first shock at being in an

English hospital. I listened and some were sure that they'd be taken out and shot once they'd been interrogated. I did nothing to reassure them. They can sweat a little until the intelligence men see them. We have more walking cases than you and they've begun to interview them in the room they set aside as an office."

"Surely the ordinary soldier has nothing of much importance to tell us?"

"We have three fighter pilots and they have been grilled. At first they tried to hide the fact that they were officers and flyers but their tags and personal belongings gave them away and now they have to answer a few questions." She raised her eyebrows. "Just questions, no thumb screws, and now they look arrogant and as if they find the situation funny. Sister said that they were well enough to go to a camp up north, so they will find it less comfortable than a well-heated ward and nothing to do but eat and sleep. Some of the men are badly injured but others, once we have sorted them out, will go away tomorrow."

"Some of ours look as if they are long stay patients. We have several amputees, and one terrible character who shouts and demands that we do his dressings. He has a knee wound and a dressing on his back but seems not half as bad as the majority. Sister told him off in no uncertain terms in very sharp German. That made the whole ward go quiet for a while as they were under the impression that none of us spoke German. If we speak to them in English they look blank, but I have a feeling that at least four of them understand and probably speak good English, but like you, are pretending ignorance."

"Have you been told that they must not know where they are in England? We mustn't talk to other nurses about our off duty and where we are going. I know they took away all the road signs when we thought we'd be invaded, but this is ridiculous. Imagine trying to escape from here in hospital pyjamas with half a pound of shrapnel embedded some place."

"They even lock the main gates now and have sentries posted there. We have to come and go by the postern gate by the lodge and show a pass to get back again. Have you been given yours?" Emma looked unhappy. "This makes the war seem closer again, just when we thought it had receded across Europe and would soon be over."

"There's a long way to go against the Japanese," Bea said. "Reading between the censored lines in Dwight's letters, they are putting in a lot of flights and trying to subdue a very vicious enemy. We agreed a code to let me know what really happens out there and it works well. He is fine and somehow I don't worry about him as much as I did. The General told me on the phone that he's keeping tabs on his movements in the Pacific and I have no cause to be concerned. By the way, we are invited to dinner next week if we can match our off duties."

"Good, I'll starve for a day before we eat there," said Emma.

"Don't we always starve? I shall go back and see if the Germans have left any fish. It looked quite good, and it was obvious that they had not had food like it for ages in their own base hospitals."

"Nurse Dewar, you will do the following list of dressings. The House Surgeon has seen them. They will take a long time to do as the dressings are badly stuck and will need irrigating to get them free. Many have shrapnel under the skin and sometimes far into the muscle, but it may not be obvious. Skin comes together after the foreign body enters, and unless we probe, we can't see more than a small hole and perhaps a piece of uniform material taken in by the metal. Remove what you can but make a note of any you suspect is deep-seated and they'll be for surgery later."

"Nurse Symes?" Emma pulled on rubber gloves and the junior nurse pushed the dressing trolley to the side of the bed. "Have you finished bedpans on your side of the ward?"

"I thought I was let off normal work as I have to be there when they want an interpreter," she replied in a lofty voice.

"If they burst from want of a bedpan, you won't need an interpreter to know what Sister says in whatever language she uses," Emma replied dryly. "Get going and hurry up. They'll call you when needed, so don't think you can get out of your routine work!"

"You might need me when you ask them about their wounds," Nurse Symes said in a last attempt to be important.

"If I do, I'll shout, but dressings are the same in any language and I have the notes here." Emma smiled over her mask. "It's hard work, I know. I've done it all! Work now and earn your caps and you'll love it." She eyed the man's back with disfavour. "At least, I think you'll like it." She cleaned and probed gently and the probe struck metal just below the skin. She eased away a piece of shrapnel about the size of a peach stone and a scrap of army uniform that had been forced in with it. She put the foreign matter aside and puffed a cloud of sulphonamide powder into the wound before applying the dressing, then tidied up some torn skin on his arm. She made a note on his chart to indicate that he was fit to be moved once the HS had seen him.

It was amazing how clean most of the entry wounds

94

were, but as the HS said, the hot metal sterilised the muscle and introduced no infection with it. That came later if the injury received bad treatment and any discharge became putrid.

"It will be difficult for any of us to have off duty today," Sister said later when she made a round of the men whose dressings had been completed. She put red stickers on the charts of those to be transferred and looked at the next man to have his amputated leg stump dressed. She pursed her lips. "Time you had a break, Nurse Dewar. When you come back, bring a shallow tray from the clinical room to put under the stump and cover the bottom bedding with a rubber sheet as you'll be using a lot of water to remove the dressing." She looked at the filthy wrapping and touched the part covering the actual wound. Her frown deepened. "They may have saved his life but they went straight through as if chopping meat and left no muscle flap to fold over, so you'll be faced with exposed ends of blood vessels and nerves, all stuck fast."

"Is there a danger of haemorrhage, Sister?"

"Every possibility, I'd say, but it will be no fault of ours," Sister Sinclair said without visible concern. "If they let their own people get away with that crude surgery, then they must take a chance with us." She began to walk to the next bed. "It might be wise to apply a loose tourniquet ready to tighten in case the femoral artery spurts; spray on plenty of sulphonamide and cover with Tulle Gras. I hope you can do a decent stump bandage. At least it can look neat from the outside and he can wait for the war to end before he has more surgery. No need for us to waste more time on him than necessary now. There are others much worse off."

Emma was reminded of Sister Cary, the cold and fierce sister at the Home on the Downs in Bristol, but she knew that what she said made good sense, and away from the prisoners, Sister Sinclair could be a deeply caring person.

The night staff came on duty and found that dressing trolleys still circled the ward. Supper for the patients was only now being cleared away as, one after another, the patients who were fit to be transferred had been taken to the office to be questioned. Two men had been to the operating theatre for the removal of huge lumps of metal and one for internal bleeding caused by more deeply embedded results of mortar fire. Emma felt exhausted, as much by the sullen atmosphere of the ward as with the urgency of the work and the trauma of the last case. It had taken two hours to do, gently soaking away the primitive dressings of coarse compressed paper and avoiding the exposed ends of blood vessels.

The man's attitude had changed from stark fear and distrust to wonder, as she patiently did her work, causing as little discomfort as possible. She stood straight, with an aching back, and surveyed the bandage once the bed had been cleaned up and he lay with the stump under a raised bed cradle to take the pressure of the bedclothes.

He thanked her again and again in German and fumbled in his locker for a shabby wallet, out of which he took two pictures of a woman smiling and two young children.

"Clear the trolley and go off duty," Sister Sinclair said harshly before Emma could comment on the pictures. "And remember, no fraternising." She spoke curtly to the patient and he sank back on the bed as if she had struck him, covering the pictures with the bedclothes.

"Any more for dancing?" Bea said as she stretched out on a settee in the common room.

Emma groaned and the Senior Staff Nurse, Acting Sister from the main theatre, threw a cushion at Bea's head. "All I need is food and a bath. I missed supper and the sandwiches they left out for us were inedible," said Seymour. "I don't think we qualify for treatment under the Geneva convention or we'd have better food."

"If you can get some freshish bread that we can toast, I have some dried egg," Emma said. "Come over to the villa where we can eat it in peace, and bring your own knife and fork if you have them as the lot they left us is awful and Bea and I have bought our own cutlery."

"I got tired of being classed as a lunatic," Bea said. "One blunt inch of cutting edge on a knife blade is a bit insulting to anyone not a resident here in peacetime. I'm a big girl now and can cut up my own food, *and* I seldom feel like killing myself, at least not until today. I had to dress the superficial wounds of a very arrogant Bosch air force officer who didn't realise I understood every word he said until I finished the dressing. He let off his own feelings by saying all the obscene things he'd have said to a Hamburg tart, and wondered how long it would be before I begged to jump into bed with him. All this as if he was saying thank you very much for all your kindness, and looking, I have to admit, very handsome."

"What did you say?"

"I broke the rule we've been told, not to talk to the Bosch. I said very clearly in my very good German, that he was a louse that I wouldn't even bother to crush under my shoe and I intended to put him on a charge for obscene language and harrassment."

"That took him down peg," Seymour said with feeling.

"I think I did a good thing. There was dead silence in the ward after that and now we get spoken to with respect and a tinge of good, healthy apprehension, especially as I did report him and they trundled him away in a wheel-chair to an isolation ward where he'll be looked after by army orderlies, so I've seen the last of him." Bea chuckled. "I can't stand that type, from any country. We have them and so do the Yanks but I don't have to take it from this lot! Did you know they are using the old padded cells for solitary confinement? Enough to give him the screaming habdabs if he has to watch those grey padded walls and the tiny observation slits in the padding over the door. They are very silent and the doors have no inside handles, although in the general civilian wards they have fitted pulleys that open and close the door from inside." Bea looked at their awed expressions. "Cheer up. I'm not starting a hate campaign and I don't intend doing anything criminal. I gave him a very neat dressing. Let's celebrate. I shall open a can of chicken and a box of chocolates that came from Switzerland and *not* from the US of A."

"Have you heard from Guy?" asked Seymour, when they were scraping the last of the chicken from the plates with the last scraps of their toast.

"Speak of angels and you'll hear their wings flap," said Bea when the phone rang and a voice called for Nurse Dewar.

"Guy?" Emma clutched the phone as if she might be able to touch him.

"You sound a bit distrait. Are you all right?" he asked.

"Fine now that I'm talking to you, but we've had quite a day and we are exhausted." Briefly, she outlined the work done in just one day and sighed. "It was almost like D-Day again but not as urgent. Just hard work and tension, and the growing awareness that many of them are like our men, conscripted even though they have no political leanings, and want only to be back with their wives and families."

"I hear that many will stay at Heath Cross for a few

98

weeks, or even months if they are not ambulant enough to go to a camp, so don't let their loneliness get to you. It's hard but they are the enemy, and the general public would be indignant if they thought they were given preferential treatment." He paused, then said, "In one base hospital they used penicillin for septic wounds and the news leaked out. It caused a nasty response and a few scuffles in the casualty department as irate relatives demanded that their kin should have priority. It was useless trying to tell one man that penicillin wouldn't touch his wife's invasive carbuncles as it was the wrong bug causing them, and they had to give her a dose or two to prove that it wouldn't work for her."

Emma laughed but it held a trace of bitterness. "Here we are, talking carbuncles when we have other things to share. Where are you?"

"I'm still at Guildford and likely to be for a few more days as they want more lectures on the uses of penicillin in surgical cases. There is still a mystique about it as it isn't as stable as we'd like as yet, and there is a limit to its usage. One or two cases of allergy, have been reported, but that may be because it's still crude and not pure enough to be non-irritant in the tissues."

"Do I see you soon?" she asked. "Bea and I have done a few things to the cottage and it's ready for occupancy."

"Great! I can hardly wait, but wait I must. I'll try to pop down for a day next week, but after that I have to do a few full lists at Beatties and give more lectures, so I can't commute between Heath Cross and London. When you have time off, stay in the cottage. Even if I can't be there, I like to think of you in our first home and you'll need a rest after this week."

But it isn't our home until you've been there with me, Emma thought as he went on to tell her about the new wing he hoped to run at Beatties after the war. She found her attention wandering until he said, "I think you met an old friend of mine who trained with me? Paul Sykes? He got in touch and asked if I knew where he could stay in Surrey as he is involved with the treatment of tuberculosis using the sulphonamides, at a day centre near Reigate."

"He could stay here at Heath Cross in the visitors' wing. There are a lot of foreign medics here so why not Paul? You could arrange it and let me know when he comes, as I owe him a dinner. Hs really looked after me when I was in Bristol and you were in Devon."

"I'll do that and I'll suggest that he gets in touch as soon as he settles in."

"Make sure they know at the lodge that he's a *bona fide* doctor. We're bristling with guards now and have to use passes. An ordinary identity card doesn't seem enough for them but it seems a bit much. Who do they think would want to break in here?" She laughed. "The staff might want to escape if this goes on for a long time but the patients are *very* comfortable."

It would be good to see Paul again, she decided. He was a link with Guy as they'd shared so much as students and Paul had a light touch with memories. She undressed and showered. A link with Guy? That was a strange thought. She didn't need a few second-hand memories to link her with him. She would see Guy soon and they were very much in touch by phone.

She slipped into bed but left the light on, suddenly wide awake. Bea's husband was far away and it was unlikely that they would be together for months and Bea was resigned to a long parting. Now it was as if Guy was far away too, but it was more frustrating. Physically, they were only a few miles away from each other but their meetings were unpredictable, often cancelled by calls of duty. The house in Epsom was waiting for him but he would not see it, sleep in it, make love in it, for how long?

"You awake?" Bea handed her a mug of cocoa. "I think I must be overtired, so we might as well drink our cocoa like good grass widows and simmer down until we feel sleepy. My body wants sleep but my mind refuses to budge." She smiled. "We can't have the best sedative God made, but who'd want to sleep when we have our men back again?"

Emma propped herself on one elbow and sipped the hot drink. "You make it sound as if they are both far away. Dwight may be in the Pacific but Guy is still close by and I may see him next week," Emma protested.

Bea slicked back her damp hair and Emma was reminded again of a smooth Siamese cat, with sleepy eyes that saw everything and an inverted triangle of a face, that could either purr or spit.

"You are worse off than me," Bea asserted. "Dwight has a fixed time out there unless something very radical happens. Guy shunts about all the time and you are like a cat on hot bricks waiting for him. You don't enjoy your off duty in case he phones." Bea looked thoughtful. "If you were married, I could understand it and everyone would take it for granted that you stayed put until your lord and master called, but as you are not, you still have freedom of choice and can do other things when you want a change."

"I want to be here so that I can see Guy as much as possible."

"You refused to come up to London with me to see *The Merry Widow* and stay for the night with the Homer Stuts in a very decent apartment. You didn't hear from Guy that evening or the next day as he was busy. What did you

101

have for supper? More fish cakes or was it unidentified meat stew and hard potatoes? They really ought to get a vegetable cook here, instead of a catering corps reject."

"It's not like that. It's my choice," Emma said defensively. "When we are together, it's pure heaven."

Bea sighed. "Probably I'd do the same, but don't pin all your attention on Guy. There's a big world out there that even an insular islander should explore, and you must keep up with old friends and make new ones."

"I know you're right." Emma thrust back the knowledge that she had at least three unanswered letters in her writing case and had turned down several good invitaions. "However, I shall come with you to Hunters Lodge whatever happens."

"You're safe there. You know very well that the invitation includes Guy whenever he can make it, so if he's here, he comes too." Bea laughed. "You seldom go to the hospital dances now even though you enjoy dancing. I go as I like to meet old friends, and as they know I'm married and some of them are married or have a lover, it makes it easy. I've been amazed by the way they accept that I'm not available, and we have fun." She looked complacent. "However I am still attractive and it's nice to know that other men still want me even when they keep a stiff upper lip and try to hide it. Good for the morale."

"What does Dwight say about it?"

Bea looked wickedly wise. "I flaunt my broken hearts and lay them at his feet. It convinces him that he's very special, as indeed he is, and it makes him very possessive and arrogant, but he's really a sweet little tiger cub at heart, bless him."

"I wonder he trusts you," Emma said.

"We have a complete understanding," Bea said in a serious voice. "Before I met him I didn't think it was possible to want only one man, especially after my parents' examples but he knows that I am faithful and so I can have a little freedom and don't have to stay dressed in black waiting for him to call."

"You know you look fantastic in black," Emma said.

"I know." Bea half closed her eyes. "I shall wear the black velvet jacket to Hunters Lodge and you shall wear your 'you may look but don't touch' expression and we'll drive every frustrated man wild."

"I'd better wear something more than that!"

"Idiot. Get some sleep and be ready to face more bits of metal and gore tomorrow."

"Oh, Bea?" Emma called before Bea shut the door. "If you hear that a Paul Sykes is trying to contact me, steer him in the right direction. He may be coming to sleep in the visitors block and wants to meet me again."

"*Oho!*" Bea put her head round the door. "Does Guy know of this?"

"He's an old friend of Guy's since student days, and he once took me out to dinner," Emma said.

"How boring," Bea said and closed the door.

Chapter 7

"Gee! If they need models for advertising British girls, then you'd be the tops," the General said. He hugged Bea and kissed her firmly, and repeated the gesture with Emma, asserting that he was an honorary uncle and so priviliged.

"I love you too," Bea said with a smile, and proceeded to ask very indiscreet questions about the war and Dwight's part in it in particular.

"We've almost reached the old Siegfried line in Europe. Dwight and his men are giving hell to the Japs from the Marianas, a group of islands in the Pacific that we captured a few months ago. It makes the perfect launching base for bombing missions." He turned to Emma. "Your RAF boys are doing well. They strafed an important set of oil refineries in Sumatra and did a lot of damage. They're pressing on in Europe with our boys, and now we have confirmation of Rommel's suicide after failing to dislodge Hitler, and General Montgomery's successes in the desert, it's all go in the Pacific and all theatres of war. Who would have thought we'd be in cahouts with the Russians? They are good friends but I'd hate to be against them. They seem to be sweeping through the Balkans like a dose of salts." He nodded as if the thought gave him pleasure. "We have a lot more that we're playing very close to our chests." He grinned. "Lots more. Don't look at me like that or I'll give away state secrets I was told in the White House. You'd be one hell of a success in interrogation, Bea! They wouldn't know what they'd said to you until after. Come and have some food. You are both far too slim."

Bea regarded the well-upholstered wives of the top American brass who were helping themselves liberally to the good buffet. "We have a secret formula for keeping slim," she said sweetly, when one of the wives remarked on her good figure.

"I suppose you starve yourselves like Imogen over there," she said eyeing the willowy blond PRO with disfavour.

"Ours is an involuntary starvation. We eat as little as we can of unpalatable food and work twelve hours a day. The surplus pounds slip away." Bea piled her plate with smoked salmon and lobster, added Parma ham and salad and topped it all with some duck pâté.

"But you are eating a lot tonight," the puzzled matron said.

"My day off," Bea said. "Back to the diet tomorrow."

Emma sipped white wine and was helped to kidneys in wine with saffron rice by a very attentive American marine officer. He looked as if he had been in a monastery for months and needed the touch of a woman's hand or more. "Down Rover!" she whispered to Bea when he turned away to bring her some more wine and was side-tracked by a large lady with an arrogant manner, marking her as the wife of an officer with a lot of rank. "I'd be as fat as the lady in pink if I stayed here for a few weeks," she said. "But it's nice to be pampered and yet feel safe. The General has eagle eyes and pulls rank when he sees someone coming anywhere near either of us with a gleam in his eyes. I think everyone in the room now knows that you are married to his godson and I am engaged to an up-and-coming surgeon!"

"Strange," said Bea. "There are at least five very good looking men here and they do nothing more than make me lonely for Dwight."

"That's love," Emma said. "There do seem to be a lot of very high ranking officers here. They can't have come all this way just for smoked salmon and lobster."

"The General was very cagey on that subject but hinted that there's to be a top level meeting with heads of staff from all the allied forces. He refused to say more, so he can't depend on me to win the war. I shall concentrate on more important things. I think we should congratulate the chef," Bea said with an air of doing good to the masses. "The kitchen staff need encouragement."

Emma nearly choked. "You aren't going to tell them to do better, are you? This is superb."

"They have a very civilised custom in the States. Ever heard of doggy bags? When they serve vast steaks and customers can't finish them, the waiter packs the rest up for the doggy back home, but I wonder who does eat it? The customer most likely and the poor nonexistent doggie has none."

"You can't ask for that here!"

"I shall just say how wonderful it all is and how much I'll miss it when I'm working on the ward, doing my best for wounded humanity while chewing a stale crust." Bea slipped away and Emma turned back to the buffet.

"Have you saved some for me?"

"Guy!" Emma's face glowed.

"Careful, you'll spill that trifle." Guy took the dish from her and held her for a moment lightly, kissing her gently on the lips. "Um, you smell deliciously of good food. Whatever it was, is there any left?"

"I left a message in case you rang, but I didn't think you'd be down today," Emma said, half apologetically.

"I found you and that's what matters," he said. "Let's sit over there and talk." He helped himself to food and carried his wine glass to join Emma on the wide window seat. "I rang here to see if you and Bea were still with the General and was asked to come for supper."

"How long can you stay?" Emma asked anxiously. "Are you going to use the cottage?" She remembered four damp dusters hanging up to dry in the kitchen and the fact that the beds were not made up. Neither she nor Bea had had time to sleep there and the linen kept aired much better in the cupboard over the immersion heater.

"I have to get back tonight. I came down to see Desmond about the local application of penicillin to wounds instead of injecting it systemically." He looked embarrassed. "I had to catch him before he left for St Mary's, so we met in Epsom before I came on here."

"If I'd known, I could have come to Epsom and met you there. Did you see the cottage?" she asked eagerly.

"There wasn't time. We had a late lunch and a long discussion and then he had to catch a train to London."

"You've been here for hours!" Emma felt deflated.

"I'm sorry, I came here as soon as I could find out where you were."

"I was off at six and the ward knew where to find me."

"I had to write up notes and I saw Mr Samson for half an hour." Guy looked hurt and embarrassed. "Don't waste time now," he said. "I'm here and we have another hour. It's a busy old life," he added reproachfully.

"I had noticed," she said coldly. "Oh, here's Bea." Emma was shocked to feel how relieved she was to see her and how distressed she felt because Guy had been in the hospital for such a long time without contacting her, as if seeing her was an afterthought to be fitted in when he had exhausted his medical contacts.

Bea kissed Guy's cheek. "Do I ask for my carriage now and leave you two together?" she asked.

"No!" Emma spoke more loudly than she intended. "Guy has to get back soon and we must catch up on sleep if we are to be fit for work tomorrow."

Bea sensed her anger and said in a mild voice, "What devotion to come all this way for such a short time, just to be with you, Emma."

Guy coughed and held up his empty glass. "Anyone for more wine?" He left them and the general caught his arm to take him over to a gleaming new heated trolley just in from the States, that was keeping food warm. Guy glanced over to Emma, his helpless expression showing he was probably trapped for a while and her frozen look did nothing to lighten his situation.

"Tiff?" Bea asked. "He hasn't been in the room for more than five minutes and you are looking as if you want to strangle him." She regarded the ormolu clock on the gilded shelf. "Look. I have a jeep coming to take us back in half an hour but I can go alone if you want to go to the cottage with Guy. Come on, whatever is upsetting you can't be important. Kiss and make up." She smiled. "That's the part I like. It's worth a little blip in a relationship just to have that afterwards. Guy is a thoroughly nice man and would never want to hurt you."

"He's been here all day and didn't contact me," Emma said. "It was more important to look up old colleagues. He thought I'd be sitting in the villa, knitting and waiting for him just in case he showed up and could spare me an hour." Tears were close to the surface. "And he had the

108

nerve to remind me that as he said, 'It's a busy old life!' As if we hadn't noticed."

"The swine," Bea said, calmly. "He should know better than to take you for granted. Anyone would think you had been married for years." She put a hand on Emma's shoulder. "Don't say or do anything rash. You do love each other but men put a lot of importance on their work. Who was it said . . . love to a woman is existence itself but to a man is a world apart? I always get quotations wrong, but you know what I mean. Dwight would be the same if I let him, but as he is completely besotted with his lovely wife, he never has a chance to stand me up for his brother pilots when I'm around and available. He has the sense to know I could lose interest and find a lover." She smiled. "Not that I would. I'd grovel to keep his love," she said and Emma gave a reluctant grin. Bea, in the elegant black velvet and heavy gold chains, looked as if she could never grovel to anyone.

Bea walked across and took the General's arm. "I've seen nothing of you tonight and Emma and I have to leave in half an hour." She gazed up at him, a bewitching smile on her lips. "Betrothed people need to say good night, as Guy has to go back too."

"Take her into the conservatory, Guy. It's heated and private. Bea will fetch Emma when her jeep arrives."

"What a man of decision," Bea whispered.

"Come and meet my cousin from Alabama. He's three times your age and has acne! You are one hell of a dangerous woman, Bea. I like having you here but you disturb far too many of my officers." He glanced at Emma's slender and shapely hips and sleek well-brushed hair as she retreated with Guy. "Between the two of you, you'd drive this lot mad, even though half of them are married."

Guy took Emma's resisting hand and led her into the dimly lit room. The smell of wet earth and exotic plants made her think of Kew Gardens. He held her close and her resentment melted away in their kisses. "If only we had the time," he said at last. "I've dreamed of making love to you in our cottage but every time I think it's possible, something prevents it. I thought that if you didn't know I was at Heath Cross, it would be better for you, but I was mistaken. I thought of you all day and took in only half of what Desmond said."

"Never do that again," she said sternly. "Even if I can't see you, at least I'll know why and I can plan what time we have together."

"There was something more I did in Epsom," he said. "The people who own the cottage were eager to sell and wanted a quick agreement so the agent acted for me and I bought it for a disgustingly low price. He said that if I didn't have it, as a sitting tenant, he could sell it at the same price to someone else quite easily."

"That's wonderful!" Emma buried her face in his jacket. "Oh, I wish we were married and I could make it a real home."

"Wherever you are with me will be home," he said simply. "The war will soon be over now; at least for some."

"What do you mean?"

"I heard from David that there's been a massacre of United States troops at Malmedy. The SS shot eighty-six prisoners in the battles round the Ardennes. I don't know why the Germans do these pointless atrocities. They must know that the war will be over soon, and questions will be asked. At least they have stopped gassing Jews in Auschwitz concentration camp, as if they want to tidy up their image and paper over the cracks before the Russians advance that far!"

110

"How do you know?"

"David has contacts with the Intelligence Corps in Paris and a friend of his came back here for a few weeks and told us a lot that doesn't get on the news bulletins."

"I suppose the General knows about everything?"

"He knows a lot more about the Japs than we do, and there are rumours that a big offensive out there will happen soon, but nobody talks about it and it remains top secret."

"I think I'll say nothing to Bea about the massacre," Emma said, reflectively. "We are nursing German prisoners now and Bea is very anti, especially after today." She told him about the German pilot and Guy's face was grim.

"She was right to report him. You must never let that sort of thing happen without taking some action, or discipline will go down the drain."

"Not on our ward, with Sister Sinclair," Emma said with feeling. "Somehow I can't see them enjoying Christmas with us. She isn't likely to make any concessions to the festival and they will have no contact with their families."

"No turkey and mince pies?" He smiled. "I wish I could take you to Devon for Christmas. My father will have a turkey and a few extras like whisky left in the surgery and my sister and her family will be there."

"Do you have time off?" Emma asked.

"Yes, but any time I have to spare from work will be spent with you," he said, and Emma lost the remnants of her doubts. "I thought that we might have Christmas Eve together at the cottage. If we go to midnight mass at the church on the way to Epsom, we can go back there until morning. I'll have my car and we can be on duty as early as necessary." His smile

111

was of a small boy planning a raid on an orchard for apples.

"It's a wonderful idea," Emma said, and couldn't spoil his anticipation. She knew that next week she would be on night duty again and she doubted if her nights off would occur over the Christmas period.

"I'll see you before then. I'm back at Heath Cross in two days time and we can have time together."

"I have a day off on Wednesday," she replied eagerly. "I can get a sleep-ing out pass the night before and make sure the cottage is welcoming."

I must make sure that it helps you get over the disappointment of Christmas, she thought as they kissed goodnight and Bea called to say that the jeep was ready.

"Everything rosy?" Bea asked, and pulled her scarf up round the back of her neck to stop the draught in the back of the jeep.

"Better," Emma admitted cautiously. "But you are right, Bea. I must do what I want to do sometimes, rather than sit about waiting for Guy to call. I've always known what his work means to him. Remember the nights before D-Day when everyone was trying to relax and pass the time, but he wouldn't join in any social activities? He even took a huge textbook to the musical evenings."

"That's because he wasn't sure if you would ever love him," Bea said. "He thought that Phil might still be in the picture."

"That's partly true but it isn't the whole picture. He lives for his work and I have to be sure that in the future I can take what's left and think it's enough just to be married to him. Do we have to forget everything we've learned the hard way and everything that meant so much to us, just to follow a man around and be there when he has the time?"

"I can't wait to do just that," Bea said.

"You will go to a new life in the States, to a very prosperous background, with plenty of social contacts and all those gorgeous horses. Dwight isn't a doctor and you'll be able to plan what you do together, and not have to give up arrangements because there is an emergency."

"Guy is near to being a consultant and will have a busy private practice. Try to persuade him to bring you to the States. He could make a million over there, and we could see each other. I shall miss you, Emma. We go back quite a way now and I've never been this close to any other woman." Bea shrank down into her warm coat as if suddenly chilled. "In fact, that's the one thing that puts me off going away; contacts with you and a few others I've met at Beatties. I hope you and Guy have made arrangements to meet again soon?"

"Guy will be back at Heath Cross next week," Emma said.

"That's good . . . isn't it? Why so glum? I'll help you make the cottage warm and neat and I'll never be a clinging gooseberry unless I'm invited."

"I didn't like to disappoint him, but I shall be on night duty all over Christmas."

"Oh dear! You seem to be . . . ."

"Fated?" Emma sounded miserable. "You were going to say that, weren't you? First, I had to cancel the visit to Devon and I doubt if Guy has told his folk that we are engaged, as he wanted to announce it when we are there with them. Then we have been posted to separate hospitals for a long time and now I go on night duty just when we could have time together in the cottage."

"Coffee and bed for us," Bea said firmly when they passed beyond the guarded lodge and hurried up the windy road to the villa. "You'll see him before Christmas, and have a night or two off sometime." Bea stopped by the kitchen. "I'll pop these into my special glass fridge box and put the kettle on," she said. "You take the other tins and I'll keep them in my room. There are thieves about," she said darkly.

"You didn't ask for a doggy bag?" Emma laughed and felt better.

"I didn't need to twist any arms. A big parcel was waiting for me, from the General, who thinks it's his role in life to make me as fat as his beloved Marj back home. He really takes his role of godfather to Dwight very seriously, and thankfully, he provides food as well as good moral advice."

Bea brought the tray of coffee cups and a large pot of fragrant coffee. She chuckled when she saw Emma putting the tins of food out in a row. "Good. He knows I adore asparagus and that looks like duck with truffles. Yummy," she said. "We'll take some to the cottage for emergencies, and if Guy manages to be there at the same time as you are there, feel free to eat the lot."

"Thanks, Bea," Emma said quietly. "You put everything into a sane perspective."

"No, this time you needed no help from me. You are no longer drifting along on a rosy cloud and it's a good thing to view your situation a little more dispassionately. Both of us have to take life as it comes just now and hope for better times in the future. We'll take our finals and be independent of Beatties if we want to leave, and my man will be back in England, or so the General hinted. Not home to the States, but here for a while before he goes back at the end of the war." She sat on the bed, hugging her knees. "That gives me such courage," she said. "I think the General will make it happen and I can go back to the States with Dwight as a GI bride."

114

"Before that, we have smelly dressings to do tomorrow and there are rumours of another convoy to replace the ones sent north."

"Just when I've educated this lot about the way that English nurses expect to be treated." She held up her hand for silence and in the distance they heard the siren and a muted crump of bombs. "V2s again," Bea said, "But far away tonight and I'm not going to shelter even if the hospital siren blows. If the ward gets hit, I hope my dressings aren't affected. I spent hours on them."

"Your favourite pilot will be all right in his cosy padded cell," Emma said.

"Get out! I don't know why I bother with you. See you at breakfast."

Shouting woke Emma at dawn and she heard the wheels of heavy vehicles. A fresh ambulance convoy of prisoners came into the hospital grounds under the escort of army personnel carriers. They stopped with grinding brakes and left the ambulances free to advance to the entrance by casualty.

She turned over in bed, pulling the bedclothes high over her ears but it was too late to blot out the knowledge that there was more hard work in the offing. She dressed and took the tin of precious coffee that Aunt Emily had sent her and went down to the kitchen. Acting Sister Seymour was there and the kettle was almost boiling.

"You heard them too," Seymour said. "I remembered that we hadn't enough sterilised gloves and thought I'd go on duty early to make sure they had arrived. I hate this kind of surgery, digging for chunks of metal and putting in drains if the wounds are infected. Some have been left for far too long and the smell is appalling at times. We had a case of gangrene yesterday and the whole theatre had to be scrubbed and drenched in disinfectant before we could do more ops. One of the surgeons was grumbling that he wasn't allowed to use penicillin and he had quite an argument on the morality of using it only on our men."

"Our civilians can't have it," Emma pointed out. "Unless it is really urgent I suppose. There isn't enough to go round, but supplies will improve and then it will be freely available, like the sulphonamides, which are so good that we take them for granted now. It's like magic dust when we puff the powder into wounds."

She made coffee and Seymour brought out some almost new cake. They sat in the small sitting room and watched from the window as the military vehicles lumbered away again and the empty ambulances were scrubbed out and aired. "Well, better face it, I suppose," Emma said as some of the other nurses arrived downstairs ready to go to breakfast.

"Nurse Dewar?" A porter handed her a note. "He rang last night and left this message," he said.

"I probably had the message," Emma said as she took the piece of folded paper. "Thanks all the same. I saw him last evening." She glanced at the words then looked again and smiled.

"Not another man?" Seymour said with ill-concealed curiosity.

"Just a friend of Guy's who is going to be here for a while and said he'd be in touch."

"A Beatties man?"

"No, he's Paul Sykes, from Bristol now, but he was a student with Guy and they've kept in touch. When I went to my father's funeral he took me under his wing and was very kind," she went on, a warm feeling growing as she talked of him.

"Is he surgery?"

"No, he's a physician. Guy says he is very bright, but

you'd never guess. He looks very mild and calm and so casual that I can't imagine him getting in a rage. Maybe the pace of medicine is slower for physicians, but they do have to be pretty brainy."

"Wheel him in. He sounds like my type. I'm fed up with temperamental casualty officers and their ilk! That is unless he has a girl friend?"

"I don't know. That didn't arise. We talked about Bristol and places we had been to and it was good. He made me laugh and forget how depressed I'd been at having to go back to my mother again, and my father's funeral."

"I look forward to meeting him. You can't be selfish and keep him all to yourself, Dewar. There are others who need a good, honest man. You have bagged the best one, so give me a chance with this one!"

"He's moving in to the visitors' block tomorrow," Emma said. "Let's have a party and make him welcome. I'm sure he'll want to meet people."

"Other than you?" Seymour raised an eyebrow.

"Of course. I'm just a friend of a friend, and he may have a girl friend somewhere, so don't frighten him off by oozing sex appeal at your first meeting."

Seymour giggled. "It usually works. Can I invite Craig and then ditch him for this new one?"

"He *has* annoyed you," Emma said. She decided that Seymour was not Paul's type, but could think of no reason for coming to that conclusion.

"The weekly hop is the day after tomorrow, so we can spread the word and bring in a few extras for refreshments if we can lay hands on something better than Spam and bully-beef. The room next to the dance will be free and we can have our party privately and dance as well. That's one of the perks to being senior. The sprogs will never dare come into our holy territory!" Seymour was enthusiastic. "I'll ring Tony and see if he can come up from the wilds. His girl friend is away and he's lonely. I saw him last week and he pines for the days when we were all in the same operating theatre and he played silly practical jokes on us."

"That's one memory lane that I'd rather not see again," Emma said. "Too much tragedy, but it did have its moments," she admitted with a wistful smile.

"I'd better stoke up with scrambled eggs. I have a feeling that lunch will happen about five o'clock tonight, if at all."

"I'll make some cheese scones for the party, and some we can have with jam," Emma said. "My aunt sent some cheese and butter and I must use it. I can't bear to waste food and I have an uneasy feeling that she sends me her rations, but she does eat at the British Restaurant where she works as a supervisor, so she doesn't really go short."

"I'll bring a can of strawberry preserve that an American boy friend gave me and I expect Bea will have something in that very private box she keeps in the fridge. Is Guy likely to be there?"

Emma hesitated. "He might be," she said as if the idea hadn't occurred to her. "I hope so, as I have a day off after the party."

"And a sleeping-out pass?" Emma nodded. "I suppose you'll stay in Epsom?" Seymour looked envious and Emma's mouth was dry. Did everyone know that she and Guy were lovers now and they had a cottage in Epsom? "I'm wildly jealous of you," Seymour went on.

"All those lovely American officers and I expect they give you a very comfortable room."

"Oh, yes, the General is very good," Emma replied

weakly, and inwardly sighed with relief mixed with annoyance and guilt that it was still necessary to hide the fact that she was with Guy, as good as married, but with a gulf that separated them in the eyes of society.

Chapter 8

"Do you do this every night?" asked Paul Sykes, reaching over to take another buttered scone.

"No, this, believe it or not, is in your honour," said Seymour, making the most of her thrusting bosom and her long eyelashes as she handed him a glass of cider. "Guy and Emma said how kind you'd been when Emma had to go to her father's funeral and it's good to see a fresh face among the usual ones here."

Emma smiled. Seymour was making her sound like a spinster of no fixed age or intelligence who needed helping across a road. Craig Lucan sulked in the background and Seymour ignored him, conscious that she was looking good in a new rayon blouse and a tight black skirt.

All the women invited to the party had dressed up and Emma wondered at the impact that one new face had on their close community. Even before they saw Paul, the invited girls had pressed favourite blouses or dresses, and used precious make-up that was in short supply. Nylons that were carefully put on, having made sure that fingernails were free of snags and hands were smooth, showed off good legs, and high-heeled court shoes usually kept for very special occasions, made an appearance.

"You look wonderful," Guy said softly as Emma went to meet him at the door of the room. The pale blue lace blouse showed an oyster rayon lining and the beige skirt was well fitting and matched the suede shoes from Switzerland that Bea had insisted were too tight for her and perfect with the skirt. "How soon can we get away?" he asked.

"We can't go yet," she reproved him. "Paul has been here only a few hours and this is a way of introducing him to our friends."

She laughed. "Have something to eat before it all goes. Seymour has her eye on Paul, as you can guess from Craig's expression, and everyone is interested to see a new British medic. Somehow Desmond and his team were a disappointment socially, and the Dutch and French keep to themselves and the people from their own wards, so we hope for better with Paul. He looks as if he might play badminton or tennis and we need a few more. I didn't realise until now how cloistered we are here, even though we move between London and Heath Cross and the place where Tony works. There he is, by the way. I haven't seen him for ages."

"Paul doesn't need any introductions," Guy said dryly. "He seems to be very much in demand. Come and dance."

"In a minute," Emma said. "Come and talk to Paul. He *is* your friend and you haven't been near him."

"I want to hold you close, if only on the dance floor," Guy whispered.

"We have a lot of time later," she replied softly. "Be sociable and mingle a little." She touched his hand and smiled. "We'll slip away at ten. Bea said she'd clear up here with a few helpers, but there isn't going to be any food left so it will be easy."

"Hello, Guy." Michael Price, one of the house physicians followed them over to Paul, emanating a familiarity that Emma knew Guy would resent from a newly

121

appointed HP "What's this I hear? You've bought a house?" Guy stared at him and said nothing. "My cousin lives in Epsom and his father is an estate agent. He asked if I knew a Mr Guy Franklin and told me you signed the papers the other day."

Bea was listening and saw that Guy looked nonplussed and annoyed. "Oh, blast!" she said, breaking the thin ice. "Now everyone will know. We'd hoped it would be a secret place for sundry hard working people studying for exams, to take their ease undisturbed by the hoi polloi of Heath Cross." She turned to the interested faces. "You needn't think you are all invited. I have bagged one room for myself and Emma has another. Guy will use the rest when he is here, but heaven help him if he invites too many people, as we want a bit of peace."

"You mean, you are involved in this, Bea?" Michael's thin face showed disappointment, and the triumph he had experienced at the thought that he might have some scandal to stir up, faded.

"Your friend is guilty of a breach of confidentiality," Guy said coldly. He raised his eyebrows and looked very angry. "What did he say I paid for it?"

"He only said you'd bought it," muttered the crestfallen man. He glanced at Emma. "I thought that a whole house seemed a lot for one man."

"So it would be," said Bea, patiently. "We don't want to go to the General's house all the time as it means dressing up and eating far too much, so this will be good. I can make endless cups of coffee and slouch around in frayed slippers without anyone being the wiser, and when Dwight comes back, soon I hope, Guy has promised that we can have the place to ourselves for a while." She fished in her purse and dangled a key in front of Michael's eyes. "See! I have a share in this transaction and I am not prepared to share it with anyone but Emma."

"You'll have to have a house warming," Seymour said. "We have a perfectly adequate gas fire and a fireplace for logs," said Bea. "It's warm enough and if you think I'm feeding the five thousand there with my precious Yankee food, you can think again." She looked at the empty dishes. "Some blighter has had the last of my smoked salmon! I left some on a pink plate over there and I thought I'd eat it later," she said in mock exasperation. "I might have known what a lot of gannets you are."

Michael hastily put the empty but oily pink plate he was holding down on the table and blushed. "Sorry," he murmured and made his escape as quickly as he could.

"Good guess," Bea said and giggled. "I don't know what was on that plate but I suspect it was that rather pungent smoked mackerel that I was glad to have eaten by anyone but me. A man of his low tastes and sensitivity wouldn't know the difference."

"Thank you, Bea," Emma said softly. Her face was pale and Guy looked uneasy.

"You'd better stay until Michael goes to bed. His pointy nose would follow you to the car," Bea said.

"I can do better than that," Guy said. "He should be doing a night round unless he has a stand-in. I'll see if he is on call. Excuse me for ten minutes?"

"Time we danced," Craig said firmly and gripped Seymour's arm as if leading her to her doom. She made a feeble pretence at resisting then followed him meekly into the room where the dancing was still in progress. Bea glanced in and said, "She's draped all over him and he has one thing on his mind. They'll be engaged soon. I see it in my crystal ball."

Tony Goldstone took her hand. "I've learned to jive

123

since I saw you the last time we danced together here, centuries ago. Come on baby!"

"Don't *you* give me that Yankee rubbish. I'll get enough when my man comes home," she said with an accent that might have come from southern Tennessee.

"Hello Emma, I haven't had a chance to talk to you. It was good of you to invite me here." Paul laughed. "I feel as if I am among friends."

"It's good to see you again, Paul. How is Bristol?" she asked lightly.

"A bit battered but still there. I can't say I miss it now. I find that many of my contemporaries have gone away to other jobs or are in the services, and I really prefer the country. This area has a lot going for it."

"Even in winter?" She seemed amused. "Most people go up to London as often as they can and hate the cold Heath at this time of the year, but of course, Heath Cross, being a madhouse in all senses of the word, has a certain horrible fascination. I'm not even frightened of the bats flying in the corridors now."

"You love it," he said.

"Yes. I think we do good work here and have more freedom than we had at Beatties and I like walking through the bracken, even when it's frozen. It reminds me of home. Small towns like Epsom are good and I'd hate to live in a big city again."

"When you and Guy are married, isn't that what will happen? He's in the running for a consultancy, very young, and that will link up with city hospitals." He grinned. "How do you fancy Manchester or Hull or even further north?"

"He wouldn't go there!"

"Of course not, at least not by choice, but there is great potential in cities outside of London, and there will be a

124

lot of rebuilding to do before some hospitals are ready for new consultants. A stint away from the main cities might be to his advantage."

"We have never discussed that possibility but he did say that he had no intention of following his father in general country practice."

"He's lucky to have that choice. I think I can just about manage to buy a partnership in such a practice. I have a legacy that's waiting for the war to end to give me freedom to choose what I do." His eyes were dreamy and Emma decided that they were not really dark brown but had golden flecks in them and she could see how someone like Seymour had been immediately attracted to him.

"You don't sound as if you are planning anything," she said.

"We all have dreams, and before I settle into a cosy country existence, I shall travel, maybe to America and study Indian medicine and find out more about healing plants." She nodded. "You don't find that absurd?"

"No. My grandfather used a lot of gypsy medicines for his horses and sheep, and even for humans, I believe, if my Aunt Emily has it right, but he'd never admit to taking medicine of any kind." She bit her lip. "At last, he had to obey the doctor and have treatment, and eventually he died of a burst aortic aneurysm."

"I'd like to take a year off to go over there," Paul said.

"You must talk to Bea. Her husband's family is important in ranching country and Dwight may be able to introduce you to a lot of useful people."

He eyed her quizzically. "Don't you have any relatives out there?"

Her eyes widened. "Not really. There was an uncle once but I suppose he's dead by now and I know nothing about him. I'd love to go there, but I have no excuse for such self-indulgence, unless Bea and Dwight persuade Guy to work there."

"Rich pickings in the States," Paul said cryptically.

"You wouldn't earn much doing research into herbs," she said.

"I wasn't thinking of me. The work would be a rich reward and I'd come back and maybe write learned papers about it which might or might not earn their keep."

"And you'd take time off in between to do nothing?" she said acidly, as if his ideas were to be envied, but inaction was forbidden.

He gave a lazy smile. "'What is this life, if full of care we have no time to stand and stare,'" he quoted. "Staring at nothing can bring knowledge," he added. "At least self- knowledge."

"Stop teasing me." She felt uncomfortably aware that he was laughing at her. "There's Guy. I think I'd better help Bea clear away. You have the phone number of our villa?" He nodded and stretched.

It's been wonderful, meeting again and seeing your friends, Emma. I have to go. My motor-bike will be freezing and it hates to start in this weather, so I must put it undercover for the night or I'll never get to Reigate in the morning."

"Give me a ring," she called after him. "I owe you a good dinner."

"I'd like that."

"You already have a ring," Tony quipped as he brought Bea back breathless and flushed from jiving.

"Not that kind, silly," Emma said. "Have you to go back tonight?"

"I'll camp out on someone's floor and get away early

126

tomorrow. The first list isn't until ten-thirty and there's nothing of great importance."

"All good little house physicians are doing their night rounds," Guy said with obvious satisfaction. "The acute civilian ward put out a call for Dr Price and he had to leave us." He glanced at Bea and turned towards the door. "I'll see Emma back to the villa," he said.

Ten minutes later, the gates were opened for the car to leave Heath Cross and Emma gave a sigh of relief. They arrived at the cottage and Emma went quickly inside while Guy put the car in the shed. She lit the gas fire and put the kettle to boil on the gas stove, then plugged in the small electric fire to heat the bedroom. She noticed with pleasure the pretty room and the bed made up with crisp sheets, warm blankets and covered with a crimson silk eiderdown that Bea had brought from her father's apartment in St James's, having told him that he needed a new one.

Bea's room was obviously her own territory, with a bookcase filled with favourite literature and textbooks and a small desk, also filched from St James's, and rugs that were old and worn and valuable. The other two bedrooms had smaller cupboards and single beds and Emma had put enough of her own things in one of them to show that it was her room, but she now shut that door and turned back the bedcovers in the main bedroom.

Guy was making tea in the kitchen. "No champagne, darling," he said.

"I hate champagne," Emma said. "It makes me miserable."

"That's a pity. I have a magnum for when we go to Devon and announce our engagement."

"I drink it if I am expected to do so, and I can even smile when I do, but it brings back sad memories of the early

127

part of the war." Guy nodded, but was more concerned with the present than any of her memories in which he had no part.

I have never told him about Evans and her brother dying, she thought, as if it was a surprising discovery. The separation of her life into segments was frightening. Would this period in her life fade away as she made new friends and moved away from London and Beatties? Worse still, would Guy be with her in ten years time? She shivered.

"Come to bed," he said softly. "You are so lovely tonight, but a little sad, I think."

"I wish we really belonged," she whispered.

"You must never let people like Michael Price worry you. Next year, we'll be married and you will never have to hide away from people like him."

"He worried you tonight, and if Bea hadn't taken over, we'd have been humiliated."

Guy switched off the gas fire and Emma watched the bars dull through dark red into grey, then picked up her jacket and walked up the stairs. The bedroom was warm and the red shades over the wall lights cast a friendly and flattering glow as she undressed. Guy came back from the bathroom wearing pyjama bottoms and his face felt cool and almost damp as he kissed her. She recalled the first time they'd made love in the bracken on the Heath when they were exhausted and horrified by the wounds they had tended in the operating theatre that hot night in June. It was my decison, she remembered. I knew how much he needed me and I wanted him, too.

He kissed her gently, then with increasing fervour and his hands caressed her body as if learning every curve and every softness. He murmured her name and she wriggled out of her modest nightdress, pushing her body close to

128

him and feeling his passion grow. This loving was more gentle but more intense than that time on the Heath and at any time in hotel bedrooms when they'd snatched a few hours together. It had the same good feeling of belonging that they'd experienced when staying with Aunt Emily, and Emma gave herself up to wave after wave of desire, uninhibited and demanding, in exultation and triumph that this man loved her and would be hers forever.

They slept and made love again and heard rain on the windows as dawn came. Guy slipped out of bed to light the fire downstairs and they lay sweetly entwined again until the first grey light had given way to watery sun.

"We'll drive to Boxhill," he said later when they'd eaten toast and some of Emily's marmalade, and drained the coffee pot. He eyed the elegant suede shoes that she had worn to the party and grinned. "On second thoughts, it's no use taking you into the country," he said.

"Bea's not the only one to stake a claim here," she replied, and put on rubber boots and a warm raincoat. "We'll climb Box Hill and find some food in that nice pub there." Her gaze was soft. "It's wonderful having you here for a whole day and night."

"We'll be here again on Christmas Eve," he said. "I saw two donkeys in the field at the back of the house." He laughed softly and she had never loved him more. "We shall see if they really do kneel down on Christmas Eve as the legend has it."

"Have you heard from your family?" she asked.

Guy frowned. "They are gathering for a couple of days and wanted us to go there, but I told them it was impossible this year."

Emma reached up to shut the window tighter as the old car bumped over rough ground and a thin line of cold air came through the gap at the top of the door. "I can't come here at Christmas," she said slowly.

He looked sideways at her. "Are you sure? Even if we can't make love, we can be together. I know I'll hate not making love when we are alone in the cottage, but being there is good on any level."

"It's not that. I have been told to report on night duty tomorrow night," she said. "I said nothing last night as I wanted everything to be perfect, and it was," she whispered. "It was perfect."

"Damn!" She saw that he was confused and angry. "This is too much. Can't you change it? Leave now and we can be married before Christmas by special licence and go to Devon for our honeymoon."

"There isn't time, Guy. I have to do as they say until I finish my exams, and we agreed to wait until then in case I have to leave Beatties for good."

"You'll do that in any case as soon as you qualify. Once we are married, you'll be there when I come home." He stopped the car overlooking the beauty spot and stared out at the misty skeletal trees and bushes. "There's no need for you to work, and if the authorities kick up a fuss, you can take a part-time job in a clinic." He laughed. "My father could do with you to sort out his files and case histories. He's a wonderful GP but otherwise he's a pretty vague individual at the best of times and hates paperwork. It's a wonderful idea! I can kill two birds with one stone and have my folk and you there whenever I have leave."

Emma stepped out into the cold wind and pulled her hood over her head. "I don't think I want to be a dead bird! They might not like me and I might not get on with them. Apart from that, I can't waste all my training on tidying desks!"

"It was only a thought," he replied in a conciliatory

voice. "Don't be cross, Emma. Let's find some food."
He grinned and she gave a reluctant smile. "Love makes
me ravenous and if I can't eat you, I'll settle for hot soup
and whatever they have in there."

"Not enough shepherd," Guy said as he stirred the thick
layer of potato on his shepherd's pie.

"I find bread and cheese a bit better," Emma said. "At
least they gave me a spoonful of pickle and the bread
isn't bad."

"Do you mind going back on night duty?" he asked
abruptly.

She looked up in surprise and saw that he was serious.
"After the first week, it becomes a habit, and in a way it's
quite pleasant." She smiled. "Especially if you visit me
after Night Sister has done her rounds and we can talk
in a quiet corner." She shrugged. "Sometimes I think I
see more of my friends when I'm on night duty, as they
relax after the day's work and drift along to whoever is
on night duty for coffee and conversation if the wards
aren't busy."

"I could ask for leave for you over Christmas," he
said.

"No, Guy. I have to follow the rules and I have no more
leave due until the New Year. It would make people look
at us with beady eyes. We've been discreet. People know
we are engaged, but we've been able to fend off men like
Michael Price who want to dig into what doesn't concern
them." She frowned. "There would be no point in making
a fuss about Christmas as we couldn't go to stay in the
cottage openly or everyone would know that it was . . .
our place."

"I wasn't thinking about the cottage," Guy said dismissively. "I have time off and we could spend Christmas
with my family and announce our engagement when we

are there." He laughed. "There are all sorts of quite silly conventions that have to be observed in a country practice. The local paper will want a picture of us and a brief history of our lives and the vicar will ask when we intend being married and what hymns we want! They do tend to jump a few stages and sweep people along towards the happy day. It keeps the village gossips happy for weeks, and the church flower arrangers busy planning for whatever month we choose," he added with satisfaction.

"I really can't have leave," Emma said, "and we haven't decided where we want to be married. I suppose that traditionallly the bride chooses the time and place, doesn't she? I hadn't given it much thought, but I think I'd prefer a registrar office ceremony with just a few friends," she said firmly. "And your family, of course," she added when she saw his shocked amazement. "You know I have very few relatives and I would hate to be married in Bristol where my mother would be intolerable. I suppose the Island is out of the question?"

Guy ordered more coffee and lit a cigarette. Emma watched the blue smoke rising and knew that the cigarette wasn't the only thing smouldering. She put a hand over Guy's and smiled but he seemed not to notice the contact. "So this Christmas we can't use the cottage as you'll be on duty, and you refuse to let me ask for time off for you. I thought I'd say that we wanted to announce our engagement to my family. I'm sure that the Admin people would have seen reason, if I asked them and they knew why we wanted to go away."

"You know you never like to pull rank, Guy, and I think you know that it would be far more trouble than it was worth. It would disrupt staff and make others resentful if they thought you used your influence, when maybe they had equally viable excuses for time off."

"How often would I see you? A couple of mornings before you went to bed, or at most an evening up until seven before you got ready for duty?"

"Why don't you go to Devon alone?" she asked. "I think I'd rather have that than to know you were kicking your heels here just to see me for an hour or so." She took away her hand and sat straight, hoping that he'd say he wanted to stay with her even if he saw her briefly each day, and she hoped he'd be a little more cheerful about it. "Whatever you decide will have to be soon. Do you realise it's only three days to Christmas Eve?"

"Tomorrow night you go on duty," said Guy in a flat voice. "The day after, you'll be as limp as a rag with confused sleeping patterns, and not much better the day after. Happy Christmas!" he said wryly. "For both of us."

"I've never seen you so disgruntled," she said.

"It's important, Emma. I don't know why but I feel as if time is against me and I have to fit in a lot that I once thought could wait. I want you as my wife and I want to show you off to my family. I love you and this waiting for a normal life pulls me to pieces when I can't be with you." He was trying to control a deep emotion. "Dwight had it right. They are separated now but even Bea has that sense of belonging, a kind of aura that is so precious, and they know that they will be together soon. What if I was called back to the Reserve again and went way for months? I'd be wondering who was getting close to you, knowing that you were not really mine."

"We haven't had a good walk," Emma said. "The sun's out now and it isn't as cold. Come on, you can decide later, but I think you should go to Devon and be with your family." She stood up. "It might be for the last time as their unattached son and they'll enjoy that."

133

"I hate to think of you working here while I am spoiled by my family," he said, slowly.

"It's part of the job and someone must be here to make life a little better over the festival." She saw his disbelief that she could accept it so philosophically. "We used to giggle at the motto of the Home on the Downs in Bristol, 'Love Serves'. But it's true, Guy. It *is* an act of love to give what we can to our patients. You know that as well as I do," she added, faintly disapproving of his dark mood.

"Marry me now," he said.

"Nothing has changed," she replied patiently. "I am going to qualify soon in the New Year and then we can plan what we want to do. They say the war is nearly over and if that's so, we shall have a wider choice for the future."

"You look cold. Let's walk back to the car and find some tea somewhere." Guy held her hand inside the deep pocket of his greatcoat and Emma felt his nearness, warm and reassuring and strong. He would be a strong man always, firm and utterly reliable, and yes, she decided, selfish when he couldn't have his own way. They agreed on so many things that it had seemed that they agreed on everything. Now, she felt exhausted as she tried to keep to what she knew was right for her. I must not give way in this, she decided. I must retain the right to think as an individual, sometimes.

Guy pushed open the door of the cafe and slipped out of his greatcoat, rubbing his hands before the log fire. He smiled. "Log fires at Christmas," he said. "Don't you love the smell of burning wood?"

"Lovely," she agreed, and gazed into the depths of white hot ashes and crimson caves, remembering not her parents' home but the house where her grandmother had lived after she gave up the shop on Coppins Bridge.

Strange, Emma thought. I didn't really know her but I do remember her kind hands.

"When do you leave?" she asked when the scones arrived with small pats of butter and a dish of plum jam. She bit into one and the taste of bicarbonate of soda filled her mouth as she chewed the over-risen dry scone.

"I haven't said I'm going anywhere," Guy said defensively.

"If you do go, we shall both be able to concentrate. You on your family and me on my job," she said, mildly. "Telephone them tonight Guy, and tell them when to expect you. I know they'll be thrilled."

"You and Bea could use the cottage and invite friends," he suggested, already half convinced that he was leaving for Devon. He smiled. "We'd be doing Bea a favour. She'd be very lonely without you, now that Dwight can't be here."

"That's true," Emma said.

"Maybe I can bring back some farmhouse cheeses and a rabbit or a duck. I suppose the oven in the cottage works?"

"I've no idea. As yet, we haven't planned on cooking there," Emma said. "After being on duty, the last thing on our minds is cooking."

"But all women like cooking," he said with a grin.

"You haven't tasted my mother's efforts," Emma said. "Aunt Emily is a race apart and even if I take after her in some ways, I need leisure and an urge to cook before I walk into a kitchen." She picked up another scone that looked as if it had erupted and over flowed like volcanic lava, and put it back on the dish. "They made these over-light but stodgy. How did they manage that?" she asked.

"Let's go back," Guy suggested and appeared embarrassed.

"You have to pack and make sure the car is ready," Emma said solemnly. "Take me back to the villa, Guy, and I can give you your Christmas present." She ran her tongue behind her teeth and found roughness from the sodium bicarbonate in the scones. "We should have had tea in Epsom at Fuller's," she said. "Could we stop there and buy some cakes for Bea?"

Chapter 9

"Brass monkeys!" the porter said as he pushed the linen trolley further into the empty side ward. "A right frost last night, Nurse Dewar. Bad on the roads. Army lorries got stuck on the hill and that new doctor came off his motor- bike on his way here."

"Doctor Sykes? Is he badly hurt?" Emma asked.

"Na, not him. Bounced back with just a few bruises and after they'd stuck on a few plasters, he sat in the small common room in the medics villa all day." He grinned. "Seemed to like being off duty and said there was nothing of importance that he couldn't handle by phone so it looks as if he's here for Christmas."

"Do you get time off?" she asked.

"Not a chance, Nurse." He tried to look self-sacrificing. "I can't get back to the Smoke where my missus is with her mother, so I'll have to put up with a bint I've found in Epsom." He grinned. "I'm better off than that lot you've got in there, Nurse. I talk to the guard sometimes, and he said one of them was crying is eyes art when they started asking questions about his home and all that."

"That would be Edwig Gesner," Emma said. "Do you know that he is only fifteen."

"Garn! He looks much older than that."

"He enlisted from Hitler Youth and I suspect they didn't ask too many questions. They're taking them from school

137

now, and telling them what a wonderful thing it is to fight for the Fatherland."

The porter sniffed. "Do they tell them what it's like to die? But I still say he can't be only fifteen."

Emma picked up a dressing towel and began to fold it, corner to corner and again, corner to corner to make a small square. "I think that anyone would look more than fifteen if he had five big pieces of shrapnel in his body and a peppering of small bits of metal everywhere. He has five drainage tubes in, and tonight I might be able to reach the piece over his liver as it does seem to be working its way out. It pushed out the drain."

"Why not get him under and remove the lot under gas?"

"These are the ones left after surgery. He couldn't stand any more," Emma said.

"Poor little bleeder, if you'll excuse my French, Nurse."

The porter pushed the empty trolley into the corridor and whistled, *Come All ye Faithful*.

Emma laid the dressing trolley in the clinical room. She pushed it quietly behind the screens that the Junior had set up round the boy's bed and turned up the light over the patient. The day staff had been too busy to do evening dressings as one man had suddenly bled from his lung and died without more than an hour's warning.

Edwig Gesner eyed her listlessly. She glanced at his chart and saw that his pulse was fast and his respirations shallow, but his temperature was not raised beyond a point or so. On the bedside locker were a few creased photographs. Emma had noticed that today, on Christmas Eve, most of the men had their family snaps out on the lockers and although nothing was said, an air of deep depression covered the ward like a pall.

The junior nurse came as soon as she was called, to

138

expose the wounds needing fresh dressings. First, Emma swabbed and dressed the ones on his abdomen, then asked the nurse to hold him forward so that she could reach the two on his back and side. When she had dressed these wounds on day duty, she had found it easier for the patient to be in that position rather than trying to lie on his wounded abdomen.

Nurse Read raised his shoulders and brought him into her arms to rest his head on her shoulder and expose his back. He stiffened for a moment then slumped hard against her as if he had no energy to resist what Staff Nurse Dewar was about to do.

Emma glanced at his face and saw that tears were running down his cheeks. She noticed how firmly and impersonally Nurse Read held him. Her breasts were taut against his shoulder and she was breathing quickly with the effort to hold him in the right position for the dressing, as he was now a dead weight. Emma worked quickly and found a loose piece of metal which she removed, then put in a smaller drain and puffed sulphonamide powder round the wound. She strapped the dressing in place and pulled down the pyjama jacket.

"Lower him on to that side, Nurse," she said. "He'll feel better without that pressure now."

"I can't. He is clinging to me, Nurse." The more that Emma tried to lever his hand away, the closer he clung to Nurse Read, as if he never wanted to let her go. He was muttering in German and sounded frantic.

"What does he say?" Emma asked the man in the next bed, who she knew could speak a little English. "Is the dressing too tight?"

"No. He calls for his mother and sister and your nurse is pretty and smells nice."

Emma picked up the picture of the woman and the girls

and the solemn faced man and smiled. "Tell him that they will be thinking of him tonight and that he will go home and see them as soon as we make him better," she said. "Boys and the chronically injured are to be sent home soon as there is no place for them in prison camps," she added, knowing that what she said was true but not for the ears of the German prisoners, in case they had more to tell the security forces.

He spoke in rapid German and the boy looked up and saw Emma's eyes, full of compassion over her mask. He half smiled and said *"Danke"*, putting out his hand for the picture. Nurse Read made her escape, her cheeks pink and her eyes wary. "He's a bit grown-up for fifteen, Nurse Dewar," she said as she pushed the dressing trolley away. "It wasn't a sister he wanted or his mother!"

The lights were dimmed in the ward and only the ward kitchen was brightly lit. Emma made a round with sleeping drugs and pain killers and the Junior took round hot drinks.

Christmas Eve, thought Emma. Guy would be getting ready to go to midnight service, while she tossed evil smelling dressings into the bin and scrubbed instruments. In London, the patients at Beatties would have helped deck the wards with greenery and any coloured paper streamers they could get. Relatives would be there long after normal visiting hours to help them make the most of being away from everything they loved at Christmas. Tomorrow, they would eat better food than many ever had at home and the medical and nursing staff would make it a time for laughter and companionship.

Even in Heath Cross, in the civilian wards and in wards where the last of the RAF boys remained with a few soldiers on traction, there would be laughter and sometimes a kiss under the mistletoe, and sherry and beer

140

smuggled into the wards. She sighed. Some of the best Christmases in her life had been in hospital, but now this dreary ward seemed full of unhappy ghosts and the staff were forbidden to fraternise with them.

The men were very quiet as if afraid that their emotions would show, and for the first time, Emma wished she could communicate with them in their own language. Gesner dozed and was less restless than she had last seen him. Was it that his wounds felt easier or had the brief physical contact with a pretty girl had more to do with it?

The man in the next bed spoke in English when she took his temperature and checked the pad over his injured eye and cheek. With no day sister there, he was more relaxed and Emma felt a tiny bond as he explained about Gesner. "He comes from a village where all the men have gone into the army and the boys have been told many tales of the glory they might bring home if they went too. Some of his friends are dead and he misses his family who are simple people and loyal to the Führer, so now he does not know what to believe." He smiled. "At least I have convinced him that he will not be used for medical experiments here and will not be shot when he leaves here. We were warned of what would happen to us if we were captured and many believed it."

"Did you believe that?" she asked.

"We did not expect to be captured," he replied dryly. "I was conscripted as many of your men were and had no choice. I work in a bank and have never been interested in politics, but it had to come." He shrugged. "You are kind and after the war I shall come back to see your country if I am allowed. I came once to camp in the Lake District and it was a good time. I shall bring my wife here if she survives the war." He looked sad. "I know that we shall not win and everything we fought for will be as nothing.

I would like to know what news there is but I know you must not tell me."

Emma shook her head. "I can say nothing, but please believe that most of us didn't want war and will be glad when peace comes." She shook the thermometer and noted that his temperature was down. Peace? she thought as she went from bed to bed. Tony had said that the face of peace might be a bitter one for many after the war.

Night Sister made an early round and saw that all was under control. She stood at the end of the ward and frowned. "Some of the staff insisted that the usual things should be observed and so we have a procession of nurses singing carols coming round the wards. They will go to the service wards and the civilians', but not in here. The patients will be able to hear them. A pity," she added. "I think the sight of nurses in red cloaks and carrying candles might be good for them and be a memory of peace, but the military say no."

"They are very quiet," Emma said. "Gesner wept and seemed very homesick and the others have their family photographs on their lockers."

"Some will be moved on next week," Sister said. "I wish we could send the whole lot home, but Sister Sinclair was a bit waspish when I suggested it, and of course, she's right. Many of our people and thousands of Jews have died over there and many are in horrendous *stalags* under awful conditions. What escapees have managed to get home, bring tales of murder and suffering and from what we've seen with these men, supplies must be bad enough for their own people now and they obviously treat our men less well than their own." She turned to go. "Any problems, just ring the office," she said, and smiled. "I expect Guy will come to see you, and tonight I don't want to know who else comes to visit the nurses."

"Guy is in Devon with his parents," Emma said. "It seemed sensible as I couldn't be off duty."

"Who needs to be sensible in wartime?" She laughed and walked away and Emma recalled that a certain RAF officer from one of the other wards was with Night Sister whenever he could get away, on crutches.

Music from a recorder sounded as if a medieval minstrel was approaching and the soft singing was recognisable as *Once in Royal David's City*. The nurses, with their dark cloaks worn inside out to show the scarlet linings, came slowly along the bleak corridor, the flickering candles sending the resident bats flying out into the night.

The guard came further into the ward, his face taut with practised suspicion as if expecting trouble, but Emma smiled and shook her head and he relaxed. The nurses paused at the doorway and Emma saw that Bea was among them, her face pale and her eyes downcast.

Dwight is thousands of miles away, but at least Guy is safe here in England, Emma thought with a sense of guilt because she had been feeling depressed and alone. When she had telephoned her mother in a sudden burst of family guilt, she had been told by the lodger that Mrs Dewar had gone to spend Christmas with a group from the chapel and wouldn't be back until the New Year. She sounded very fed-up as she had been left alone, unable to get home to Scotland for the holiday.

The singing faded, leaving a blank silence in the ward but Emma knew that the men felt affected by the music. She sat in the office, writing report, then heard more music. She put down the report book and listened. It was a harmonica, played with skill and feeling and it came from a bed at the far end of the ward.

Tears pricked her eyes as a gentle humming from the

143

other patients made an accompaniment and a man began to sing softly in German, *Stille Nacht*.

The bare floorboards and dull blackout curtains seemed even more bleak as she listened. She missed Guy, she missed Aunt Emily and she missed the Island. She wondered if Bea would go to the cottage tomorrow and she wanted someone to give her warm companionship. Guy would be in the village church by now, exchanging Christmas greetings and maybe even glad to be alone with his family. She bit back the rising self-pity and walked into the ward to make sure that the guard did nothing to stop the music as being bad for British morale, but he too was listening, fascinated, and Emma went back to the office.

"Hello, Emma."

"Paul! What are you doing here? I heard you were slightly wounded."

"I really am," he said, touching the small plaster on his cheek and making an exaggerated limp towards her.

"You look fine to me," she said with complete lack of sympathy. "What can you expect if you will ride that terrible bike on ice?"

"And there I was, hoping for coffee and sympathy." He grinned. "I think you are the one to need that. You look a bit peaky. I heard the music. He's not bad. What a pity he's a Hun and we can't ask him to play for our dances." He laughed. *Silent Night* wouldn't go down well. Does he know any jazz?"

"This is Christmas Eve," she said, trying to look serious. "We have carols on Christams Eve, not jazz."

"That's better. You're smiling." He sniffed. "I was right, you have coffee brewing and I've brought some candies that I begged from a guy in the service medical ward. I told him he was putting on weight and I'd help him

144

by eating his candy. He can get more as the Yanks send in masses for their men. Bea said to tell you that she has a hamper from the General for tomorrow and she'll open it at lunch time for a few select friends, so you'd better stay awake for it."

"Great! I shall starve when I come off duty and really enjoy the treats. Warmed up chicken and potatoes was not what I was looking forward to tomorrow night."

As if on cue, Nurse Read brought in a tray of coffee and two cups. She raised her eyebrows when she saw Paul as she'd expected to see Guy Franklin. "Do you need another cup, Nurse Dewar?"

"No, Mr Franklin had to go away," Emma said.

"I'm really Father Christmas," Paul said and handed her a packet of chocolate. "Hide it from Nurse Dewar as I have some for her too, but share it with the other nurse, and Happy Christmas." He planted a kiss on Nurse Read's cheek and pushed her out of the room.

"What was all that about?" Emma asked.

"She'll be too busy telling everyone that I kissed her, to worry about you, without Guy, spending hours with me in your office."

"Hours?"

"Why not? I have nowhere to go, I'm lonely and I need a fresh crepe bandage on my ankle, so this is an official visit."

"Sure you don't want a bed in the ward? Nurse Read would love to give you a blanket bath."

"Just a bandage put on by your own fair hands," he said lightly. "Coffee first and some sweets."

Emma poured coffee and saw that he was watching her. "Sugar?" she asked.

"Thanks honey," he said and grinned, and she found her lips twitching in an effort not to laugh. The office

145

felt cosier and the distant music went on, now including German folk songs and some Bach.

"I suppose it isn't allowed," she said. "But what harm can it do? I hope that Nurse Read has given the guard some coffee and a piece of cake. This one is more relaxed than some I've met and the men in the ward never play up when he's here, as they like him."

"Do they play up?" Paul asked.

"Some did at first when they were really frightened at what we might do to them, but two were taken away under guard to be looked after by male orderlies and the rest simmered down. Do you know, I shall miss some of them when they are sent north." She glanced at her watch. "Nearly midnight and Christmas Day. You should be in bed, Paul, and I have to go down to my night meal and an hour off in the ward day room. Nothing urgent is likely to happen here and Nurse Read likes to sit in the office and pretend to be very senior if anyone comes round."

"I want to stay with you," he said quietly. "I'm not tired, I had a nap earlier and I can sleep tomorrow."

"Thank you," she said.

"Don't thank me. I am being selfish. I want to stay with you even if you wish me far away so that you can think of Guy."

"Guy will be in church now," she said. "He is with his doting family and I'm sure that he'd rather be there than hanging about here for just an hour or so with me tomorrow."

"He could be here now just as I am. You sound as if you don't mind."

"I do, but I accept it. Guy loves his parents. I envy him that, but I don't resent it and we shall have all the time in the world together when I finish my training, and that's very soon."

146

"Do you have to go down to the dining room with the rest? Bea sent some rather nice pâté sandwiches and there are enough for two. We can eat them in the day Room."

She shrugged. "It's an iron rule that we leave the ward for our meal time, but I'll hurry back and join you. Save me a sandwich as I don't think our meal will be very good. Nobody here has achieved the skill of serving warmed-up food in an appetising way. They don't consider night staff to be humans with healthy appetites." She sighed. "I must stop the music now. They need rest and it's gone on for long enough. I don't want them bursting into patriotic songs and getting all het-up. I'll make a quick round before I go."

She walked into the ward and addressed the man who understood her. "Tell them that they may have one more song and then silence. Do you understand?"

"Yes, Sister. I will tell them, and they wish to thank you. This night will be remembered."

He spoke in a loud voice and she felt that as a sergeant, he had a lot of influence on the other men. Emma went from bed to bed and Nurse Read collected and replaced urinals until the ward was quiet, then the harmonica began to play again. Emma, and Paul who listened from the office and the guard who was sitting at the end of the ward, were lost for words. Emma almost wept as the song that had swept Germany, France and Great Britain and even the forces in the desert and in the Pacific, on all sides of the conflict, *Lilli Marlene*, came softly across the bare floorboards and simple iron bedsteads then died away into silence.

"I shall go for meal now, Nurse Read," Emma said in an unsteady voice.

"Yes, Sister, I mean Nurse Dewar." The girl managed a watery smile. "I think I'll keep away from Gesner or I might want to hold his hand," she said. "Did you see him? He had a fit of the sobs again, and no wonder, poor boy."

It was a surprise to find many of the night staff in a festive mood, but most of them were nursing British civilians and service personnel and everything possible was being done for them to make Christmas brighter. Two nurses asked if Guy was at Heath Cross and seemed surprised to learn that he was in Devon.

"Had a tiff?"

"No, of course not," Emma replied sharply. "Nothing like that, but with me on night duty, we would have had very little time together."

She wasted no time in the dining room, finding the determined jollity stifling. It might have been better if we had been having a tiff, she thought as she wandered back to the day room. Am I being too bloody understanding? She was startled at her own vehement thoughts and let her latent resentment surface. Paul had been with her for a long time tonight and would be with her until she made the next round of the ward. Tomorrow, he suggested, they might listen to music or the radio, and if his ankle held up might walk a little way on the Heath before she went to bed.

Paul was only a friend who she had known for a very short time but he had filled a very empty space in her Christmas Eve, and he made her laugh.

She pushed open the door and blinked in the dim light of the day room which appeared to be empty. He's gone to bed, she decided, and was suddenly lonely. The packet of unopened sandwiches lay on the table, and lying on the settee, Paul was fast asleep, looking exhausted and pale, and the plaster on his face was damp as if it needed cleaning up. Emma covered him with a red army blanket and went into the ward.

148

"Dr Sykes has gone to sleep in the Day Room," she explained to Nurse Read. "Leave him as I think he looks as if he might be suffering from delayed shock after his accident. You can go for your meal now. I shall sit in the office so that he is undisturbed and he can have something to eat when he wakes."

"Is he married or anything?" Read asked.

"I don't know." Read looked surprised and Emma laughed. "You must ask him. I know very little about him except that he was a student with Mr Franklin and I met him in Bristol when I went to a family funeral."

"He's nice," Read said and collected her stiff cuffs to wear in the dining room.

"Cold ham and pickle," Emma told her. "Avoid the so-called mashed potato. It has huge lumps in it and is a nice shade of grey. What wouldn't I give for a helping of tiny, hot new potatoes with lashings of butter and a sprinkling of parsley"

"Bread for me," Read said firmly. "And I saved some chocolate to eat afterwards. Let me guess. There's swiss roll in jelly for pud?"

Emma laughed. "The Germans like it, even though they have it at least three times a week."

"I suppose our men over there in the camps have far worse," Read said. "Sister Sinclair says . . ."

"Don't! It's bad enough knowing they are prisoners, and if we thought too deeply about it we'd never be able to nurse the men in there. Forget what Sister says and try to be objective. You nursed VD patients at Beatties, didn't you? This is no different. We have to treat all patients alike whether we enjoy it or not."

"Yes, Nurse." Read walked away, her back showing a kind of anger and Emma knew that she must have sounded pompous. She smiled wryly. Would the habit of

149

"Love serves", the motto of the Home in Bristol, never leave her?

She doodled on the memo pad and tore off the top sheet. Love *did* serve in her profession and she would always be the type to need people to care for. Like my Gran, she thought. Aunt Emily had told her about life years ago and made her envious of the love and caring that the woman she had known only as a vague shadow bending over her pram had showered on her family and friends.

"Runs in the family," Emily had said. "It passed over your mother and Lizzie but it's there in the rest of us; even your uncles were not bad in their own ways. My brother Sidney cared when he was allowed to, but it was difficult for him."

"He was the actor?"

"Quite famous in America for years and he kept in touch with me and sent us all presents in the early days before he lost his fiancée, Lucy Dove. I think he may be dead, too. I haven't heard from him for two or three years and my last letters came back 'address unknown', but I have a feeling that it was sent back by his manager who resented any contact with his family."

"Why would he do that?"

"Jealous," Emily said. "He was more than Sidney's manager as far as I can tell, but Sidney was a good man and a loving son and brother," she said firmly, and changed the subject.

Read and the other nurse on duty on the ward came back from the dining room and said that they'd peeped into the day room and Dr Sykes was still asleep. "Looks as if he's here for the night," Read said. "Shall I put the oatmeal on now, Nurse?"

"Yes. I suppose it will be porridge again for the patients even on Christmas Day." Emma glanced at the almost innocent expression. "If you eat too much of that you'll put on weight, Nurse, but make plenty tonight as we may all want some in the early hours, and I have some real brown sugar that my aunt sent me."

The coarse oatmeal was covered with water and put to simmer in a double saucepan so that it could be left to cook slowly without being stirred all the time. The oatmeal was fresh but took a long time to soften during cooking. The result was far superior to the pallid porridge made from quickly prepared rolled oats which had a floury base to thicken it and very little flavour. The night staff had the task of cooking the breakfast porridge and had found that during the terrible four o'clock chill, it was delicious, much better than the solid slab cake provided for the four o'clock snack. They made far more than was needed for the ward so that they could have a share of it.

At three-thirty, Paul Sykes woke and went along to the staff lavatory. He splashed cold water over his face and combed his hair before presenting himself at the office, looking shamefaced and still sleepy. "Must have dropped off," he said and yawned.

"Christ! Is that the time?"

"You became a patient last night and we let you sleep," said Emma. "I shall put a fresh dressing on that nasty cut on your face and bandage your ankle, then I shall take your TPR just in case you really are suffering from shock."

"I feel fine," he protested.

"You've made your face wet and the sticking plaster is peeling off so you might as well let me do you, or we won't give you any porridge," Emma insisted. "Sorry we ate the sandwiches but you were flat out and I doubt if that gorgeous pâté would be good for shock."

151

"You offer me *porridge* instead of that lovely food I brought you?"

"You haven't tasted Heath Cross oatmeal," she replied and pushed him into the clinical room. "Sit there and be quiet. I have to start the day soon so I'll do your face first." She stripped off the old dressing. "I hope it doesn't go septic," she said anxiously. "It still looks full of grit."

"It will be fine. I managed to get some penicillin and I had a massive dose in Casualty. It really is a wonder drug and I wish it was more easily available for everyone."

He walked into the kitchen and Nurse Read set a bowl before him. He eyed the steaming porridge with distrust then put brown sugar over it and tasted it. "Will you marry me, Nurse Read?" he said. "Unless your other nurse made this, in which case the offer to you is closed."

"I thought you were married," Read said with wide eyes.

"Not yet. I am still looking for someone worthy of my charms," he said, and glanced at Emma. "All the best ones are spoken for and I am very fussy."

At six o'clock, when the patients were being washed and minor treatments were to be given before the day staff appeared, Paul limped down the corridor to his room in the medics' villa, saying he'd be awake again by ten and would meet Emma in the common room soon after.

Work seemed light and the mood of the ward was more optimistic, with an exchange of laughter and more conversation than usual. The change of guard and the arrival of Sister Sinclair did nothing to damp the atmosphere.

Emma sank into a chair in the common room and listened to the wireless. News of fighting in the Ardennes continued but United States troops, reinforced by the British, were moving up to take Bastogne and on other fronts the news was good.

Bea appeared by her side and listened to the announcer stating in clipped, correct and impersonal English that the United States Air Force had bombed strategic positions in the Pacific and there had been a certain loss of aircraft. "I'd rather listen to Lord Haw Haw than that mealy- mouthed announcer," Bea said. "At least I know that Lord Haw Haw is lying, and the boys think that Tokyo Rose is a joke."

"No news from Dwight?"

"Nothing. If there was anything, the General would let me know," Bea said. "He's in London now but he promised to keep tabs on Dwight wherever he goes." Bea made an attempt to laugh. "I'll have to take a lover," she said. "What about Paul?" She turned away to go to her room to change her apron and have coffee. "Not that he'd look at me with you about. See you at twelve for lunch in my room. Sister says that I can invite Paul and you and miss lunch. The hamper won't cater for more and we'll be cosy friends together. I'm off this afternoon. Bring a knife and fork for Paul."

Chapter 10

"Neither of you seem very happy," Paul said. "All this lovely grub and you haven't eaten much." He reached over and took another slice of Maryland ham and a bagel.

"Help yourself," said Bea dryly. "It's obvious that you have no food prejudices. Bagels and ham?" She picked at a chicken drumstick and sipped her white wine.

"Why don't you both blow your tops and admit how you feel?" Paul said with an amiable grin. "You feel neglected and neither of you have heard from your man."

"I had a call from Guy," Emma said defensively. She picked up a lobster patty and chewed the pastry. It wasn't as good as Aunt Emily's and had a background taste of herbs that didn't go with the lobster. "He isn't coming back tomorrow," she said. "I did mention that I had two nights off."

"Did he say why he can't get back?" Bea asked. "Why not go down to Devon and then you can come back together. Trains will be running again after Christmas."

"No, he is tied up with his family and I'd feel in the way," Emma said. "I've never met them."

"He's your fiancé!" Bea said. "He's the man you are going to marry in a few months time so how can you say that?"

"Leave it, Bea," Paul said quietly. "Well, you'll have to make the best of it," he added cheerfully. "His loss is my

154

gain. Tomorrow, after Emma has had a sleep, and I think you are off duty too, Bea, I shall borrow a car and take us down to a nice little place I know where we can have tea and see the river. My ankle is good enough for me to drive, but if not, one of you can take over. I need at least two skilled nurses to look after me. If the weather is OK we might stay for dinner too, after we've seen what they have to eat." He laughed and carefully selected a cheese biscuit. "Isn't it strange that life after duty gets tied up with food?"

"Not strange at all for those of us who have nothing more to do to fill the time when our men are away. I could get as fat as a pig if I didn't work so hard." She smoothed down her slim hips and looked provocative. "What do I care if Dwight is away? You are an angel," Bea said. "I shall tell Dwight to go to hell and live with you."

He held up his hands in mock horror. "And have me dragged before the American courts for un-American activities? Besides, from his photograph, he's bigger than me."

Emma giggled. "I love cowards."

"Is that a promise?"

Paul stirred his coffee and didn't look directly at her but Emma knew that he was aware of what she said and did. She yawned. "I'll have to get some sleep," she said. "One more night on duty and then time off."

Bea packed the rest of the food into the fridge. "I'm on at four as Sister wants to get off early today, but that means I can have a half day tomorrow, so your idea is wonderful, Paul." She glanced at the plaster on his cheek and his bandaged ankle. "If you need any help, pop in to the ward."

"I have a nurse, thank you, Bea." He smiled at Emma.

155

"Go to bed and I'll see you tonight about ten if you would be kind enough to do my dressing."

"Of course I will." Emma helped Bea to clear the small table and put the note that Bea had written, in a conspicious place, inviting anyone who wanted food to use up the rest of the hamper before it went off. "No use keeping it and I'd rather not waste it," Bea said. "I must write to my dear husband and tell him that fighting a war is no excuse for neglecting me."

Emma undressed and pulled the curtains together to block out the daylight. She thought of Guy, who didn't have the excuse that he was fighting a war to make him stay away from her. On the telephone he had said, as if it was a major breakthrough with his family, "I've told them all about you and the fact that we are engaged and they can't wait to see you, but I think they feel that once we are married they will see less of me, so I'm giving them this time. My mother said that it may be the last time I stay here alone, just as their son."

She had hardly heard the rest, even though he said he missed her and loved her. What if I suddenly announced that I must go to see my mother and stay for a week, when he had time off? He is very lucky, she decided. He will never have any need to consider my family, except for Aunt Emily. I hope I shall never be pushed into working for his father, as dogsbody and filing clerk.

She slept, with drying tears on her cheeks and woke late and had to hurry on duty, with her head aching and the mild disorientation that comes with night duty after sleeping in the daytime.

"Where are they?" she asked Sister Sinclair.

"They collected six ambulant patients and three wheelchair bods, so we cleared one room and brought the rest into the main ward. I'd hoped they'd get rid of the lot of them but we are stuck with a few who can't be moved, and may have to expect more if they send them from France." She looked at her watch. "You should have a quiet night if the V2s keep away. I want to go now to hear the news and *itma*, as we can't use the wireless on the ward. That's just one restriction that these men have brought me!" she said as if it was a conspiracy aimed entirely at her.

"Tommy Hanley makes a bright spot in my week."

"Any dressings to do, Sister?"

"All done," she said briskly. "Good night, Nurse Dewar."

As usual, there was a sensation of relief when she left the ward, felt by staff and patients alike. Even the guard decided that it might be permissible for him to sit at the end of the ward instead of standing clutching his rifle.

Coffee was keeping hot in a large jug in one of the instrument sterilisers when Paul limped along the corridor. Emma had a dressing tray ready and was surprised to see how clean the gash on his cheek had become. "I had more penicillin today," he said in explanation. He rubbed one buttock. "Three doses today, as they say it has to be topped up every four or five hours to be lastingly effective, but it really is marvellous. I doubt if I shall be able to pretend I have a romantic sabre scar on my cheek." He grinned. "They say that penicillin might be given for specific conditions, mostly streptococcal infections, but it would probably cure a lot of things you didn't know you had!"

It was good to laugh again and Paul lingered over coffee and teased Nurse Read a little, before leaving them to get on with their work. "See you after lunch tomorrow," he said. "Also, I've plans for the following day."

The empty time off was now looking less bleak and Emma found the night shorter than usual and the patients

157

cooperative, as they were thankful not to be chosen to be transferred, even with Sister Sinclair in charge of them during the day. Porridge at four in the morning was eaten in peace and the ward was neat and quiet when the day staff came on duty. Report was short as nothing of importance had happened during the night and Emma hurried off duty, had a helping of baked beans on toast and went to bed, setting her alarm for noon.

Bea was wrapped up in a chinchilla fur coat and matching hat and Emma added a thick scarf and the ocelot-printed rabbit-fur hat to her blanket coat and the woollen gloves that Aunt Emily had knitted for her.

"You obviously think you'll freeze in this car," Paul said. "We aren't going to Russia."

"You strike me as being the kind of man who would take a girl wearing high heels, walking across a ploughed field," Bea replied sweetly.

"Isn't that usual?" he asked innocently. "That comes later."

"Sit in the back and put your foot up," Bea ordered. "I'll drive for a while."

"She's right," Emma said when he protested. "You can navigate from the back, and woe betide you if you find fault with the driving."

"Turn right at the gates and head for the main road," he said and settled his leg on a folded rug on the back seat.

"Aren't we going through Epsom?" asked Emma. "I thought I might call in at the cottage to see that everything is all right for Guy when he comes back. It will be cold."

"As he's not coming back for few days, it can wait," Bea said firmly, and added dryly, "It will be a nice cool contrast to all that family comfort and log fires."

She drove on, following Paul's instructions until they came to the river. The glint of water was silvery in the thin afternoon sunshine and remnants of snow clung to the banks of rough grass. Bea shivered but Emma climbed out of the car and watched the reeds moving against each other making faint, harsh music above the ripples. "The sedge is withered on the lake and no birds sing," Paul quoted softly. He regarded her with a dark brown stare, the golden flecks invisible. "*La belle dame sans merci* has me in thrall," he added. A moorhen scurried across the water and the rank scent of the river came sharply, not the sea but at least flowing water, and she smiled.

"Where now?" Bea said. "Get in before you freeze," she ordered. "The chauffeuse wants her tea."

"About half a mile further on," Paul said, and after the car was parked and Paul walked stiffly into the café, Bea relaxed. Tea was served in pretty china, none matching but showing signs of the time when the café was full of genteel ladies, and tidy children with uniformed nannies.

It was late for serving tea but the woman in charge seemed glad to have customers and they stayed for over an hour. It was dark when they found the one big hotel a few miles away where Paul had ordered dinner. "This is good. I must remember it when Dwight comes back," Bea said as they lounged in deep armchairs and looked into the depths of a huge wood fire.

"Can you hire boats on the river?" Emma asked.

"How can you even think of that, this weather?" Bea sounded shocked.

"The woman in the tea shop said that a few hundred yards up river they hire out canoes and skiffs in summer. We must do that some time," Paul said.

"That would be wonderful," Emma said, then realised that Paul wouldn't be there and Guy might not enjoy canoeing.

The hotel served jugged hare and really creamy mashed

159

potatoes and after good bread and butter pudding which indicated that the proprietor had a secret supply of eggs and butter, they lingered in the shabby, comfortable lounge and smoked Bea's Sobranie cigarettes while they had coffee that did not, as she said, taste of ground acorns and dandelion roots.

"Time to go," Paul said at last. "I'll drive now; my ankle is fine for a one way trip and it's Emma's turn to take a back seat and snooze. You look as if night lag is catching up with you."

"I'll be fine tomorrow," she said, but sank into the back seat of the car and left Bea to chat to Paul. She half listened to their laughter and dozed, but wondered if Paul preferred the company of Bea, who was very amusing when she liked people, and she did like Paul.

There were no notices for any of them in the porter's lodge and Emma went to bed, pleasantly tired but with the warm knowledge that tomorrow would be another good day. After a full night's sleep with no interruptions from buzz bombs or alerts, her eyes were bright and her cheeks pink and her limbs felt loose and free of tension. She dressed in a new skirt of blue and mauve checks and a favourite jumper that matched the blue and smiled when she considered shoes, as Paul might just be as Bea suggested, the type to take her walking over rough ground regardless of whatever she had on her feet, so she wore well-polished brogues.

As Bea wouldn't be there to outshine her with a good fur coat, Emma pulled on her fake fur jacket and picked up a knitted beanie hat and scarf that matched her jumper.

Paul had been pleased with the recovery of his ankle when she had renewed the bandage and she had suggested that he should leave the bandage off in bed and exercise the joint as much as possible in a passive way, and when he called for her at the lodge at ten a.m. he was walking well and insisted on driving.

"Sun will be out by eleven," he said with assurance when Emma glanced up at a threatening sky.

"Where are we going?"

"Never you mind. This is a mystery tour." He grinned. "It will be if I lose my way, but I think it's straightforward. Peel me a Minto," he asked when they had reached the clear open road south and the sky *did* seem less grey. They sat radiating peppermint and contentment.

"Where are we going?" she asked for the third time as the miles fell away and she knew they were travelling a fair distance.

"Brighton," he said, then almost apologetically, "not quite your kind of seaside, nor mine, but at least it's the sea."

"How did you guess?" her eyes were misty.

"I remember what you told me about the Island when we were in Bristol and I thought you might pine away if you didn't see a drop of sea water, so being a good physician, this is your treatment for the day," he said lightly. "We'll have some food and walk along the beach if we are allowed on the shore, and if it rains we can sit in the car and watch the waves."

"It's a wonderful idea, Paul. I've never been there although I know several people who have sailed there from the Island before the war, and I'd hoped to join them but it wasn't possible."

"You say that you dislike your family, except for one aunt, and yet your roots go deep, Emma. Everything you do stems from the Island background. Do you think you might go back there to live?"

She sighed and was silent for a full minute, then said, "How can I think of that? Guy will work in London, I expect, and I shall have to be with him. We might be able to take a cottage or something, but staying there on holiday isn't like living there and being a part of it. Places mean so much and even if many people fade from my memory, you're right, my roots are strong and I miss it terribly at times."

"If you work with Guy after you are married, you will have other interests, but your work means a lot too, doesn't it?"

"It's been very important and I was determined to get my SRN badge, but I wonder if I'll use it once I'm married? Guy will be a consultant by then and I shall be a surgeon's wife."

"You will have a lot in common," he said. "Surely your training will be of vast importance?"

"When we were working together in theatre during D-Day and after, it was wonderful. That's what brought us close together. Thinking back I noticed that the wives of the consultants handed out coffee and food in an emergency canteen every night, very pleased to be of any use at all. Some were trained nurses and they actually envied us all that tragic mess and gore, as they had given up their profession once they were married to important men."

"Most doctors would give their eyeteeth to have a wife with all that experience," Paul said, with a force that she found alien to his usual calm manner. "You are a very good nurse and you must not waste it."

Embarrassed by his manner, she laughed. "Maybe we shall follow Bea and Dwight to America, and I shall learn to love being idle," she said.

"I can't see Guy doing hernia repairs on rich fat men for vast fees, and neglecting his research into new procedures."

She laid a hand on his arm. "Cheer up, Paul. None of us

162

knows what will happen. I might not pass my exams next month, the war may go against us at the last minute and I might have to go into the Naval Nursing Service or the QAs. I think the Navy, as they have such a lovely uniform and I might be stationed by the sea."

"And Guy?"

"Let's not talk about it. Even Guy is uncertain of the future and he says he can never look far ahead." She cried out with pleasure. "I can see the sea! Oh, Paul, thank you for bringing me here."

He parked at one end of a plot of rough ground, as close to the beach as possible but the stony shore was forbidden. Coils of barbed wire cut off many sections of the foreshore, while a row of rusting spikes far out in the water showed the extent of the sea defenses. Emma pulled on her hat and clutched her jacket close against the keen wind. The salt in the air made her eyes smart and her cheeks felt as if they were being gently stroked with sandpaper, but she breathed deeply as if she couldn't get enough sea air into her lungs. She swayed as the wind gusted and nearly threw her off balance and Paul put an arm round her shoulders to steady her.

She pulled away as if she had not noticed the contact. "We can walk along there," she said. "Can you manage a hundred yards?"

"Sure, but you'll have to take my arm," he said solemnly. "Just in case I'm blown away."

The stunted grass that in pre-war summers had been a carefully nurtured lawn where visitors could take their ease in deck chairs and listen to the band playing, and where the daily promenade of holiday-makers made a colourful procession to watch and to stimulate comment, now lay flattened by army trucks and a barrage balloon sat uneasily on its hawsers by an anti-aircraft gun.

"Look!" Paul began to laugh. "If I had a camera, and if I didn't think I'd be arrested for taking pictures in a sensitive military area, I'd take a snap of that. Doesn't it sum up a lot of what it's like here in wartime?"

Emma peered beyond the barbed wire and smiled. A menacing gun peeped out of its camouflage covering of green nets. It was sheltered by what had been an amusement kiosk, sitting snugly inside it with the long gun muzzle exposed. Round the doorposts were the remnants of a halo of fairy lights, now shattered, and the name in fading lettering, "FAIRY PALACE".

"What fun it must have been," Emma said wistfully. "Do you think they'll have slot machines after the war? I used to save up all my ha'pennies to make my money go further and I preferred the ones that gave me my money back if I scored high enough."

They argued happily over the merits of the pinball machines and the crane that promised to pick up a cigarette case but slid off to pick up one brightly coloured licorice allsort.

The Lanes, full of picturesque old buildings and narrow alleyways were mostly silent. The only cafe open was too dreary to sit in for any length of time, so Paul asked a shop- keeper where they could eat.

"It may not look much, but the British Restaurant gives the best value and the food's hot," she said. "I often go there. The ladies who run it really like their work and it gets quite full."

She pointed to the church and said that the restaurant was behind the cemetery. Paul hung back but Emma pulled him along. "My Aunt Emily is in charge of one," she said. "It's not a soup kitchen for tramps and a lot of people use them now as they get government supplies way above some food supplied on ration to cafes."

The Nissen Hut was warm, with a couple of tortoise stoves belching out coke fumes and heat and misting up the windows. They ate thick vegetable soup and corned beef fritters with crisp batter, and chips. The brown sauce was too spicy and the tomato ketchup was a very bright orange and tasted only of salt and oil, but the meal was filling and reasonably tasty.

Emma insisted on paying as she didn't want to be under further obligation to him now that he had already been so generous with his time and care for her.

Paul smiled lazily. "OK. You pay, as your puritan soul tells you that you owe me a meal."

"It's not that," she said quickly.

He put down his cup. "What then? Do you think that Guy would not approve of me kidnapping his fiancée for a day?"

Emma drank some more of the bitter coffee. "That's silly. You are Guy's friend," she said.

"I am also a man," he replied so softly that she wondered if she heard him correctly. "I wonder where they keep the loo? Don't go away, I'll be back."

She watched him as he crossed the room. He was slim and slightly taller than Guy. His hair was smooth and healthy and his shoulders gave an impression of latent strength. She remembered his warm hands when he had shielded her from the biting wind, and the brackeny scent of good tweeds. When he came back, she bent to pick up her bag, suddenly too shy to meet his gaze.

"It's too cold to stay here. Do you mind if we go back? I thought we might end our day in Reigate and I can pick up a few things from the unit that I need at Heath Cross and can't carry on the motor cycle. A car is quite useful at times, but I'd hate to give up the bike, and the car goes back tomorrow."

165

"Do you really intend using the bike again in this weather after what happened?"

"Why not?" He shut the passenger door and went round to the driver's seat. "I love that old boneshaker and I have only myself to please. If I come off again, does it really matter?"

"I'd worry about you," Emma said.

"Thank you for that, and thank you for today," he said. The fleeting brush of lips on cheek was barely a kiss and he crashed the gears as he started the car.

Emma gulped and stared ahead. Why did she feel as if that was important? Dwight kissed her on the lips each time they met and so did many of the friends she'd made in hospital. Tony hugged her and held her hand when they talked, and the easy affection was friendly and no more than mutual appreciation and a warm "Hello".

The country roads were dark, and the muted lamps on the few cars they passed did nothing to light the way as darkness came, but gave warning of their approach. Hedges that badly needed a winter trim swayed against the gloom and the moon rose to help the blacked-out countryside, shining brightly as the clouds dispersed.

"A bombers' moon," Emma said.

"Why do you say that with such sad conviction as if it is important to you? Do you know many RAF boys?"

"I grew up with a boy who went into the RAF and is now in South Africa," she said. "But I was thinking of Dwight. Do they have huge moons in clear skies over the Pacific? I know that Bea sleeps badly now and worries the whole time, but she'd never admit it."

"She's a good sort," Paul said, then heard her chuckling.

"What's funny? She's your best friend, so you know she's all right," he said.

"I have never heard a man say that about Bea," she said. "Most men fall over themselves to gain her attention and they think she's far more than all right. They fall at her feet like flies."

"I'm not a fly, and I'd hate to be swotted by an elegant blonde who is madly in love with her husband."

"Very wise," Emma said crisply and kept her eyes shaded so that she could look out at the road. "We seem to be coming into a built-up area. Is this Reigate?"

"This is it. Do you want to stay in the car while I fetch my things? No, on second thoughts, you'd better come too as I might meet someone who wants to rabbit on about work and you'd freeze."

The medical unit was situated in part of the old college and had an air of solid calm, unlike Heath Cross. They went to the library and Emma found a pile of medical journals with interesting articles in them. She sat by a desk and read while Paul went to his room and brought back a case of books and papers. He also introduced her to another doctor who eyed her with interest. "So this is what we are missing here," he said. "I heard that Heath Cross had a lot of beautiful nurses but they keep us away from them."

"Engaged to a surgeon," Paul announced as if that made Emma a leper. "A different breed entirely, James."

"Pity. I thought at last I'd found out about Paul's love life."

"Are we busy?" Paul asked. "If so, I might have to beg a couch here as I can't ride my bike until the frost goes away and the car I borrowed is needed tomorrow. My ankle is better and I can't say I need sick leave."

"Don't rush it. We have empty beds and no tests

167

imminent so take your time and ring through each day to see how things are here. You'll do more good getting the gen on the new drugs and penicillin. I have a theory that we ought to try it on our chronic bronchitis patients, and of course it's been miraculous with pneumonia. No crisis, and clears up in a few days."

"I could use the time following the team from St Mary's around," suggested Paul. "Once they go back to London, I may not see them so often."

"What are you doing now? This evening I mean?"

"I have to feed Emma and take her back. You've no idea how hungry these surgical nurses at Heath Cross can get."

"Why not eat with us? The food isn't bad here as they equipped a new diet kitchen before the war and we have a very good cook who was refused army service because of flat feet. He dreams of the time when he can go to France and work in a high class hotel. Meanwhile, his curries are spectacular and his pastry is a wonder. He begs extra rations on the pretext that this is a physicians' experimental unit and he needs the extras for diets."

"Why not?" Paul regarded Emma with amusement. "Fancy being a guinea pig on special diet?"

She hesitated, then smiled assent. She was off duty and the nagging feeling that she ought to go back was stupid. Guy was far away and she would have nothing better to do than to eat more fish cakes or something equally unappetising, and listen to music or read for the rest of the evening. "It depends on the special diet," she said. "Our supper at Heath Cross would take a lot of beating for lack of flavour and we had corned beef for lunch."

James shuddered. "Never mention that word to our

168

cook, Reg. He's sensitive." He saw what she was reading. "Interested in becoming my assistant in a diabetic clinic after the war?"

"I have yet to take my finals, and you've no idea if I'm any good."

"Beatties trained and you say that? You have only to say the magic name and you'll have a queue of medics panting after your services in hospital and in the private sector. Put me head of the list." He saw her disbelief. "I'm really serious."

"I know we have a very good training," Emma said slowly. "I had no idea that we rated as high as that. You are just being polite."

"He's not, but I'd hoped to hide the fact that you were all that a doctor could desire, in case you change your mind and are free to be my slave labour and fellow researcher." Paul laughed but it sounded false. "She is engaged to a surgeon who will never use her nursing talents and she'll fade away," he said. "I shall hang around to pick up the shrivelled remains and save her from all that."

"Idiot," Emma said but her cheeks felt warm. "When do we eat?"

"I'll take Paul away for half an hour if you are happy here and we'll pick you up at seven."

"Fine." Emma sat back and began to read, becoming absorbed as she found an article that filled in a few blanks in her information about neurological diseases, which might be useful in her exams.

"Interesting?" She sat up startled.

"It can't be that late?"

"Just eight, and I'm sorry to leave you here so long."

"The time just flew past, Paul. I found this very useful."

"Come on, we can eat now. I've ironed out a few problems that took more time than I imagined, but now I'm free for a day or so until the frost eases off and I can ride again."

The dining room was well-lit and modern and the food was very good. "I can't think why you opted to stay at Heath Cross when you can live like this," she said.

"There's a room shortage here as it was intended to cater for daytime work in clinics, and the patients we now treat have taken all the staff beds. I like to get away from my work and not talk shop when I'm off duty, so I made the great sacrifice. Heath Cross has definite compensations."

Emma looked anxiously at the time. "I ought to go back," she said. "We do have a curfew for nurses in training although they are much more flexible about it than they are at Beatties."

"It will be nearly midnight when we get back," he said. "You are off duty, so why not go to your cottage and stay there for the night? You can walk back in the morning and will have broken no rules." He laughed. "It's either that or hide under a rug while I go past the gates. A bit infra dig if they found you."

"What a good idea. I keep night clothes there and the immersion heater on all the time now to keep away frost will have kept sheets and blankets warm."

"Well, let me have your key to make sure there are no ghosts under the bed," Paul said when they drove into the small front garden of the cottage.

"That isn't necessary," Emma replied firmly and unlocked the door.

"Good night and thank you for a wonderful day," Paul said. He held her by the shoulders and looked down into her face, dim in the moonlight. Instinctively, she closed her eyes, convinced that he would give her the kiss of a loving friend, but he merely sighed and said as he put her away from him, "What a pity I'm in love with you, *belle dame sans merci*."

Chapter 11

Bea must have been there. Emma took off her coat. The living room was still warm although the gas fire was out and a washed mug drained by the sink in the kitchen. She looked in the fridge but it was empty except for a piece of stale cheese and a slice of ham curling up at the edges. She shrugged. Black Camp coffee would have to do when she woke up as there was no fresh milk and it wasn't economical to open a tin of evaporated milk for one. If she needed breakfast she could walk back early to Heath Cross.

She showered and got into bed, using the small room and not the room she slept in with Guy. The immersion heater was in the linen cupboard at the end of the bedroom and kept the room off-chill.

In the night, she woke and heard a vixen calling. She drew the bedclothes high against the primeval sound, but a part of her mind relished it. Perhaps she'd put out the ham for her if she came scrounging for food by the refuse bin. She felt oddly disturbed as if she had forgotten to do something vital, but dismissed the thought as imagination stimulated by the vixen's cry.

She listened but heard nothing more and was going to sleep again when she remembered that Bea had not been off duty the evening before, so would not have been in the cottage that late. Mildly annoyed, she turned in bed to face the now brightening dawn. It wasn't like Bea to give the key to just anyone and she knew that Guy wanted to keep the place as private as possible, but someone had been there during the evening and she couldn't think who it might be.

She made coffee and checked the other rooms but none had been slept in and the double bed was still unmade. She swept the earrings that Bea had carelessly left out on her dressing table, into a drawer and pulled the blind down in the kitchen for no reason at all other than she thought that someone might look in.

She raised it again, deciding that the house looked more lived in with it up, and knew that as Bea's valuable earrings hadn't been taken, there had been no burglary.

She walked briskly along the edge of the heath, the dry frozen bracken crunching underfoot and the first signs of new gorse flowers among the remnants of last year's storm- tossed blooms regretting their venture out into the cold.

She followed a group of daytime cleaners in through the gatehouse, showing her pass, and went straight to the dining room as she was later than she'd intended and was hungry.

Nurses were leaving the hall to go on duty and there was nobody from her ward there. She helped herself to fried bread and dried egg scramble and sat alone, unable to decide what to do. If she had to be on duty later, for the night, she ought to rest a while but now was too restless to stay in her room.

Guy would be back tomorrow, she thought, and considered returning to the cottage to take a few tins and a packet of dried milk in case he looked in and wanted coffee. She drank a second cup of coffee and wondered if Paul had taken the car back. It had been fun with him and she had felt more relaxed than she had done for a long time.

The sun was out and she knew that she couldn't sleep again, so she dressed warmly and went across the heath to the first dew pond where, in summer, water lilies bloomed. The ground was boggy and the water high after the winter rains and the lily leaves looked muddy. She turned back and walked into Epsom to look in the one dress shop that still flourished, even if the clothes all bore the "Utility" label, lacked style and were skimped on material. She bought sewing thread and buttons for a dress she was making from a pattern that had a pre-war style full skirt and well-cut bodice.

The public library was empty and she browsed through the newspapers supplied each day, until it was a reasonable time to have coffee in Fuller's cake shop and cafe.

"Hello! Did he find you?" She swung round and stopped as Nurse Read called to her.

"Who?"

"Mr Franklin, of course. He seemed a bit narked that you weren't there with a bunch of flowers to greet him and he went off to Epsom in a huff."

"When was this?"

"Yesterday afternoon."

"But he couldn't have been here! He was in Devon," Emma said stupidly.

"Either him or his ghost," Read said. "He said that you might be at the cottage with Nurse Shuter and went away. I saw him again last night when I went down for my midnight break and he seemed worried and asked if you'd left any messages in the ward." She laughed uneasily. "I tried to be bright and said that you must have run off with Dr Sykes, and I thought he'd explode. I must learn that some people can take that sort of a joke and some can't."

174

"Did you mention that I had nights off? He did know that and I wasn't expecting him back, so I went out all day," Emma explained.

"You did right. Catch me hanging about for a man who isn't coming to take me out even when he does have the time," Read said and tossed her head as if she knew the scene from personal experience.

"I'd have stayed here if I'd known," Emma said and felt her tension and annoyance rising.

"He ought to have phoned to let you know he'd be back. Surely he didn't expect you to wait around and twiddle your thumbs for two days?"

"I'll get back and find him," Emma said.

"I know it's a cheek as you are far senior to me, but could we have coffee together and let him stew a bit longer? You need to calm down. It wasn't your fault, it was his, and you shouldn't feel that you have to apologise."

She ushered her Senior Staff Nurse into the cafe and ordered coffee and cakes. Emma regarded her with interest. No wonder the patients liked Read and her downright manner and sensible ideas.

"I'll catch up with him in the dining room at lunch," Emma said and felt a guilty relief that she had no need to meet her beloved fiancé just yet.

"Gesner was in tears again yesterday," Read said in a conversational tone. "They took him away and he didn't want to leave us."

"Didn't want to leave you, you mean," Emma said with more humour.

"He says he'll learn good English and come back after the war to find me." Read laughed. "He'll forget all this soon and wonder who the girl in the snap was!"

"You gave him your picture?"

"The same one I gave to that commando in Ward Four

175

and the sailor with TB in Six. Safety in numbers and you'll find my face in a good few wallets. It shuts them up and gives them something to treasure, but I think they really know it's only a gesture and they haven't a hope of contacting me again. I must get a few more printed in case I find another man dying of love for me."

"I can't decide if you are completely heartless or just a very warm person," Emma said.

"I don't want any of them, but they need a bit of a boost now and again. No skin off my nose to have my picture next to a few fast beating hearts," she added calmly.

"What if they all come back after the war at the same time?" Emma chuckled, and Read looked approving.

"With any luck I'll be married by then and have six kids."

"You expect the war to last that long?"

"I intend having my babies in threes," Read said firmly. "My sister has four, all singly and I couldn't stand all that morning sickness for years, but I do want a family. How many do you want?"

"Me?"

"You do intend marrying that dishy man, don't you? He'll want to pin you down with children, especially after yesterday when you escaped for five minutes."

"I have exams next month and then we get married, but we haven't thought about children." Emma took the bill and payed.

"You'd better think, then." Read yawned. "I'm on duty tonight so I'd better get some sleep. Thanks for the coffee. If I see him, I'll say I saw you sitting lonely as a cloud in a cafe in Epsom. Stay there for a bit longer and have some more coffee, and if you aren't as broke as I am, buy some of the cakes that just came into the shop, before they all go. If you order them now as a customer in the cafe, you are allowed to jump the queue and have first pick. There's nothing to beat them and we could do with a change from porridge at four." On her way out, she spoke to the waitress and Emma found herself ordering more coffee and a whole lemon sponge sandwich to take away.

She was smiling. Read would make a formidable ward sister in time, if marriage and children didn't catch up with her first. She lingered over the coffee and the last mouthfuls were cold. Marriage and children? She had worked on the children's ward for a short time and found it interesting but not as fulfilling as theatre work and she had no memories of any particular child who had tugged at her emotions.

Guy would expect her to want children, just as he expected her to want the same things as he did for their future. She dismissed as absurd the idea that she was being manipulated. They had so much in common; music and poetry and books and of course their work. Physically, they were just made for each other, and suddenly she longed for him.

She pushed back her chair and picked up the sponge cake in its greaseproof paper bag. As she walked back to Heath Cross, wondered at what point during the war Fuller's had to give up using the elegant stiff cardboard boxes for their cakes.

The porter handed her a slip of paper and she glanced at it as she walked to the villa. "Came back early as you were off duty but no Emma! Call me if you have time before you go on duty tonight. Guy."

Very restrained, and because it was, she felt more guilty than if he'd said, "Where the hell were you?"

She tidied her hair and went to the dining room. Lamb stew and overcooked vegetables were piled on her plate

177

and she took it to a vacant table apart from those occupied by chatting nurses and doctors.

She mashed the lumps from her potato and attempted a mouthful of lamb. "There you are!" Guy sat down beside her and kissed her briefly on the cheek. "Did you go to Bristol or the Island?"

"Of course not," she said. "There wasn't time for that."

"You were off for two nights and not to be found here, so where did you go? I checked on the cottage but you weren't there and by the bleak look of it, nobody could stay there just now in any comfort."

"Bea and I went down to the river for dinner the first night," she said, "and I went to Brighton for the day after."

"By train, all alone?" His eyebrows shot up.

"No, Paul took pity on us and borrowed a car. He was off too, as he'd come off his motor cycle and needed treatment and time off."

"How . . . nice of him. What did Bea think of Brighton?"

"She didn't come with us there as she was on duty," Emma said.

"I see."

"It was very cold," she said. "We had lunch in a British Restaurant and came back fairly early."

"Not to Heath Cross. I tried to find you here and then went to the cottage and when I came back, you were still away." He eyed her with displeasure. "I asked the night staff if they'd seen you in the dining room, and by midnight it was clear that you must be sleeping out."

"Paul wanted to fetch some things from Reigate so we had dinner there."

"Dinner? And after that?"

"Guy! What are you suggesting?" Emma's eyes were

hot with anger and she wanted to cry, but anger won and she retorted, "Where do you think I slept? Not with Paul, if that's on your mind. He took me to the cottage as it was too late to come back here. It was midnight, so I slept in the cottage, quite alone, and yes it was bleak and comfortless and very lonely, but I made the best of it. If it wasn't for Paul this would have been quite the unhappiest Christmas of my life."

"Let's get out of here. People are staring."

"No, I'm staying here. I have nothing more to say, Guy. I have nothing to hide, nothing of which I'm ashamed, and I make no apology for not being here when you whistled. You told me you would not be back, so I made sure I didn't waste my precious off duty waiting around just in case you phoned to tell me what a wonderful time you were having!"

"I came back to be with you," he said. "Isn't that enough?"

"You told me that you were staying for two more days with your family. I was disappointed but I tried to see their point of view. You could have phoned and I would have waited for you."

"I thought you'd be here," he said. "I had no idea that you'd go far."

Emma took deep breath. "I love you, Guy, but I need a longer leash. When you gave me *The Prophet*, I thought you and I agreed with most of what was written, but he said, 'Let there be spaces in your togetherness . . .' and you obviously don't agree with that, but I think he's right."

Guy pushed aside his plate. "This food is disgusting." He went to fetch some pudding and Emma was confronted once again by a glass dish of red jelly with a slice of swiss roll suspended in it.

"We had better than this on Christmas day," Emma said demurely.

"Don't tell me that this place ran to decent mince pies?"

"No, but we had lots of goodies that the General sent to Bea as he was in London and couldn't invite her to the Epsom house. We both consoled ourselves with good food. What did you have? Turkey and homemade puddings and lots of champagne?"

"Ducks," he said shortly, avoiding her slightly mocking glance. "I wish you'd been with me, darling. I did miss you very much and I longed to be with you in our cottage."

"Did your family finally give up the idea of you marrying the girl they'd picked for you?" she asked. He had mentioned this a long time ago and dismissed it as a joke and she'd forgotten it until now. "I take it she was there, all ready to be kissed under the mistletoe?" She couldn't stop and knew she was being a bitch.

Guy flushed. "Yes, she was there and no, I didn't kiss her. I told her that I was engaged to be married and if you want to know, it was the first time I'd mentioned that we were really engaged and would be married in April. My mother was upset that I broke the news in that way and not with her in private." He added hastily, "It wasn't the engagement that she minded but the way I told them all before she could talk to me."

"And talk you out of it?"

"That wouldn't have been possible, and they know that now. I said I'd stay for two extra days to let them get used to the idea but I had to come back. I love you Emma. I want you so much just now that I can hardly keep my hands to myself. Give up your job and be with me wherever I go. If we are married we can live in the

180

cottage until we move on to better things and I'll have you all to myself."

Emma got up. "I must have some rest before I go on duty tonight. No, don't follow me, Guy. I need space." She smiled sadly. "I'll not be coming to the cottage for a week. I feel as if the curse is coming on, so you'll have to wait. You might as well have stayed in Devon."

She twisted her engagement ring as she walked away. Such a small piece of jewellery to make such a difference to her status. Even that was a kind of barrier, to keep other men away and to show people that Guy was taken. She hadn't worn it to Brighton but put it on when she thought she might meet Guy again, as a personal reassurance that they were bound together and that he really loved her.

And I love you, she thought. I shall always love you whatever happens. She shivered as if, as Aunt Emily would say, a goose walked over her grave. Her head ached and she felt bloated. Wasn't her coming period enough without it making her feel psychic? She had heard that in certain tribes women saw visions and foretold the future when they were that way.

To her surprise, she slept well and woke feeling released and her body less full. She laughed softly. The other nurses would be glad that she was in a good temper, now that her menstrual tension had broken. She even faced the meal that was served before she went on duty without thinking that it was silly to be having breakfast this late in the day. Breakfast? It could be any meal where baked beans were included.

The Night Sister met her at the door of the ward. "Nurse Dewar, I want to speak to you." She looked pale and Emma braced herself for bad news, perhaps of a new convoy of Germans being admitted or casualties from the latest V2 bombs that fell short of London. "It's to do with Nurse Shuter." Night Sister shut the office door. "I want you to go back to the villa and stay with her. I can send another nurse here and there is nothing more than routine tonight, so they can cope without you and I'll look in frequently."

"What's happened?" Emma's mouth was dry. "Has she had an accident?"

"Her husband's godfather rang to talk to her, and as he insisted that it was urgent, Matron allowed the call to go through." She smiled slightly at the thought that anyone would dare forbid the General anything. "I don't know details but Shuter's husband has been injured. As you are her best friend, I feel that you should be with her just now." The Sister's face tightened with emotion. "Poor lamb, she must be feeling terrible with him so far away. I know I'd be frantic if it was my boy friend."

"How badly?"

"I don't know. I've heard nothing more than I've told you. Stay with her for as long as you think she needs you and if she manages to get to sleep come back here later, but go off early in the morning to take her some tea when she wakes."

Emma almost ran to the villa. The Night Sister was reputedly a very sentimental woman when tragedy struck in the wards under her care, but she would not have made this gesture if she didn't think that Bea might be distraught.

The door to Bea's room was shut and Emma hesitated before tapping and calling, "Bea are you there? It's Emma."

"Come in." Bea sat up on the bed, her face tearstained. Emma ran to her side and put an arm round her shoulders. "I'm all right. I'm fine, Emma." Bea took Emma's hand as if she was the one who needed comfort.

"Dwight?"

"He fell from a roof. They were doing parachute exercises and had to land and roll in a safe manner. His harness broke before it should have released him on the way down from the roof of the aircraft hangar and he came down hard. I'm not crying because he's badly hurt, I'm crying tears of relief."

"But he *is* hurt?"

"Broken leg," Bea said with almost normal cheerfulness. "Isn't it splendid? He was so lucky! Just a badly broken leg and he's strung up on a Balkan beam under traction."

"You sound pleased!"

"I am, oh, I am! Don't you see? I can sleep at nights knowing that he is no longer on those awful night ops. The only thing to worry me is the depth of the cleavage of the average American nursing sister."

"He must be shocked and in a lot of pain," Emma pointed out reproachfully.

"Sure he is, but that will pass. I shall have him back here safe and sound on sick leave, and isn't it lucky that I know all about orthopaedics?"

"You think he'll come here, to England?"

"The General will swing it, and as his wife is in England, doing a wunnerful job of work for the war effort, yes sir! they will put no obstacle in his way. He was due to come back after the tour of duty ended, so he's coming back only a few weeks earlier."

"I was sent to cheer you up," Emma said, "but instead, you need calming down."

"My mind is buzzing with plans. The General said that Dwight will have to go to an English-based American unit hospital first for treatment and assessment and then have sick leave. We can use the cottage if Guy is willing, and not

183

be entirely in the General's pocket when he's in Epsom. It will be a second honeymoon, if we can make love without a great plaster cast getting in the way." She frowned. "That's a bore. He'll be in plaster for a long time if the fracture compares to many I've nursed."

"I'll make some coffee. No, looking at you, it might be too stimulating. What about cocoa? That would calm us both down."

"If he had to break a leg, this is the best time for it. My mind will be at rest for the exams and he won't be available to cloud my judgement, and afterwards I can take the promised three weeks' holiday that we get after the exams, while we wait for results."

Bea washed her face and annointed it with expensive nightcream while Emma made cocoa and brought it up to the room in a jug, with some of Aunt Emily's crumble biscuits. "If Night Sister can't contain her curiosity and pops over to see you, for goodness sake look sad and take that idiot expression off," Emma said, "or I'll have to go on duty PDQ."

"Your men will wonder where you are," Bea said. "Guy will be there, waiting for coffee and sympathy, and the others who drift by to take a glimpse of the delectable Emma Dewar, will have to put up with less."

"Oh dear!"

"Something you want to tell Auntie Bea? How was Brighton, by the way? Did it come up to its reputation for unbridled illicit passion? That man has great potential, so don't lead him on."

"Lunch in a British Restaurant and a biting wind off the shore?"

"Why, the 'oh dear'?"

"We got back late so I slept in the cottage, while Guy had returned early in a fit of guilt and expected me to be there. He was a bit peeved, having dragged himself away from his family and I have a feeling he might go to the ward to see me tonight and so will Paul. Nothing happened, Bea, but I feel almost as guilty as if something *had* happened between us and I ought to explain it away."

"Wish I could see the stags crashing antlers."

"Don't. I think I'll go back and report that I've soothed your fevered brow and tucked you up for the night. When you emerge tomorrow, for goodness sake look as if you care that your husband has broken a leg." Suddenly, it seemed funny and they rolled on the bed in a fit of giggles.

"You'll have to come to America with me, Emma. There's no other person who will laugh at the same things as I do and they'll think I'm mad."

"What makes you think you aren't?" Emma took a deep breath and tidied her cap. "I'm going. I have problems of my own."

"Convince everyone that you have worked a miracle and you think that I may sleep for a while on a tearstained pillow. No visitors as yet, please, as I'm far too fragile."

Emma called in at the main administration office on her way back to the ward, knowing that the Night Sister would be bursting with curiosity and suspecting that she might come to the ward, probably at an awkward time when Emma was having coffee with the drifting medics.

"It's bad enough but not as bad as I thought," Emma said solemnly, after she had described the accident. "Nurse Shuter is very brave and I left her sleeping."

The Night Sister shuddered. "How terrible to feel that you are falling from a great height. Poor man, he must be in a considerable state of shock, apart from the pain. Thank you for letting me know, Nurse. I've been to the ward so I shall not need to come again until the morning round."

And by morning, the whole of Heath Cross will have heard Sister's exaggerated account of what has happened to the brave American pilot and the terrible shock it has been to his wife. Emma was still smiling when she reached the ward and saw Nurse Read hovering to hear the latest news. "Just a broken leg," she told her staff. "Nurse Shuter is fine. In a way it's a relief as she knew that a lot of big airforce operations have been happening in the Pacific and she consoles herself that he can't take part in any more for a while."

"Wise lady," Read said and bustled off to do her bedpan round for the few bed patients left after the last convoy went north.

Emma sat in the office to read the day report and to check on what treatments the night staff would have to do before they went off duty. It was boring being so slack and she sent the Junior Nurse for her meal and told her to take an extra half hour. It was almost as bad as the time when they waited for the balloon to go up before the advent of D-Day, but she couldn't imagine that happening again, once the wards were full of civilian patients and the hospital was busy with the usual admissions and discharges once more.

The war had to end soon. The defeats of the Italians and Germans in various theatres of war and the lack of supplies that were obvious from the state of the prisoners coming to Heath Cross, pointed to a limit to future hostilities. Hungary was out of the war and a president was once more in charge of Greece under the Allies. Many people thanked God that the Russians were on the side of the Allies as they advanced relentlessly through the German defences. Churchill continued to rally the nation and

186

persuaded the Americans that they needed to help Britain even more with supplies and men fighting with the British Army and the RAF in the Pacific and Europe. Gains were made in Burma and the Far East generally and everyone in all the countries involved were tired of war and privations and a lack of normal family life.

The office door opened and Guy stood there, wearing a white coat and looking tired. "I thought you must have gone to bed," Emma said, glancing at the clock.

"I looked in earlier but you had gone over to see Bea," he said. "I seem fated to miss you."

"Bea's fine after the first shock. She is being very sensible and recognises that this will keep Dwight away from the fighting for a while, so she feels he is safe." She cleared some charts from a chair for him to sit down. "Did you have a case?" she asked.

"A civilian emergency from a car crash," he said. "A fracture similar to Dwight's I think, if what the General said was true. He spoke to me on the phone as he wanted my opinion and he quoted from the details of the notes they radioed to him. Bea will be familar with the treatment so he may be able to be flown over as soon as he's off traction, if no complications occur."

"He'll go to an American hospital at first," Emma said.

"So he said, but where's the need? Bea can leave here as soon as he returns to England, and she can take over."

"Bea has exams in a week or so," Emma said. "She can't give up everything like that when there's absolutely no need, and I don't think Dwight would want her to do so."

Guy looked blank. "But they are married and it's her duty," he said. "I think that you and Bea are very foolish. You could be at leisure or at least not working as hard as you do. I mentioned to my father that you would be very useful in the practice and he was enthusiastic. I think it helped to make them come to terms with the fact that I am about to marry a girl they've never seen."

"We discussed that," Emma said as patiently as she was able. "I made it clear that I didn't want that kind of work and I want to make sure of my SRN registration. Bea thinks as I do, that even if we use our skills less in future, we will have the satisfaction of knowing that we succeeded and have the status of trained nursing sisters. It isn't only these years of training, but the effort we put into the work in Bristol, too."

"Is there any coffee?" he asked as if she had not spoken.

"Of course." Emma left the office and went into the ward kitchen where Paul was talking to Nurse Read.

He raised an eyebrow and instinctively she shook her head. Paul grinned, made a thumbs down sign and crept away from the ward in exaggerated careful silence as if he was afraid of being seen. She wanted to call him back, feeling guilty that she'd contributed to his conspiratorial attitude. Guy and he were friends and there was no reason for Paul to stay away from the ward. Medics visited any department where they liked to have coffee with staff, so why not with Guy?

"The milk's a bit blue," Emma said as she handed Guy a cup. "I think Sister Sinclair waters it down for the patients and uses the rest to make milk puddings for her and her friend from Casualty."

"When are your exams?" Guy asked. She told him the dates and the venue and the fact that she would have to stay overnight in London with Bea, at the St James's apartment that her father had made sure would be available for them for as long as they wanted it.

He nodded thoughtfully and Emma felt that he was reconciled to her taking the exams and maybe having some say in what she did after she qualified. "I have a long holiday due after that," she said. "Bea is talking of going over to the States to fetch Dwight as the American airforce will take her and bring them both back. What it is to have a General for a godfather. If she has taken her exams she can rate as qualified, and she can be registered as his nurse if there are any offical objections."

"Fine," he said and she knew he wasn't really listening. "I shall be busy, too. I've been invited to a symposium on the care of crush syndrome in fractures, and it means I shall be in Birmingham for a week. I think that Easter would be a good time to get married. We shall have fulfilled all our commitments and you can have worked your notice."

"What about my holiday? It's due to me and I want to take it. I thought we were getting married during that time? The exams are the important factor. Once they are over, we can marry before the results come out."

"I thought it was later," he said. "If we did marry then it would be a very dull affair as I doubt if my parents will have everything arranged before Easter, and the church there frowns on any show during Lent."

"Nothing has been said to me about having to leave if I get married," Emma said. "I did mention it to one of the sisters in admin and she hinted that times are changing and I might be allowed to stay on as they'd lost far too many good nurses by such wastage, so until they kick me out, I'm not giving in my notice." She regarded him with reserve. "Did you tell your family we'd be married in Devon?" she asked. "I thought we'd discussed that and decided that it was my choice, as the bride, that mattered for wedding arrangements."

"What arrangements had you in mind? Nothing really constructive if I recall rightly."

"Certainly not a very elaborate wedding with the organ playing and the place full of people I've never met. I want a simple ceremony in a quiet registrar's office with a few friends and relatives there and afterwards a drink and sandwiches in a local hotel."

Guy looked disbelieving. "You'd be doing a lot of people out of a wonderful day," he said. "Think what they'd say when you eventually went to live and work among them."

"But that won't happen. You said that there was no way that you'd ever follow your father into general practice, and so I'll not be there either."

"Don't you want to be married in church?"

"I'm not a hypocrite, Guy. As far as I'm concerned, we are married now and have only to have the union legalised. I really can't see myself walking up the aisle in white, with a bouquet of lilies."

He stood up, looking angry. "You are obviously in a bad mood. We'll discuss it when you are less tired and in a better frame of mind."

"So what do I do with my three weeks' holiday? Sit in the cottage and wait for you to have time off?" Her lips trembled. "If we don't get married then, I shall go to the Island alone, or somewhere where I too have people who like to see me sometimes."

"You might as well, as I have a lot of work lined up and I'll be away for most of that time. I've heard of a consultancy that will occur soon and I want to enquire a little more deeply into it before I commit myself."

"Where?"

Guy looked embarrassed. "We needn't stay there for

190

ever," he said. "It's a start and a very good one. It's in Doncaster."

"So you'd be in Doncaster and I'd be a filing clerk in Devon if your family have their way?"

"Don't be silly, you'd go to work with my father in Devon only if I stayed in London, otherwise, you'd be with me," he said.

"Good night, Guy," she said and walked out of the office, afraid to say another word. The Junior Nurse reported back from her meal and when Emma went to fetch notes from the office, Guy had left.

Chapter 12

"Where's Guy?" Paul sounded cautious. He draped his long body over the arm of a fat armchair in the common room and settled his shoulders as if they were stiff.

"Not scared, are you?" Bea asked with a mocking smile.

"Scared? Who? Me?"

"Yes, you. I think he's convinced that you didn't seduce his fiancée in Brighton and he's a very reasonable man, I've always thought," Bea said.

"There does seem to be a slight chill when we meet now. I think he believes that I've influenced Emma in some way to be a bit bolshy about some of his ideas for their future."

"About time," Bea said mildly. "I'm fond of Guy but he has a trace of the Ironside about him, and he wants everything to be as it was when his parents got married." She giggled. "Emma was speechless when he handed her a veil that his mother had worn at her wedding and said she'd be hurt if Emma didn't accept it and wear it at her wedding."

"But Emma told me she had refused to have a church wedding," Paul said.

"'Much dripping weareth away stone'," Bea said dryly. "That seems to be the policy, hoping that she'll say, 'All right, have it your way,' give in and be miserable but

192

pliant." She handed Paul her box of candies and he popped one in his mouth. He encouraged her to go on and she frowned. "What Guy doesn't realise is that Emma's grown-up now and I doubt if she wants to be smothered by other people's plans. I know I'd be furious if I was forced into something I'd hate to do, and once other people take over for one thing, they think they have the right to do so for ever. I used to think that they'd be very happy together but I'm beginning to doubt it."

"You do?"

"No, not really. Stop eating all the hard centres and *stop* looking like that. You haven't a chance there. Emma really does love him and Guy is mad about her. That is certain and once they've stopped being mad in another sense, they'll come out of this and live happily ever after, but I hope that she doesn't let him rule her in everything."

"Are you really going to America?" Paul asked enviously. "How did you manage that?"

Bea shrugged. "I just looked helpless, said I was very worried about Dwight as he was so far away, and left it all to the big brave General to arrange, and now that we've finished with those grisly exams I'm free to go next week."

"Can I come too? You'll be lonely on the plane with all those rough men," Paul said hopefully.

"I need a chaperone, not another man," Bea said. She laughed.

"Men are funny. I suppose I am travelling as a VIP but not in VIP conditions. The plane taking me is a troop carrier and the one on the return flight will have a first-aid compartment for Dwight on the way back."

"So?"

"I'm a very experienced nurse who has seen a lot and

193

heard just about everything, but I'm also the wife of a high ranking officer who has the Purple Heart and who has the General for a godfather, *and* I'm the daughter of a man who has a voice in British Government, so they worry that I might hear some nasty language or be goosed by a less than polite Yank on the way over."

"I'd like to see someone try," Paul said and grinned.

"Who asked for your opinion? I'm a very soft woman at heart, easily upset by rough men."

"What are you cooking up now, Bea?" he asked with obvious delight.

"I don't know what you mean," she said, but her eyes were pure Siamese cat and her smile a purr. "If a call comes for me, will you say you'll find me? I'll be in my room. How hot will it be in California? I'd better look out some pretty flimsy things." She smiled at him. "You can eat the rest of the candies. They are the ones I never touch."

"Bring me some back when you return. They do my ankle a power of good."

"You are a fraud. There's nothing wrong with your ankle, and even Emma knows that now. I hear she's given up massaging it and being sympathetic."

"Did wonders for me," he said.

"*Je crois!*" she said and swept from the room.

Paul picked up a book and tried to read, but one after another nurses came to talk to him and he made all the right replies without really listening.

Guy would be negotiating soon for a consultancy which could take Emma far away for ever. Apart from his own feelings, Paul was apprehensive for her, as he knew how much she needed to be near the country and preferably by water. Two possibilities that Guy had mentioned were in big cities, now war torn and depressed but offering a

194

wide range of surgery and work in hospitals as well as good opportunities for private practice. There would be no need for Emma to contribute anything to the family exchequer. One city had been Bristol, a good choice, with plenty of green spaces and the beautiful River Avon winding through the Gorge, if Emma could bear being in the same town as her mother, who featured less and less in her plans and who never wrote to her.

Paul read again the letters he had received, with details of partnerships and apointments of assistants in various general practices, all of which needed some investment of capital. It would be a struggle but not impossible, he told himself, and some were in very pleasant surroundings. One sounded pathetic. The ageing doctor with chronic emphysema, wanted a young partner and offered very attractive terms, but the snags would come later. If the doctor died, then his share of the partnership would be retained by his widow and she would expect to be supported until she could be bought off, which usually meant probably for the rest of her life if she refused to sell and lose what amounted to a good pension. This would be at the expense of the young doctor, who would need to pay for an assistant or take a fresh partner.

Regretfully, he put this letter in the envelope with the "impossibles" to whom he must reply politely but with definite refusal. He smiled ruefully when he read again the letter from the Isle of Wight, offering him a partnership in a village near Newport. That too would be impossible. Once Emma was married he must never see her again or his life would mark time and he would miss the possibility of a happy marriage and a contented mind.

"Come to stay for a weekend," the letter said. "Even if we aren't what you want, it will be good to meet you and talk shop that must be more up-to-date than data I can find here. Not that we are archaic. I am preparing a paper on tuberculosis among children on the Island and would value your comments."

Paul absent-mindedly fanned his face with the letter. Maybe I'll go, he thought. I can't take the job but I'd like to see what Emma loves about the place and then I can go to some remote spot to work and say goodbye.

The letter fluttered to the ground and as he bent to pick it up, Emma came from behind his chair and got there first. "Throwing away your love letters?" she said, teasing him. "Oh!" The bold letter heading made her look again. "You didn't tell me you had friends on the Island," she said.

"I haven't."

He took the letter and folded it carefully. "But I know that doctor," Emma said. "He's a very nice person and a good doctor. He came to see Aunt Emily when she had a burned arm and they've been friends ever since."

Her curiosity was evident and Paul knew that some explanation was necessary. "He's writing a paper about TB and I hope to do some work in the same area of research," he said, slowly.

"You should go down and see him," Emma said. "He can take you to the Hospital for Diseases of the Chest at Ventnor, which is one of the leading sanatoria in England." She laughed. "It's strange. I almost went there to do a TB nursing course before I was old enough to come to the Princess Beatrice or some other London hospital, but I was afraid of catching TB and so I went to the Home on the Downs in Bristol. Just think, my life might have been completely different if I'd done that: I'd never have met Bea or Guy . . . or you," she added. "Where is Bea? She said she'd be here this evening."

"She's being mysterious. She looks like a cat with the cream and she's expecting a phone call."

"I'll wait here. I was planning to go and tidy the cottage but she said she wanted to see me about an urgent matter so I put it off. Anyhow, it's raining and I didn't fancy walking all that way and getting wet. Guy is away for a few more days so he isn't likely to be there for a while."

"It's a busy time. He has a lot of interviews in the offing," said Paul.

"So have you, haven't you?"

"As yet, mostly by post. Guy has to see the people and be seen by committees before he's chosen. I have to choose which of several partnerships I buy into, and then go to see them. I make my own short list. In a way I have an advantage as the choice is mine where I go. Guy might have to take a job where he wouldn't normally choose one, but can't afford to miss the opportunity." He smiled lazily. "I am never going to be as high-powered as Guy and I can take my time over my choice. There are plenty of older GPs wanting new partners, as many young doctors have been killed in the war or have been invalided out of the services and can't return to their work."

"You have your Fellowship, Paul. There are lots of jobs in teaching hospitals and you could easily get a medical consultancy.

"I want time to breathe and make up my mind what to do next. If I'm caught up in red tape and endless clinics, I could lose my way and never do the things I dream about, so I'm going to buy a partnership and do research as well, possibly taking on an assistant so that I can get away to follow up on my chosen subjects without neglecting my patients."

Emma laughed. "Doctor Sutton would be perfect for you," she said. "You share the same interests in medicine, he likes sailing and walking and food, and you like the country. What a pity he doesn't need a partner."

"Isn't it?" Paul replied cryptically. "Now what has Bea been doing? I distrust any woman with that look in her eye. She flares her nostrils like a horse scenting battle; a very beautiful horse of course, but whatever it is, she'll win!"

"Oh, there you are, ducky." Bea said with a smile that could make golden syrup a bad second in sweetness.

"Careful, Emma, she's about to ask you to do something you'd normally hate to contemplate."

"Paul, *shut up*," Bea said, but her smile stayed. "It's not much to ask a friend and Guy will be away, so Emma, poor lonely girl, will have time to waste and nowhere to go as I can't stay with her. I am going to the States," she announced as if they didn't know. "California, to be exact. Dwight was transferred there a week ago and has a bright new plaster but no traction so he can come back to the UK with us in under two weeks."

"Us?" said Paul.

"Not you, dear. Just Emma and me. The General said he was very relieved that you'd said yes. The alternative was his personal PRO who I can't stand and he can't spare, so this fits in well. You have the time off, we have free transport and a look at how the other half live in wartime and I bring my beloved Dwight back safe and sound in one piece, with me. What more could any girl ask? The General sends his love and hopes we have a pleasant time in God's own country."

"The key word is *ask*," Emma said. "I don't remember that bit, and the answer is *no*."

"Why?" Paul said quietly. Emma looked at him in amazement. "I asked why you can't go. Give me one good reason why you have to turn down an offer that

198

most girls with any sense of adventure would give a lot to have."

"But, I can't!"

"That's not a reason, that's just a coward's way out of something unfamiliar."

"Guy would blow his top." Emma faced two pairs of eyes that gave her no comfort. "I can't tell him I'm going to America at such short notice. He may want to talk about his new job if he gets one settled."

"He isn't here and no committee is going to make a decision that quickly," Paul said. "You have the time and I really do think that you'd be doing Bea a great service."

His eyes were gentle and the flecks of gold more noticeable.

"Bless you." Bea leaned over and kissed him. "Your patients are going to love you." She dropped her flippant manner and her lower lip trembled. "I do need you, Emma. What if I am lost and out of my depth over there? What if Dwight has gone off me and I need a female shoulder to cry on. What if . . .?"

"Pigs could fly," Paul said scathingly. "But I do think you need a companion, and Emma knows all your funny little ways."

"Thank you very much! I don't need a psychiatrist," Bea retorted but gave him a grateful smile. "The General is seeing to our passports and other details. All we have to do is to get into the car he'll send and drive to the air force base to catch the plane. We stay in a good hotel and visit Dwight for a few days until he's given the all clear to travel, and then we come back and he goes to the American Air Force Hospital for a while. I shall stay on the base as a guest and it

199

will give me time to get used to the American way of life."

"I have nothing to wear," Emma said.

"Typical," Paul said. "When all else fails, a woman falls back on that excuse."

"I thought of that and decided that we can buy clothes over there, off ration! We were both planning what to buy for the summer so this fits in well. You can buy that present for Aunt Emily that you moan about. There's sure to be something nice over there that isn't Utility and hasn't been bombed, and we'll have time to see a few sights and do shopping." Bea's delight was infectious and Emma relaxed, convinced more by Paul's support than by Bea's impulsive demands.

"I'll have to tell Guy," Emma said.

Bea hugged her. "I knew you'd help me," she said. "You can't back out now; it's all fixed and we can forget about exam results until we come back."

"What a lot of changes are ahead," Emma said seriously. "Real changes, not from ward to ward or between Beatties and Heath Cross, but changes in our lives. I've put it off and signed on here again for a while as Junior Theatre Sister at Beatties until Guy finds what he wants to do, but you'll go with Dwight, Bea, and Paul is looking for a country practice."

"Persuade him to take a job in the States," Bea said. "I can't bear to lose you all."

"I'll look you up when I do my research into Indian folk medicine," Paul said.

"You were serious about that?" Emma asked. "How can you do that if you go into general practice?"

"You have to make things happen if you are ever to do anything you want," he replied. "I'll do it one day and find a way round the obstacles."

200

"It sounds exciting," Bea said. "Be sure that you let me know when to expect you and I'll help as much as I can. Dwight is sure to have masses of contacts who will make short cuts in communication with the people who matter in this kind of work. It could save a lot of your time."

Emma felt excluded and bereft. Who could take the place of Bea? She regarded Paul's animated face and knew she'd miss him, too, but as soon as she heard Guy's voice on the phone that night, she forgot him. To her surprise, Guy was enthusiastic when she outlined Bea's plans. "You might as well go as I shall be away for most of that time and I want to do some work at Beatties too."

"Guy was quite happy about me going with you," Emma said later.

"I thought he might be," Bea said, with a cynical twist to her mouth.

"Why? I thought he would object."

"He's away a lot and Paul is here," Bea said. "You'll be safer in America."

"He can't be jealous of Paul!"

"Why not? The man's in love with you, and don't forget, he said that if you want something badly enough, you make it happen so don't be taken in by those soulful brown eyes. They remind me of a setter I once had who could get his way every time if he looked at me like that. I've taken him out in the pouring rain lots of times, just to placate him when all I wanted was a comfortable chair and a good book."

"It takes two to tango," Emma said. "I'm going to marry Guy and he's the only man I'll ever love."

"Let's make lists of what to take, and some clothes we can share as we are the same size, even if I am taller than you. I'll take that silk suit that my father

201

sent. It's really too short for me and as it's a lovely dull turquoise which is your colour, you're welcome to it." She laughed. "Stop looking po-faced. I'm not doing you any favours. I want that lovely blouse you made and embroidered. There's nothing to touch it in the shops and it really is *my* thing. Dwight would love it. Swap?"

"But the suit must have cost the earth."

"And the blouse didn't? Take the time it took to make, your own design and all that silk embroidery and we have an exclusive model worth far more than one suit that isn't unique."

"Swap," Emma agreed and they picked out the clothes most likely to be worn in California if the weather was hot.

"I shall buy lots of underwear over there," Bea said. "The black set that Phillip gave you, and you never wore, silly girl, is getting threadbare. I think you might have had the decency to keep Phillip in tow a bit longer to supply me with those lovely things."

"I'm very sorry," Emma said sarcastically. "You wouldn't care if I had to sell my body for your cami-knicks? I shall buy a good swimsuit. I have only the ones I wore at school, all modest black with hardly any shape, but I saw some gorgeous styles in the American magazines you brought me."

"You're beginning to enjoy the idea," Bea said with satisfaction.

"It will be wonderful and now that we seem to have cleared enemy ships from the Atlantic, it's probably as safe as we can get it travelling by air. I've never flown. Do you think I'll be sick?"

"Put paper bags on the list, but if you are never sea-sick, you will be all right."

202

"I must telephone Aunt Emily. I hinted that I might be able to stay with her for a while but it seems that most of the time will be taken up now. If I can be back early enough, I'd like to go there for a week," Emma said.

"Does she know about the American trip?"

"Only that you are going. I'll ring her now as she is usually in at this time."

"Are you still there?"

"Still here and unlikely to be cut off," Emma said later and laughed at her aunt's apprehensive voice when faced with a call on the telephone.

"I hate these contraptions," Aunt Emily said.

"I have to cancel my visit, I'm afraid," Emma began and went on to tell her what Bea had arranged. There was silence on the other end of the line when she finished, followed by a sigh.

"Are you all right?"

"Yes, it's just a shock hearing that. It's been my dream to go there one day to find out about my brother Sidney, but I know I shall never go there now."

"The actor?"

"Yes. He was quite famous when the moving pictures started and they liked his English accent when they began talkies. He was engaged, you know. The girl went out to find him and Lucy was killed in a car accident."

"I remember you telling me, but my mother never mentioned him. That's his picture you have in your bedroom, isn't it?"

"Yes, he was very handsome in those days."

Emma recalled the picture of a young man with thick dark hair and arresting eyes, wearing a white shirt open at the neck with a loose silk tie flowing down the front.

She had always thought he looked sensitive and almost effeminate but his mouth was warm and generous and indicated humour. "Do you still write? Is he alive?"

"That's what I don't know. He had a big house and wrote regularly to me. He sent pieces of jewellery to us after he began to make money and sent some to all of us girls, including your mother."

"I've never seen any at home that came from him," said Emma. "I've seen your gold chains and bracelet but Mother never said she had anything of his."

"She wouldn't." Emma heard the derogatory sniff and smiled. "He sent a lovely pendant on a chain to your mother with a heart picked out in marcasites and I think real diamonds, but she was jealous of him and gave it to Lucy to tease her, saying that he'd sent it for her. Lucy thought it was a love token and followed him to America."

"But they did get engaged," Emma said. "It was all right, wasn't it?"

"My mother thought so and that's what mattered," Emily said. "Sidney had to move into a sanatorium a few years ago as he'd contracted TB, and the last letters I sent were returned 'Not known at this address'."

"Did he die? Surely someone would have written to you if he had?"

"You'd think so. I think he may be still there and his manager, who seemed to see to all his affairs, thinks he is better off without us."

"You mean he intercepted your letters?"

"And the ones that Sidney wrote."

"Did you write to the person in charge of the sanatorium?"

"I thought about it, but what good would it do if Sidney is so dependent on that man?"

"Where is he?"

"Wait a minute while I look."

Emma heard rustling and the phone was almost dropped on the table. "Hello," she said softly.

"Are you there?" Emily was almost shouting and Emma said she could hear her quite clearly. Emily dictated an address in California and gave her the name of the medical Superintendent in charge.

"I don't know how big California is, but if I can I'll try to contact the place and maybe learn something," Emma said.

"If I knew, I could feel at peace about him, and if he's dead, then I want to know where he's buried."

Emma found a map of America and Bea saw the name of the town where Dwight was in hospital. Quite close, only about twenty miles away, was the place where Sidney Darwen had been admitted as a patient in a very smart sanatorium. "What fun! You can do some detective work," Bea said. "Dark deeds, do you think?"

"Jealousy, I suspect," Emma replied. "Aunt Emily once said that her father had called Sidney a pansy and I think this manager has been with him for years as a devoted friend. A bit outside of Aunt Emily's experience but I think Uncle Sidney was, shall we say, a trifle precious?"

"So you'll be safe if I let you off for a visit."

"Quite safe. I'll be interested to see an American sanatorium. I'll look about me if I go there as Paul might want to know how they treat TB patients over there."

"Well I'm relieved that you'll have a mission which will satisfy your puritanical streak and not feel that all is fun and games!"

205

The last few nights on duty went by slowly and the news spread that the two nurses were going to America. Sister Sinclair was acidly approving and declared her intention of living there after the war as she saw it as the only country unscathed by bombing, where she could forget all that had saddened her and made her bitter over the past few years. "They can't send this rubbish over there for honest women to nurse and wait on," she said with vehemence, but went about her duties among the Germans with icy but meticulous care.

"When you come back we must set a date for the wedding, some time after Easter," Guy said, on one of the rare nights when they slept in the cottage. "I wish you weren't going," he said wistfully. "I shall miss you so much."

Emma laughed softly. She felt warm and fulfilled but also amused. "You will be here for about two nights during the whole three weeks I have off," she reminded him. "If I'm back in time, I shall stay with Aunt Emily, but you know you are welcome there if you can spare a weekend."

"We could go to Devon."

"I owe Aunt Emily a visit and I don't want to go to Devon just now to be persuaded to make arrangements against my better judgement. We haven't decided where we are to be married, and I want to discuss that only with you."

"You're right. Make what plans you like and I'll go along with them. All that matters is that we can be together like this and have a home of our own." His eyes were dark with passion and she knew that at that moment, he would have promised her anything. He kissed her and she melted into his embrace again until the dawn light made her stir and think about food and getting back to Heath Cross. As

206

she dressed, Guy came behind her and cupped her breasts in his hands. His lips on her throat were almost rough. "I almost wish I'd made you pregnant before you have your exam results. That way you'd have to marry me now and leave to come with me."

"Soon," she said tenderly, but added, "No babies yet, Guy. I don't think I'm ready for that."

"It would bind you closer to me," he said.

"Spaces, Guy. Spaces and patience and a whole future before us with time for everything."

Chapter 13

"I'm scared!" Bea eyed the huge transport plane with horror. "It's so *big!*"

"You can't be scared." Emma spoke bracingly. "If anyone is entitled to be scared it's me, as I'm only a part of the luggage. What happened to that stiff upper lip and Bea Shuter poise?"

"You really aren't afraid," Bea said as if discovering a miracle. "Well at least they haven't lost our baggage. There it goes into that deep dark hole. I hope it isn't the loading bay for bombs or we could lose all our neatly packed clothes over the Atlantic if they sight enemy shipping. What a shock for Hitler to have your sweet blouse and my expensive perfume landing on the deck of a submarine."

"Ready to go, ma'am." The smartly dressed officer saluted and led the way up the lowered companionway and into the maw of the plane. The interior was stripped, apart from basic seats and bunks and a galley that had a steaming pan of soup and the promise of good coffee. A huge refrigerator payed homage to the insatiable appetite for ice cream of the average GI. At one end was a curtained-off area behind the pilot's cabin towards which they were taken, far away from the rear guns and a pile of equipment belonging to the crew and men going home on leave or for rehabilitation after wounds.

"I hope you spent a penny before you left," Bea whispered. "It all looks a bit matey."

There were two folding beds and two chairs and a cubicle for ablutions inside the curtained-off part. "Just like the Ritz," Bea said. "I just adore the decor."

The plane slowly taxied along the runway and they could hear the dull sound of voices in the cockpit exchanging information with the control tower. "Everything in order, ma'am?"

"It's just lovely," Bea said faintly as the plane lurched for take off.

"There will be food in an hour and coffee whenever you want it," the officer said and looked round the compartment to check that they had all the essentials.

"What's that?" asked Emma, pointing to what she thought was a bulky rucksack belonging to one of the crew or one of the other passengers.

"Parachute, ma'am. If we think it necessary, we'll tell you when to put it on. Here, let me show you. I don't expect you ladies have worn one of these?"

"No." They listened with awe as he instructed them in the art of parachuting. "One easy lesson," as Bea said after he had gone. "And no need to leave the plane."

"Let's hope it stays that way." Emma eyed the package with misgiving and decided that she wasn't keen to look out at the sea far below them. "Coffee, and then I'm going to lie down and try to sleep the flight away," she said firmly. "I don't want any food."

"Not feeling squeamish?"

"No, just excited, I suppose. I wish I'd brought ear-plugs. It's a bit noisy here and the boys back there are getting lively."

"I would have been lost without you," Bea said. "I almost expect you to brush your teeth and climb into your nightie and wish the boys good night." Bea peered out through the curtains and laughed.

"Either they think we are spies who need watching or they are protecting our virtue. Whatever it is, they have a guard outside, so I shall follow you and go to bed at eight in the morning, but as I never did like night duty and sleeping in the day, I brought these." She found a packet in her purse. "I asked Paul for a sleeping pill and he said these would knock us out for a few hours, so let's hope we don't have to parachute yet."

They woke briefly at Gander where the plane refuelled and were wide awake when they reached the airforce base where they were to land. Warm air greeted them, laced with the stench of hot engine grease. They said a polite thank you to the pilot and the crew and were soon clear of the landing strip. Packed into a large car with their luggage and bound for a hotel, they fell silent until Bea said, "I don't believe it! Look at all those lights!"

"It had never occurred to me that America would have no blackout but it was silly to think there would be any over here. Isn't it lovely? All those twinkling lights as far as we can see them and houses with no drawn curtains," said Emma.

"Look!" Bea pointed again. "There was a swimming pool in that garden with people sitting round it, in the warm air. I suppose we slept for a long time and there was the stopover at Gander and now it's another day, or evening, rather."

They were taken to a hotel for the night and in the morning were flown in a small army aircraft for the rest of their journey. It was like a dream and Emma drank in strange sounds and sights and the fact that everywhere was freshly painted, smart and secure. The huge steaks served to them for the, first dinner had been far more than the meat ration for a month at home, and they both had to leave some. The lavishly decorated iced pudding was not as good as it looked and they felt superior. Emma declared that Aunt Emily could do better on one of her off days.

The hotel where they would make their base was opulent and there was soap and bath essence and fluffy towels in abundance in their suite. "The General has done us proud," Bea said. "I know he's fond of Dwight and now me, but this is ridiculous. We must be a nuisance but he insisted that Dwight had earned the right to have me here for a few days and that you needed to be with me, so who am I to grumble? I've found that most Americans are very generous and eager to make a good impression. They really can't still believe that we resent them; after all, they *did* come into the war and have pulled out all the stops to help since Pearl Harbour."

Bea was able to have a call put through to the hospital and to Dwight from the small sitting room of the suite and Emma went into her room and closed the door until the first ecstatic greetings were over.

"I can see him tomorrow and stay there for lunch, but after lunch he has a lot of physio so I shall come away and do some shopping with you. Can you amuse yourself until then?" Bea asked when at last she surfaced from her delighted exchange.

"Fine. I shall try to find out about my uncle without saying who I am. How do I use this phone?"

"You ring reception and they'll get your number and there are phone books under that shelf."

Confused by the warmth and the difference in time, they had an early supper and went to bed to recover, to emerge bright eyed to a sunny morning which called for flimsy clothes and light jackets. Bea was trembling as she left the hotel. "I feel as if I'm meeting him for the first time," she said. "How do I look?"

"Elegant and composed as usual and he'll adore you. The silk blouse was just right with a sand-coloured skirt and pale suede shoes.

Emma went back to the suite and examined the phone book. She found the number of the private sanatorium and noted that the name of the medical superintendent was the same as the one that Aunt Emily had given her. It was comforting to know that the place hadn't closed down or changed hands and she asked to be put through to the reception clerk.

"Can I help you?" The voice was sharp and disinterested.

"Do you have a Mr Sidney Darwen there as a patient?" she asked.

"We surely do," was the reply.

"Does he receive visitors?"

"Well, that depends. Are you a fan of his? We get a great many calls from fans who remember him from the movies, and loads of mail, but his manager comes in each afternoon to visit and to see to all that, and lets Mr Darwen see only a few callers at his discretion." It was obvious that she fielded many calls from women who wanted to see him but had never met Sidney Darwen and were never likely to do so if it could be avoided. "Why don't you send a few flowers and a note, honey? I'm sure he would appreciate that, but he's sick and not able to see everyone."

"I may do that," Emma said. "Does he receive a lot of mail?"

"Since they reissued some of his early films we've been inundated, as the Press gave away the secret of where he is staying."

"Thank you," Emma said.

"You're welcome."

So he really has been a famous actor, Emma thought as she sat and wondered what to do next. If she went to the sanatorium and asked to see him she knew she would get no further than the foyer and if she rang again, the receptionist would recognise her English voice. At least he was alive!

Bea was full of her visit. She danced round the room singing, "He loves me, he loves me!"

"Of course he loves you," Emma said. "What did you have for lunch? I asked for a sandwich and they brought a huge stacked affair surrounded by enough greenery to last me a week. The wastage here would turn Aunt Emily's hair grey."

"Lunch? Oh, something with chicken, I think," Bea said. "I don't think we ate it and now I think of it, I'm starving! Let's go out and buy coffee and doughnuts. Dwight used to keep on about them when he was in England and I want to try them."

"How was the hospital?"

Bea screwed up her face. "Fine, I suppose. All white and gleaming and the uniforms are super but not as pretty as ours. I think our black stockings and tight belts are far more attractive than pale stockings, white dresses and white shoes, but perhaps they want to keep the temperature of the patients down. It was all very relaxed too, and I wonder if a bit more discipline might not go amiss. I saw nothing wrong," she added hastily. "But after our rigid rules and routine, I did get the impression that there was not enough channelling of work and there were some staff lounging about looking lost as if they hadn't been told what to do."

"I always did say you were a Beatties ward sister at heart." Emma laughed. "We shall never be able to suffer

213

slackness in others and however hard it's been at times, I think they have it right."

"Did you telephone?" Bea asked when she had eaten her second doughnut. "I shall never get the spelling right here," she said, looking at the menu and the variety of "donuts" displayed.

"The place exists and he is a patient there but I can't think how to get to him without his manager knowing. It was made clear that he vets all the mail and says who can and who can not see Sidney Darwen. They still have fan mail and so it's easy for him to avoid any contact with people he personally wants to exclude."

"I'll make the next call," Bea suggested. "I won't mention your uncle but ask for an appointment to see the Medical Superintendent as if I am enquiring about the possible admission of a relative to become a patient."

"That would a relief. It would be terrible if I was in the area and didn't contact him."

After an exhausting afternoon window-gazing at the displays of extravagant clothes and accessories and buying a few modest garments as if they were unsure if they were entitled to them without clothing coupons, Bea led Emma back and picked up the telephone.

In her most autocratic and English voice she asked for a swift appointment with the head of the sanatorium and the secretary asked if ten a.m. the following morning would be convenient. "Yes, a morning would suit me very well," Bea said, lazily, with a triumphant glance at Emma. "Good! That means you will not be interrupted by this manager, whoever he is, as you said he goes there each afternoon to sift through the mail."

"I suppose you can't come too?"

"No, I'm having a date with a handsome flyer but I'll be back after lunch. Have you proof of your own identity, and some indication that he really is your uncle? They must get a few deranged females who pose as relatives to see famous or handsome men and so they may ask you for something."

"Aunt Emily gave me the last letter that she had returned to her, marked address unknown, which will prove she sent it there and it was received. It has her name on it: Emily Darwen, as she never married and changed it. I also have an early picture signed by him to his dear Sister Emily. That should do it."

At a few minutes to ten, the following morning, Emma said goodbye to her driver , still unused to being treated as such an important person with an army driver to take her wherever she wanted to go. She mounted the shallow steps to the foyer of the sanatorium. She knew that her arrival had been observed and noted through the wide windows, and that she passed as another wealthy, influential visitor. She silently thanked Bea for the beautiful Swiss silk suit and walked slowly into reception.

"Mr Jarvis is expecting you, Miss Dewar," the girl said and from her accent Emma knew that this was a different receptionist from the one who had answered the phone the day before. The elevator sighed down to the thickly carpeted floor and a nurse in spotless uniform took her up to the administration offices where she was shown into a waiting room decked with tropical plants and fine pictures.

A heavily built man emerged from the office and held out a hand in greeting. He eyed Emma from head to foot and she felt that he was registering both her figure and the price of every item of her visible clothing and probably made a guess at her underwear. "Miss Dewar? Now should I know the name?" He looked arch. "I just know you have to be in pictures."

"Actually, no," Emma said, formally. "My uncle Sidney was but he's the only one of the family to act." She pulled out the old picture. "He is a patient here, I know, but the family were worried because they had heard no news of him for over a year and wondered if he was still alive. As I am on a fleeting visit from England, I promised I'd find out why they have heard nothing." She fixed him with an accusing stare, sensing that the man might be a bully and the best defence was attack. "Surely if he was unable to write, someone should have written to his sister? My Aunt Emily exchanged letters with him on a regular basis for years and it was only after he entered your establishment that the letters ceased and she received this." She put the returned letter on the desk in front of him. "My aunt gave me your name as the head of this sanatorium, so you were here at the time."

"My dear Miss Dewar, there must have been some awful mistake," he began.

"This isn't the only letter returned," she went on relentlessly.

"I am here to see him and to sort this out." Sister Sinclair would be proud of me, she thought as her voice took on a hard, professional edge. She stood up. "I'd like to see him now."

"His manager sees to his visitors and he isn't here just now," he began .

"And sorts his mail?" Her smile was cold. "Thank you, but I wish to see him now and alone."

"I was told that the last of his relatives had died," Mr Jarvis said, and beads of sweat appeared on his brow.

"His manager told you that? He was very much mistaken. Mr Darwen has three sisters and a brother still alive and I am his niece." Emma picked up her purse and looked expectantly at the door.

Wordlessly, she was led to a spacious room decked with flowers and with wide open windows. "Thank you, Mr Jarvis, I'll call in at your office again before I leave," she said clearly and dismissively.

"An English voice! And a pretty face," said a soft voice from the bed and Emma saw that under the emaciated features, the film actor still existed. She swallowed hard. Not only had she found Emily's brother, but an uncle who she had never known.

"Hello Uncle Sidney," she said. "Aunt Emily sent me to find you and sends her love."

For a moment, he covered his face with his hand, then said, "Ivor told me she was dead."

Emma sat by the bed and they talked about the family that he'd left years ago when he went to make his name as an actor. She told him about herself and that Emily was still living on the Island.

"She mentioned you often in earlier letters," he recalled. "I came to think of you as her daughter."

"She's been more than a mother to me," she said.

"I can imagine. Your real mother was never very warm." He tried to raise himself from the bed but fell back again. "Look in that drawer and bring me the small leather case."

He opened it and took out a collection of gold studs that would be suitable for an old-fashioned dress shirt front and a diamond studded watch. He found a pouch of chamois leather, tipping its contents on to the coverlet. Emma gasped. "Is this what you sent to my mother?" The marcasites and diamonds glinted in the gold setting of the heart-shaped pendant.

"It caused a lot of bother but in its way put me on the road to stardom when I became engaged to Lucy," he said thoughtfully. "I never wanted your mother to have it again

217

but take it for Emily and she may find that you can have it some day. It is all I have left of Lucy, the girl I was to marry. Tell Emily that I loved Lucy as much as I could love any woman and it was a real love."

Emma saw the hectic spots on his cheeks that showed that his tuberculosis was acute and he was becoming tired. He had coughed several times into a handkerchief while they talked and his lips had a blue tinge. "I have to go now," she said. "I'll write and so will Aunt Emily, and we'll make sure you get the letters."

"You are a sweet girl. I don't want trouble as I depend so much on Ivor, but I would like to hear from you without anyone knowing." He took the photographs that Emma had brought with her of Emily and her house and one of herself in uniform, and put them under his pillow.

"Mustn't kiss you," he said, and held her hand for a moment.

Emma asked the nurse at the outer desk to take her back to the office. Mr Jarvis was waiting and looking apprehensive. "We discussed family matters," she said. "No recriminations as he is too ill for that, so if you promise me that you personally will see that he receives any mail with an English postmark and make sure that when he dies, my aunt is informed at once, we can forget what his manager has done, obviously through jealousy."

"He sees to all Mr Darwen's affairs," he said.

"He does not have to see the English mail," Emma insisted. "In my country there is a law about tampering with the Royal Mail. I hope there is such a one in the States as well."

"I give you my word."

"I shall not come here again. If I am not mistaken, he has a very limited time left and I want no harm for him. Let

218

him continue to be looked after by someone who obviously must love him but make sure he gets my letters."

He took the proffered note of Emily Darwen's address and put it carefully in a file. "Thank you for coming here, Miss Dewar. It will give him a lot to think about, and I know he fretted over what he thought was his sister's death. I shall say nothing to his manager of your visit unless you wish me to do so, and I have a feeling that Mr Darwen will not mention it either." He coughed. "Some people have low flash points and carry a load of jealousy and I don't want Mr Darwen's last days to be troubled."

"I do understand." Emma smiled more warmly. "I wonder if your receptionist could call me a cab? I don't want to trouble the army again as the General has been more than helpful over this visit."

"The General?"

Feeling no embarrassment as she disliked the man intensely, she watched him seem to grow smaller when she explained who the General was and how she came to be in America in wartime to visit a very important American Air Force pilot. Emma felt that she had made a lasting impression based on borrowed power, and left with an air of elation.

"You said all the right things," Bea agreed. "It wasn't boasting to mention high connections. The Americans respect that as they rate money and self-achieved power above everything. In a way it's healthy as they think that given a break they can all be President, and so have a few dreams."

"When does Dwight get the all clear to fly back?"

"We have five days left here and then he will be ready," she said. "They wanted to keep him but I explained that we are both highly qualified nursing sisters, I hope, but didn't mention that we were waiting for our results, who had left our urgent war work to come to escort him. They were impressed. Mention war work in bombed Britain and they come running," Bea said. "They were more impressed by that than the fact that he is my husband!"

"What's wrong?"

"Nothing really. It's just that Dwight was a bit depressed as they've announced that the Russians have liberated a huge and terrible concentration camp in Austria called Auschwitz. Thousands of Jews and political prisoners, but mostly Jews, have been exterminated there in gas chambers and by shooting, and the survivors were starving so they've dropped plane loads of food and medical supplies to help the situation."

"We've heard rumours of these places but never details," Emma said. "I wonder if we'll have some of the sick to nurse at Heath Cross? I doubt it as Austria is too far away. I can't see Sister Sinclair being even polite to the Germans after this. She has enough trouble controlling her hate now, and is icily correct, rather like some of the Germans. Of course, her origins are partly German-Jew so it's hard to disassociate her from either side, and it must be difficult for her."

"Come on, we'll shop for goodies to take back and if you are going on to Aunt Emily as soon as we land, you can take her a few luxuries from me and Dwight for lending you to us."

Emma bought dress material and trimmings so that she could make her own clothes at a low cost, and a warm jacket for Emily. "I doubt if she's had anything really new for years," she said. Bea added a huge box of biscuits and another of chocolate candies to the gift and on the day when they went to fetch Dwight, they were full of warm feelings for America and yet

220

had a longing to get back to the shabby place they had left.

"Emma!" Dwight seized her and kissed her. "It was real good of you to come with Bea. I know she would have been very much alone without you and I sure appreciate it."

"Down boy!" Bea said. "She's only the hired help."

He grinned. "OK. How's Guy and when do we come to your wedding?"

Dwight was in uniform, with a split trouser leg to accommodate the plaster cast and a khaki sock on the toes of the affected limb. His cap was on at a rakish angle and his teeth gleamed with health and humour. "Doesn't he look well?" Bea gloated, and touched his hand as if she couldn't believe that he was real.

He was put in a carrying chair in spite of his protests that as he had a rocker fitted to his plaster he could walk on board the plane with the help of elbow crutches, but he said nothing more when he saw the angle of the gangway.

"I feel like a woman in purdah," Bea said later when she sat with Emma in their own quarters. Dwight was whisked away to join a party of high ranking officers on their way to Europe to set in motion a supply treaty with the Allies and the dropping of more food to the now liberated but starving prisoners in the concentration camps. There were also three doctors assigned to the camps and the body of the plane was filled with medical supplies.

"They're sending medics and nurses to help out over there," Dwight said later. He looked at Emma with a trace of anxiety. "They have called some doctors from the Reserve and if they volunteer, they are being sent to Germany with anti-cholera jabs and supplies of the new penicillin."

221

"Guy is doing important work in England," Emma said. "They wouldn't send him."

"I hope that's so," Dwight said. "I am going to a desk job while I'm unable to fly, based in London or Bath and dealing with refugees as I speak a few languages." He smiled at Bea. "D'you know, I've longed to be back there again. I shall end up a real Limey. In the States I felt guilty at being out of the action and guilty about being away from Europe where it's all happening. We have far too much of everything and very few people think it wrong. The news of Auschwitz did make an impact, especially as pictures are coming through and they see the real horror of the Nazis' regime, but we have a long way to go."

"I know what you mean," Bea said. "I want to be in the States with you, after the war is over, but now, I felt as if I've wandered into a fairy land that was all paint and paper and tinsel. Apart from the people who have boys in the American forces, there's a complete lack of understanding about what we go through at home."

The plane landed at a south coast airport near Haywards Heath and an ambulance came to take Dwight and Bea to the American military hospital. Emma packed herself into a taxi to take her to the Isle of Wight ferry, after telephoning Aunt Emily at her job in the British Restaurant to announce her arrival.

She sniffed the salt air and smiled, eager to see her aunt again, to tell her about Sidney Darwen, and glad of the mild spring sunshine and the freshness around her beyond the rusting sea defences and the broken seaside huts.

Tears formed in Emily's eyes when she heard Emma's account of what she had seen and what was said in the sanatorium. "Did you only go there once?" she asked.

"Yes. I didn't want to meet Ivor, his manager, as I was convinced that he would cause trouble and Uncle Sidney is in no fit state to have any fuss." She opened the chamois leather bag. "He wants you to have this and maybe pass it on to me if you wish," she said.

"It was sent to your mother," Emily said uncertainly.

"He was very definite that you should have it and you must not tell mother."

"Put it on. There, it looks well on you so you'd better keep it, Emma. It's enough for me to know he is alive and cared for, even if he is dying."

"It will be a gentle death," Emma said, softly. "He has a collapsed lung with fluid in all the wrong places, but that makes a cushion and he feels comfortable and without pain. He'll just fade away unless they do something drastic, but I think it's too late for that." She sighed. "I shall remember him always. He said his one regret was that we couldn't get to know each other, but I feel as if I do know him."

"You would have got on well. He was my favourite brother and we were close as children."

Emma left her staring into the fire and went to make strong tea into which she tipped a tot of whisky before she handed it to her aunt.

"Just as your Gran would have liked it," Emily said, and Emma was aware of her lost family everywhere, watching in a friendly, approving silence because she had been to see Sidney.

Chapter 14

"I thought that as soon as I heard my results I would leave and never set foot in the place again," Bea said. She fingered her hospital badge and the other badge announcing that she was a State Registered Nurse and had a number to prove it.

"I know which one will be more important," Emma said. "Every teaching hospital turns out SRNs but not many hand out these pretty hospital badges. It's good to have a visible sign that we are Beatties trained as it gives us a good reputation all over the world."

"I might as well stay at Heath Cross as they say they need me," Bea said. "Dwight is busy with refugees, working in Military Intelligence, and his leg isn't fit to allow him on active service again for a while, so we meet only at weekends. If I can work part-time and live in the cottage, we can be together quite a lot." She eyed Emma with reserve. "Are you sure it's all right to take over the cottage? Guy has been very understanding but it means that you and he will be cramped when you stay there and I hate to do you out of the best bedroom."

"Just as well if people do think we are two single people who happen to stay at the cottage in separate rooms," Emma said.

"Dwight will want to have friends visiting and certainly the General will need to pop in from time to time, so this

224

will be fine. We did have a little time together before Dwight left hospital and we shall do so again soon, when we are married, so don't let it bother you." She smiled and nearly believed her own words, but under her acceptance lay a thin layer of resentment, not towards Bea and Dwight but because Guy had been so instantly willing for them to take the cottage as if they owned it.

"I am very tied up just now," he explained. "I have the surgical unit to fix up now that we have been given an extra ward at Beatties that is no longer used for soldiers."

"When shall I see you again?" she'd asked after a wonderful weekend that had made her forget her fears for the future and left her convinced anew that Guy was the most important person in her life.

"If you'd leave Heath Cross and come to London, we could meet more often," he said.

"What would I do all day?"

"Marry me now and we can take a flat close to the hospital. You can meet your friends and do lots of things," he added, rather lamely. "I could live out and we'd be a really married couple."

"I'll think about it," she promised, but knew that the arrangement wouldn't work out. "We haven't decided where we are to be married," she added. "And I haven't been fully qualified for more than five minutes. They want me to start as soon as possible here as Junior Theatre Sister and I really would like to do that for a while, but until I take up the appointment, I shall work as a relief sister."

"Try to postpone your appointment. After Easter, I shall expect to see more of you. We can get married and have a proper honeymoon," he insisted. "You have your qualification and can find a part-time job here if you hate being idle."

*   *   *

"Do you ever get the feeling that some things just aren't possible?" she asked Bea.

"You mean, you and Guy?" Bea eyed her with anxiety. "Nerves, dear," she said. "When Dwight and I got married we had no time to think and rushed into it, thank God!" She laughed. "Once you are married, you will forget all the doubts and settle down to a life of bliss, like me."

"Not like you, Bea. I love Guy and I know he loves me, but I want more than a life of caring for a house and maybe children, and having no other stimulation. When you go to America, there will be lots to fill your time and satisfy you. You mentioned the letters that Dwight's family sent, telling you of the horses and social life there. When I am married, I shall have a modest flat or small house in a strange city because that's where the best research is done. The only social life will be at the parties that occur in every medical faculty and a few meetings with old friends who will treat me as someone they once knew who gave up nursing."

"He may take a job in a small town or somewhere surrounded by lovely country," suggested Bea.

"Like Devon?"

"It's a wonderful county."

"I know it is, but I'd be swamped by Guy's family. Close relationships with parents and brothers and sisters are so foreign to me that I dread being sucked into a situation where I'd have to do as the others think I should do."

"You need never do that," Bea said firmly. "I have no intention of doing anything that puts pressure on me to change my opinions."

"I feel the pull from here even though I've never met them. I sensed pursed lips when I refused a full-scale marriage in their village and said I would wear a suit to my wedding. So Devon is out as far as I am concerned."

"You'd change your mind if he wanted to work on that damned Island that we hear so much about," said Bea.

Emma laughed. "That reminds me. I had a letter from Aunt Emily."

"Open it and tell me the news. I have a share in her too you know, and Dwight wants to visit the Island soon to get some of that awful fresh air."

"She still writes about Sidney Darwen and hopes I can go down to her again soon." She stopped reading and stared. "'I had a visitor who might know you. My doctor called in for more of a social visit than the need to check my blood pressure, which I may add is now normal, and he brought with him a young man from a London hospital, who he hopes may join him in the practice.'"

Emma laughed. "She forgets how many hospitals there are in London and she forgot to mention his name but she's sure I know him!"

"Call for Nurse Dewar!"

"Might be Guy but I doubt it," Emma said and rushed out to the phone. "David? How nice to hear from you. I thought you were in Germany."

"Can't stop, Emma. Can you give me Guy's number? I thought he was at Heath Cross. If he's back at Beatties I need to get in touch in a hurry. I haven't the number here."

Emma told him the number, a growing sense of panic forming inside her. "What's wrong, David? It's something bad, isn't it?"

"Keep it under wraps for the present, Emma, but . . . what the hell, it will be all over the news later, so it doesn't really matter. They are calling more medics from the Reserve to go to Germany. They've liberated another concentration camp and need help urgently. It's a place called Belsen and it's bloody awful. I've just come from there and I've been detailed to bring a party out by air as soon as possible."

"Why Guy?" she asked faintly.

"He's needed. Top priority, and we are taking even final year medical students and anyone remotely useful. They are in a terrible state and we must get there quickly before many more hundreds die. The gas chambers killed thousands, and starvation and disease are killing the rest." His voice shook. "I'm also organising a visit from the leading newspapers and television. This has to be seen all over the world, or nobody will believe it. It's inhuman, and I feel worse about this than I did about the wounded of Dunkirk."

White-faced, Emma told Bea what had been said.

"It isn't fighting," Bea reminded her. "Just doctors doing what they do best, helping the sick. Dwight said that there were other concentration camps likely to be freed soon and he mentioned Belsen. Some of the German officers in charge have been making soothing noises to the Allies, trying to excuse themselves from being accused of atrocities, but they'll all be arrested once we get in there."

Soft April rain teased the curtains at the open window and Emma shut it out. Spring, and what for children would be the Easter holidays, now seemed a mockery. She picked a wilted daffodil from the vase on the dressing table and crushed it between her fingers.

"He'll be all right," Bea insisted. "What can go wrong? I almost wish I could be there to help in any way I can."

"You've had your period of waiting," Emma said. "You've earned the right to have Dwight here in safety. You must be right. What can happen?" She bit her lip. "Have I been selfish, putting off my wedding so that I can be independent for a while longer? Guy's asked me

228

often enough and now I have an awful feeling that we shall never marry."

"Certainly not this Easter," Bea said. "But as soon as he is back again you can go ahead with your plans and they say the war will be over in a week or so."

"Do you really believe that?"

Bea shrugged. "Some people think so. The Yanks are already planning great celebrations in Berkeley Square and in all the American air bases over here."

"I doubt if Guy will be back in time," Emma said. "It will take a long time to sort out the mess over there, and he will stay until the last patient is treated and the last body buried. I know Guy."

"Ring him and find out what he's planning," Bea said. "You might be able to see him at the railway station. No, silly me! He won't exactly take the boat train to the Riviera! They'll fly him from Northolt or somewhere close and so you'd better hurry if you want to contact him."

The lines were busy as if everyone knew about the latest developments and wanted to telephone someone, but at last Emma got through to Beatties and asked for Guy. The girl in the exchange was sympathetic but vague. "He's passed on his work to his deputy registrar and left here in uniform half an hour ago. Hold the line a moment. Nurse Dewar? He left a message for you to say he'd telephone before he left England if there was any chance. He tried to get you but the lines were full."

"I noticed," Emma said wearily. "I was trying for ages to get through. Thanks for the message."

"You can't sit by the telephone all night," Bea said later.

"I'll read in the small reception room. It's not all that cold now and I can wrap myself in a rug."

Just after three in the morning when the first birds

were stirring and the grey light turned pinky white, the sharp bell made her start from a fitful sleep. "Miss Emma Dewar?"

"Speaking," she said quickly.

"We'll link you now, sir." A crackling and a lot of back ground noise almost obscured the voice, then Guy's voice came over fairly clearly.

"This is a radio link," he said. "Thank God you were there darling. I have no time but I had to hear your voice before I landed in Germany."

"I love you," Emma said as if she might be cut off before she could say the words. "Be careful and come back soon so that we can be married straight away. I know now what is important and I want to be with you for always."

"Bless you. I shall take that promise with me for ever," he said.

"Just until you return," she corrected him.

"Goodbye, darling Emma. I love you to bits."

More crackling and then an apologetic voice saying that the connection was broken and Emma walked stiffly to her room, suddenly cold and very miserable.

Civilian surgery made Heath Cross seem almost normal but the guard posted outside the ward with the German prisoners was a reminder that the war was not over. Sister Sinclair went about her work with tight lips and requested a different ward. She said quite frankly that she would do someone a mischief if she had to work with the Germans for another day, and the administrators, knowing her family history and seeing how close she was to a breakdown, sent her on leave for two weeks and promised that she could take over another ward on her return.

The newsreels produced utter silence in the dark cinemas when they showed the emaciated figures dragging themselves round the empty spaces of Belsen and the mounds of bodies, already skeletal before death, awaiting burial in huge pits which now were being dug by the German guards who were in turn prisoners, made to clear up the hellish mess that was the camp. Disbelief turned to horror and as the full understanding of the atrocities sank in, many people were physically sick and all hurried away from the cinemas unable to speak of what they had seen.

"Desmond is back from Belsen," Bea said after a few days of wondering. "You were scrubbed-up so couldn't see him and he left after about an hour, but he saw Guy who sent his love and said he'd be staying for a while."

"Did he say what it's like there?" Emma asked eagerly.

Bea looked uneasy. "He didn't say much."

"What did he say? Why is he here?"

"He came back for blood tests and when I asked what it was like there, he said, 'I don't want to talk about it. If you must know, we found bunks with shit five feet deep and bodies in it, so leave me alone.'"

"Blood tests?"

"There's a lot of disease and they thought he might have amoebic dysentery. There's also typhus in the camp from the rats that are everywhere, but they are clearing it up," Bea added when she saw the frozen expression as Emma realised how bad it was.

"If only I could hear from Guy," Emma said. "I feel like going out there myself."

"You should be a journalist. They are swarming over there but the authorities are taking care that they don't catch anything or they would be just another obstacle for the medics to tackle."

"But the doctors and nurses are exposed to all that."

"They take care. You know that, Emma. All we can do is to get on with our work and be ready to welcome them when they come back safely."

"Just when the war seems to be over," Emma said sadly. "There's talk of a victory parade in Whitehall when the Armistice is signed and soon they'll be demobbing the soldiers and trying to pull the country out of all the restrictions we've endured for so long."

"My father has a supply of real champagne ready and was quite hurt because I refused to bring back a magnum when I was last in London. I can't equate champagne with victory even now, can you? I drink it socially but it would choke me to drink it in celebration, remembering how Evans died. It seems ages ago now yet only yesterday when I think of her being bombed that night in Bristol. I've had war up to my eyeballs and I really do look forward to living in a country that doesn't bear the scars."

"I shall end up in a city full of bombed sites and tottering churches," Emma said. "I'm determind to like it wherever we are and it does seem that Guy is interested in Coventry or Birmingham."

"Persuade him to come to America." Bea laughed. "I saw Paul yesterday in town. One of Dwight's buddies has a lot of books about Indian folklore and herbal medicines and he gave me one to give to Paul. It was nice seeing him again. He is waiting for peace and then he'll decide what to do, but he's promised to come to stay with us for a while in Texas."

"I haven't seen him for ages," Emma said and felt slightly left out and envious.

"He asked after you of course," Bea said. "He'll be at Beatties for a few weeks so we may see him if we go up for the victory celebrations."

"Guy will be back by then," Emma said. "Has Paul gone

back to London for good? I heard that they'd closed the other place and are making it ready to be a hospital for the permanently disabled."

"They've given him a medical department at Beatties. He's very bright under that lazy exterior and the patients love him, but he still says he wants to go into general practice."

"He's a good sort," Emma said.

"I'd put it higher than that. His staff nurse nearly lies on the floor for him to tread over her."

"Are they serious?"

"She is," Bea said cryptically. "Can't say what he thinks as he still carries a torch for you."

"Don't be ridiculous," Emma said, but her expression softened and she smiled.

"He said he might pay us a visit," Bea said. "I reminded him that we still have hospital dances and I have a hop-along-Cassidy for a husband so could do with a partner."

"I had a letter from Guy," Emma said as if she must take her mind off Bea and her prospective dancing partner. She held it away from her. "It reeks of disinfectant. All the air mail letters are treated before they let them come into the country. I'd rather have the miniaturised copies that are clean and easy to keep as they are so small."

"How is he?"

"He says fine, except for the runs, which seems rife as the food isn't good and the means of preparing it is a bit suspect. He didn't say a lot and I think he's a bit miserable. I can't wait to have him back here and look after him."

"How long does a letter take to get here?"

"The postmark's blurred but the last one took six days. I doubt if he'll be here for Victory In Europe Day after all."

233

"Paul can take us. Dwight won't risk the crowds and Guy will be away. Paul has offered to take me, so he now has two lovely ladies to escort. We can stay in St James's, in armchairs if the beds are taken, but at least we'll have a base. So cheer up. You can't bring Guy back overnight, and you've done your share of waiting around for him in the past, so we'll forget our men and go on the razzle! I shall quite shamelessly wave the Union Jack and the Stars and Stripes, and yell for the Royal Family to come out on the balcony of Buck House."

"Do you think they might? What fun. I've seen plenty of royals at home when they come to sail, but never dressed up on formal view." In spite of the empty feeling due to Guy's absence, Emma began to enjoy the prospect of Victory Day, and when it was announced on May 8th 1945 that the end of the war in Europe had been signed and terms agreed, the country went mad.

"Come on," Bea called and Emma grabbed her jacket and followed her down from the apartment in St James's to meet Paul who was waiting by the edge of the road.

"I parked in that cul-de-sac," he said. "It's walking or nothing tonight. The crowds are unbelievable. Let's make for the Palace first and then try Whitehall in case they have a statement to make from the Foreign Office." He seized Emma's hand and Bea clutched his other one as the crowd swept them along Pall Mall towards Buckingham Palace. Church bells rang out all over the city, as they triumphantly celebrated peace and had no need to warn of invasion. Slowly, as if they couldn't believe it was allowed, lights appeared from behind swept-back blackout curtains and shutters.

"I'm flying," Bea shouted as she was taken off her feet and carried forward on the impetus of the crowds. They climbed the monument in front of the Palace and joined with the rest of London in calling for the King and Queen.

"We want the King!" shouted one woman. "Don't you ever forget! They stayed with us during the Blitz. They never ratted and went to Canada. They stayed and got bombed the same as us in the East End. God bless 'em!"

The Royal Family came out three times in half an hour and the crowds roared in a wave of affection and triumph. Spotlights showed the balcony and the bright clothes worn for the occasion with uniforms glinting with insignia and decorations, and the Queen waved delightedly with the two princesses, Elizabeth still in the drab uniform of the ATS in which she had served as a mechanic on heavy vehicles.

"Let's go to Whitehall," Paul said and they pushed a way through the bushes in St James's Park as more and more people came towards the Palace. Once more, they had no choice of movement when they came to Whitehall but were pushed towards the Cenotaph where another crowd waited, expectantly, and rumours spread that Winston Churchill was inside and would appear on the balcony of the Foreign Office.

A drunken sailor hammered on the huge door and shouted in parody of the famous Churchillian speech, "Never have so many waited for so long for so little. Come out Winston! Show yourself you old so-and-so!"

The crowd laughed and called the name that had meant so much to the country in the dark days when victory seemed impossible. At last a light shone on to the balcony as one after another members of the government filed into the brightness with the family party which included the incongruous presence of Vic Oliver, the comedian married to Sarah Churchill. Slowly the great man appeared, cigar in place and a beaming smile on his face. He waved slowly and often and his gaze swept the faces below as if seeing them all as friends. He took the cigar from his lips and waved it and gave the V for victory sign with the other hand, and the crowd loved it.

"What a showman," Paul said with amusement touched with awe and admiration. "What a thorough showman he is." Beside him the other ministers looked grey and insignificant, even though they were all smiling and enjoying the reception. Like a real pro, Winston left the stage before the crowd had had enough and the lights were turned off, with an air of finality.

"We've seen history tonight," Bea said. "I wish Dwight could have been here. They could never have a night like this in the States."

"Don't tell him that," Paul said dryly. "Remember they still have to sign Victory in the Pacific and with Japan. That's when the Yanks will go mad."

Bea looked smug. "They won't have Winston. He is ours and without him we could have lost."

"You're half American now," said Emma, "so you'd better choose your loyalties with care."

There seemed no end to the singing and shouting and the good humour of the masses of people, but Bea said she was exhausted and they left the main scenes at midnight and found a cellar bar that was open and crowded with service personnel. "No champagne," Bea said firmly. "Anything but that."

"At least you're cheap to feed," Paul said and brought sandwiches and beer from the bar.

Bea peeled back the bread and sighed. "I shall miss National bread and Spam when I'm forced to eat caviare," she said.

"Are you staying at Beatties?" asked Emma.

236

"Just filling in before the new consultant arrives," Paul replied. His expression was serious. "Most people say I'm mad to give up such a lucrative career but I want to get back to research, with access to a university between surgeries."

"That means London? So you could stay at Beatties," Emma said.

"Not necessarily. I thought of Southampton University and a practice somewhere close where I can get some sailing in my spare time and breathe pure air."

"It sounds heavenly. I wish . . ." But she didn't say more, suddenly feeling disloyal when she contrasted Paul's future with her own.

"It could be," he said and the flecks of gold made his eyes almost overbright.

Emma looked at her watch. "It's hardly worth trying to sleep. I think I'd rather get back to Heath Cross if there's any transport."

"I'll take you," Paul said. "I can beg a couch for a few hours and be back here by tomorrow afternoon."

"We can all sleep in the cottage," Bea said. "Tomorrow, Emma can take the suitcase that she packed with all Guy's things as he will be living in London for a while. He said we might need the cupboard space and Emma can keep it for him until he comes back from Germany," Bea said.

The outskirts of London were dotted with lights and more street parties and even the villages were well-lit as if glad to shake off the darkness of war. The cottage was cold but they didn't bother to light a fire. They tumbled into bed and slept.

"Wake up!" Emma opened her eyes. "If we go now we can have breakfast at Heath Cross. There's no food here and I'm hungry," Paul said firmly. He was staring at her and she drew the sheet higher, suddenly vulnerable and with the odd temptation to hold out her arms to him. He bent to kiss her on the cheek and his face smelled of Bea's good soap. "Time to go, Sleeping Beauty," he said and left to wake Bea.

He put Guy's case in the back of the car and when Emma looked back at the cottage, it was just a place where she had stayed and had no lasting vibrations of Guy's presence. She shivered in the early morning air and didn't look back again.

"I'll park the car and take the suitcase into the villa," Paul said. "You can walk to the dining room from here and set up some food for me. I'll be there in five minutes."

"That looks like David's old banger," Bea said. "I hope whoever borrows it has asked him first. He's touchy about it but has to leave it here for long periods while he's in Germany."

"David's here," Paul said when he joined them in the dining room. "Can you come, Emma? He wants to talk to you."

"He's been with Guy?" Emma pushed away her plate of porridge and almost ran to the door. Paul bent to say a few words to Bea and hurried after her.

Paul caught up with her and led her into a small side room that had once been an office. She took one look at David's face and sat down hard on a wooden bench. David nodded as if the words had already been spoken and understood. "He's dead, Emma. He died of typhus five days ago, and I came as soon as I could."

She looked as if she was made of stone and her eyes were dry. "Five days ago? Why wasn't I told? They could have telephoned."

David looked embarrassed. "I came on my own," he said. "This is unoffical. You and Guy were not married,

238

so they told only his next of kin, his parents in Devon. I thought you might have heard from them."

"I've heard nothing. Where is he?"

"They buried him in a war cemetery the day after he died. They have to do that because of infection," David said.

"His parents? Were they there?"

"No. Just his friends in the service."

"I'm glad," Emma whispered. "Do they know you are here?"

"No, I came as a friend. I promised Guy that I'd see you. You'll hear nothing from the authorities, and he seemed to think that his parents might close ranks against you," he added bluntly. "I've met his mother and she is a typical matriarch who is jealous of anyone who comes between her and her family and doesn't toe the line."

"Come on, Emma. You need rest," Bea said. "No Paul, leave her to me now, but don't go far away. She'll need you later."

Chapter 15

"I'd write and tell them what I think of them," Bea said with a vindictive pull at her belt buckle.

"What's the point? They were annoyed when Guy chose me instead of the girl they'd looked out for him, and so they didn't want me when Guy was alive. They certainly have no part in my life, now, thank God, so I need never see them ever. Not ever!"

"It's been three weeks since you heard and they haven't had the decency to tell you that your fiancé is dead! For Christ's sake, Emma! You were going to marry the man in a few weeks' time!"

Emma gave a cold half smile. "One of them has to see me," she said. "They sent a message to his commanding officer asking for his effects and he asked David if there were any to be sent from here. David explained about me and said that I might have something of Guy's as we were engaged and about to marry, so the officer, who was appalled to think I had received no formal message from them, sent a curt note to the family telling them to contact Guy Franklin's fiancée, but the onus was on them to collect anything. He also sent me a very nice personal letter of sympathy which I treasure."

"So you have heard from them?"

"After that message they knew that I have been informed and there was a call for me when I was busy in theatre, saying that a Miss Imogen Franklin would call this afternoon to see me."

"It's two o'clock and you are still in uniform. No, you've changed into a spotless fresh set and you look quite formidable, as well as the French *formidable*, as usual."

"I feel more sure of myself like this," Emma said. "I shall meet her in the small music room and keep everything impersonal, but very polite for Guy's sake. I've removed a few snaps and books from his case but they are welcome to the rest. I feel as if that part of my life is over and I don't want to be reminded of this time." She moved restlessly. "I heard today that Guy had made a will when he went to Germany, as if he knew he would die. Quite simple but legal. He's left me the cottage and a few shares. The deeds are with the lawyer in Epsom, so that's very straightforward, but I never want to go into the cottage again, Bea."

"Sell it to me," Bea said. "It will save a lot of fuss and we can use it as a *pied-à-terre* in England. I shall enjoy having it redecorated and refurnished and when it's changed and quite unrecognisable, you might find you can stay there with us and forget what it was like."

"I've decided to go to Aunt Emily for a while. The powers-that-be have been very good and will keep my job open for three months while I decide what to do, but everything reminds me of Guy and makes me feel guilty that I didn't marry him when he wanted me so much."

"Why not look elsewhere for a good posting? Beatties may be the best but there are other places. I know that my time here is nearly over and I'm eager for the next stage in my life in America. Let's face it, we've had everything; good work, pleasure and some pain and more experience of people than most could get in a dozen lifetimes." Bea

241

sighed. "It's over, Emma. We'll never forget and it's good that we should remember it all, but in our own time now, without hassle and with a lot more understanding."

Emma nodded. "How right you are, Bea. Many things will haunt me for the rest of my life but strangely, I feel that I am now ready to look ahead. I've wept for Guy, and I shall cry again, but I think marriage would have been the end of us and not the beginning."

"Take a deep breath! I'm off," Bea said as they heard footsteps in the corridor.

"Sister Dewar?" The nurse smiled and stood back so that the visitor could enter the room.

Emma nodded and the woman who approached saw her calm poise and looked embarrassed. "Miss Dewar . . . Emma?" she said.

"I am Emma Dewar." She paused. "I take it that you are a relative of my late fiancé."

"I'm Guy's sister. Maybe he spoke of me?"

"We didn't discuss his family," Emma said.

"We asked . . . that is, my mother wanted anything of Guy's that he left here, to remind us of him," she said, awkwardly, and added as if the thought had only then occurred to her. "If you can spare them, of course."

"I have enough memories of Guy without having to possess everything he left behind," Emma said. "Guy loved me and we were to have been married this week or next." She held out her hand and the rubies glowed. "I have his ring and his love, so take what clothes and things he left in our cottage. I have no use for them. You are not depriving me of anything."

"Your cottage?"

"My cottage now. Guy asked me many times to marry him but I put off the date so that I could be sure it was right for me. Make no mistake. I loved him and will

242

love him forever, but I love my work too, and knew I couldn't sacrifice everything I've worked for and live in comparative idleness. We were lovers by my choice and that was complete, and for me enough, until recently when I agreed to get married."

"You were lovers?"

"Yes. He needed my love when we coped with the D-Day wounded." Emma smiled. "His case is over there. Take it. We shared something that even his family could never imagine. I have never met your parents and I have no desire to do so. Even if they offered no hint of compassion for his fiancée, I do offer my sympathy for their loss of a son, as I would for a relative of any patient after bereavement."

"I'm sorry. I don't know what I expected but I might have known that Guy would choose someone special; too special for my mother," Imogen said wryly and looked sad. "I wish I'd met you and got to know you. Do you think we could meet, sometime later?"

"No, for me, none of you exist."

Emma picked up the case and put it at Imogen's feet. "Good bye," she said and went to her own room.

Bea found her dry-eyed and almost elated. "You did well," she said. "I can see it."

"No need to think of them again," Emma said. "I feel much stronger now and I'm off to the Island tomorrow."

"I've a message for you. Paul wants to drive you to Southampton if you can cross to the Island from there. No, don't refuse. He's going that far himself and wants the company, and from the look of your luggage, you'll need him or a tame porter to carry it all."

"I'll finish packing. What time does he want me?"

"About nine." Bea lingered and helped fold a few blouses. "Going for good?"

"I don't know. I shall store some things in the luggage room and let Admin know later when I'm ready to come back."

"You'll be lonely if you return. Dwight says we must leave in two weeks for Texas. He still needs physio and will have a desk job until he has his discharge." Bea laughed. "When you come to stay, he'll be wearing chaps and a six gallon hat!"

"I shall have time to think," Emma said. "Space, that I was afraid of losing."

"I'll say goodbye now. I hate waving people off and I know I'll weep buckets tonight for everything and everyone I love here." She hugged Emma with a fierceness that almost shocked her. "If I was queer, I'd be in love you with you, Dewar."

"I know. It's because we've shared so much, and there have been so many good and bad times."

Bea smiled damply. "Like when my twisted cousin nearly raped you?"

"Even that. *Au revoir*, Bea. See you on the ranch." They were both weeping and when Bea had gone, the catharsis of tears washed away more than sorrow at their parting, and eventually, Emma was calm.

"Is that all?" Paul was comically aghast. "Who else is coming?"

"Just me."

"Going away, miss?" he asked. "Going for ever?"

Emma shrugged. "I have to see the sea and hear the wind on the cliffs before I decide," she said, half laughing.

"I want to call in at the University. We can have lunch there," he offered. "It's fairly new but they are going to build and soon they'll have a fine place for

244

research and medicine and I hope a unit for neurological disorders."

"You can drop me off by the ferry," she suggested.

"With all that luggage? I've decided I'll have to come with you all the way and hand you over to your aunt unless you want a hernia."

"I lift very heavy people," Emma protested. "Ladies get far less hernias than men and I don't even have varicose veins as most surgeons have from all that standing."

Paul gave a vulgar whistle. "I'd noticed," he said, and slammed the lid to the car boot, making sure it was shut firmly. His own bag was on the back seat with a huge parcel that he said was for Aunt Emily from Bea.

"What's in it?" Emma asked.

"Food mostly, I think; tins of biscuits and a sticky cake. I do like a nice biscuit," he said with an uncanny resemblance to Emily's voice.

Emma eyed him with suspicion. "Anyone would think you'd met her."

"Would they? Bea said she enjoyed what she sent once a long time ago. Oh, no, not army convoys! Don't they know the war's over?"

"They have to bring it all back," Emma said and they waited by the side of the road until the column of grey vehicles had passed. "They must be off a troop ship. I wonder if the men being demobbed will get their jobs back?" She laughed. "Have you seen the government issue of demobilisation clothes? Three men from Bea's ward had to be invalided out and went to get them from somewhere in London. One Irish boy begged Bea to go with him to choose as he'd never possessed a real suit, but she tactfully said that her husband would object, much as she'd like to go with him."

245

"Did she regret it when she saw the vision of elegance that emerged?"

"He paraded for her benefit and she had to think of something very sad for five minutes as he was so pleased with his choice and she couldn't laugh. Imagine a suit made of quite good cloth but in a shade that they call ox-blood, with a green porkpie hat and a tie that matched neither shirt nor suit. The others had done better with dark grey suits and white shirts and trilby hats. Good for job interviews, one said."

The huge dining room of the University was seething with students and men from the Air Service Training faculty. Emma was surprised to see so many Indian students and others from mixed ethnic groups, mostly studying engineering, but it made a lively scene and she contrasted it with the dining room at Heath Cross which was much quieter and less vibrant. She chose curry from the section serving Indian food and found herself laughing really sincerely for the first time since Guy died.

They went to the new medical faculty and it was obvious that Paul was known there, and she found, highly respected. "Coming to join us?" asked a doctor, eyeing her with great approval. "You'll like it." He looked at her left hand, now devoid of Guy's ring, and raised an eyebrow. "You'd better snap her up Paul. The opposition is fierce down here."

"I'm working on it," Paul said cheerfully, and steered her away to milder men. "I booked the ferry for five," he said.

"You planned to come to the Island all the time!" she accused him.

"Of course. I like the Island. You don't own it!"

"I feel as if I do," she replied more humbly.

"Let's get you home," he said when the ferry docked

and the cars were unloaded. "Nice ride through Newport and we're nearly there."

"I do know." She saw harbour lights and the whole of Newport before them, lit up as she had not seen it for nearly five years.

"You love it here," he said gently. "Why not stay? I hear there is a need for a very good casualty sister at the main hospital." He leered at her. "If you play your cards right dear, I'll put a word in for you."

"Stop joking. Is there, and how did you know?"

"The last time I was here I found out and my friendly doctor who treats your aunt Emily, was very anxious to help."

"So it was you she wrote about!"

"Nothing bad I hope."

"No." Emma forced herself to remember what Emily had written and her mouth was dry. "Have you been looking at partnerships here?"

"One here, one in the north of Hampshire and one in Brighton, but this would be convenient for Southampton."

"I see."

Emily welcomed them with open arms and a wicked twinkle when Paul embraced her as an old friend. "I've made a pie," she said as if that was welcome enough.

Paul left to stay with his friend, and Emma made strong tea with a dash of whisky for Emily.

"That's good. A nice cup of tea and a biscuit have solved a lot of problems in the past and will do in the future, I'll be bound," Emily said. "Still raw?" she asked. "You don't look too bad. Are you staying? You could do worse. That applies to a lot of things," she added with a tilt of her head towards the doorway through which Paul had disappeared earlier. "I like a man who can laugh and has that kind of a mouth. I know it's too early, but

247

don't turn him away, Emma. I have a feeling I might finish that bedspread at last and if you don't mind, I'd like to do it soon before I'm too old to hold a crochet hook!"